AGENT
UNRAVELED

BOOK FOUR
OF
THE RELUCTANT ASSASSIN
A HUNDRED HALLS NOVEL

THOMAS K. CARPENTER

Agent Unraveled
Book Four of The Reluctant Assassin
A Hundred Halls Novel
by Thomas K. Carpenter

Copyright © 2019 Thomas K. Carpenter
All Rights Reserved

Published by Black Moon Books

Cover design by Ravven
www.ravven.com

Discover other titles by this author on:
www.thomaskcarpenter.com

ISBN-10: 9781090126450

Other Hundred Halls Novels

THE HUNDRED HALLS
Trials of Magic
Web of Lies
Alchemy of Souls
Gathering of Shadows
City of Sorcery

THE RELUCTANT ASSASSIN
The Reluctant Assassin
The Sorcerous Spy
The Veiled Diplomat
Agent Unraveled
The Webs That Bind

This book is dedicated to Kai
and her coming adventures

AGENT UNRAVELED

Chapter One
Somewhere south of Invictus, August 2016
Even a good helmet can't protect everything

The Yakari motorcycle purred between Zayn's legs as he tore down Hwy 202 towards King of Prussia, where he'd turn north towards the city of Invictus to begin his fourth year at the Academy of the Subtle Arts. The eastern horizon glowed with the expectation of morning, leaving the industrial parks on his right cast in shadow. The occasional bug splatted against his face shield, which was annoying but not as bad as the hailstorm of June bugs he'd run into somewhere north of Atlanta. One of the little buggers had snuck under his chin-strap, smacking him right in the neck. He didn't bother to check, but he was sure he had a bruise.

Zayn zipped past a couple of beat-up sedans carrying groggy workers to the D'Agastine factory complex at the next exit. The blur of passing made him check his speedometer to find he was going two hundred and forty-five kilometers per hour. He'd been running hard, taxing his imbuement to keep up with the sensory inputs, but now that traffic was staring to thicken, he pulled back on the throttle, letting his speed burn off like morning mist in the sun.

Around the time his speed drifted south of one-sixty, a migraine hit him like a thunderbolt. He went blind with pain, and flashes like hallucinatory Northern Lights reflected across his vision.

It felt like an icicle the size of a javelin had been shoved behind his eyes. Zayn fought with the Yakari, over braking, his back tire fishtailing, trying in vain to remember if his lane was clear.

Something large and boxy passed him on his right. A semi, maybe.

Just when he thought he might be able to open his eyes, a second stab of pain hit. He felt nauseous, but held onto his stomach. Through the agony, he clamped down on the brake, deciding it would be worse to slam into the back of an SUV than to get hit from behind. He hoped his fellow drivers recognized his distress.

Since the second stab of pain wasn't as bad as the first, after a few seconds he could open his eyes enough to navigate to the gravelly side of the road.

He climbed off the Yakari, yanked off his helmet, and stumbled down the embankment to get fresh air.

It was the fifth migraine he'd had this week, and easily the worst, not just because it'd almost killed him.

Zayn pulled off his backpack and riffled through his stuff to find a small bottle at the bottom. The bottle was full. He'd gotten the prescription in Selma two weeks ago, but hadn't bothered to take a single pill.

He popped it open and stared inside for a few moments before snapping the lid back on. He couldn't understand why he'd bothered to go all the way into Selma and see a mage specialist—highly recommended by one of the Watchers—just to ignore the medicine she'd given him.

"Why don't I want to take you?" he asked the bottle, before giving up and shoving it back into his backpack. The mage specialist had told him it would unblock whatever was causing the headaches.

The rest of the ride was completed at safe speeds, allowing Zayn to consider the implications of what he'd agreed to with Lady Arcadia.

If you can bring me good information next year when you return to the Academy, I'll loosen the reins.

It'd seemed a good idea at the time: giving up his quest to kill her in return for a long and healthy life. But then he'd pushed her for privileges for his family. He couldn't take her deal without giving them freedom as well. In retrospect, it was a mistake, but a deal was a deal and he wasn't going to go back on it. But now he had to give the Lady of Varna information about Priyanka, and he sensed deceiving her would be fraught with danger.

He mulled over his options as he drove into the city, which was awake on this Sunday morning. He smiled as he saw the tourists wandering the sidewalks, heads full of magic as they gawked at the city skyline. The Spire was in full brilliance, reflecting the sun like a great jewel.

The constant sounds—the honking, the shouting of taxi drivers, the roar of illusionary battles coming from the second ward—these had bothered Zayn when he first came to the city of Invictus, but now they were comforting. He smiled as a hot-dog vendor shot a spray of sparks after a kid who'd snagged a chili dog before disappearing into the crowd. At other locations, lines of tourists formed at famous shops and at vending kiosks dispensing trinkets that could perform minor magical effects.

He found the Sunless Shore Restaurant without trouble. Classes didn't start until Monday, so his team had agreed to meet for brunch and catch up on their summers. The restaurant was named after a lake in the Undercity. Murals depicting scenes of students battling strange beasties near the water's edge or from the decks of boats covered the walls.

Zayn found the team in a back room, drinking mimosas and chatting. Marley, the striped callolo, leapt into his arms and pressed his furry cat-like face against Zayn's.

"Hey Marley, I missed you too," said Zayn.

The callolo signed: *Missed Zayn, love.*

"Have you been behaving?" he asked the callolo.

As Portia got up to give him a hug, she said, "I got here last week, and I've spent half my time returning the expensive stuff he's stolen from the neighborhood."

While they'd moved back into the Honeycomb for their fourth year, they'd kept the house in the seventh ward as their home away from the Academy. It served as a place for Marley to live since he wasn't allowed in the Honeycomb.

"Marley," said Zayn, lowering his voice to be disapproving. "You know we talked about this."

The callolo signed his acknowledgement and buried his head in Zayn's neck. The gesture made him smile.

The others gave hugs before returning to the table. Zayn threw his helmet onto an open seat and unzipped his riding jacket.

When he sat down, he caught Keelan staring at him. They hadn't hung out much during the summer, after his cousin and aunt had moved into the Gardens. But there was something more, a shadow in Keelan's gaze that felt familiar, because it was the same concern that Zayn had in the past when he looked at his cousin. But now it felt like their roles had reversed, even if he didn't know why.

Zayn opened his mouth to ask, when Vin handed him a mug of coffee.

"A little pick-me-up after your ride," said Vin.

He caught the smirk on Vin's lips only a moment before the bitter drink touched his tongue and the surface of the coffee exploded in a tiny mushroom cloud. Zayn threw the mug away from him, expecting coffee to go flying everywhere, only to see an empty mug tumbling over the table and landing in a bowl of cherries.

Vin slapped his large hand against the table, filling the air with a boisterous guffaw. Eyerolls from the others suggested that he'd performed this same trick on them.

"It wasn't funny the first time, Vin," said Skylar as she scooped up the coffee mug and tossed it to Zayn. A faint outline of runes lay on the side of the cream surface. Zayn turned the mug over, looking for more powerful enchantments that could have hid the coffee, then he scratched the runes off with his fingernail, the chalky ink flaking away with the slightest touch.

"Rocky's Rockin' Runes," said Vin, holding out a booklet of rub-on runic tattoos. Each page showed a different rune. "These things are the best."

The runes confused Zayn because they were a different construction than he was used to, older perhaps. And at least half the runes were superfluous, having no purpose to the resulting magic, but he had to admit they looked impressive. Whoever this Rocky was, he was a showman, or showwoman.

Portia threw a cherry pit at Vin, who knocked it away with a spoon. "Only the best if you like being a jerk, but whoever designed them is making a killing. Those purple kiosks are everywhere in the city."

Zayn remembered the line of tourists outside the nearby kiosk.

"Only takes a touch of faez to activate it," said Keelan. "Enough anyone with even low talent can muster."

Zayn motioned to throw the booklet back to Vin, but he gestured for him to keep it. "So who did everyone get for their mentor?"

"O'Keefe," said Keelan, "but I think everyone expected that."

"Me too," said Skylar, and when Zayn gave her a questioning look, she added, "I figured she's the best one to help me with the shadow cloak. I haven't done anything with the threads Prince Orráine gave me because I'm afraid to screw them up."

"I got Pennywhistle," said Vin, arching an eyebrow triumphantly. "She only took three students this year."

"What about you, Portia?" Zayn asked as he grabbed a piece of crispy bacon from a tray.

"Instructor Allgood," said Portia.

"What? How? I thought he was in charge of the first years?" asked Zayn.

"It's Instructor Minoan this year," said Keelan, shaking his head. "I feel sorry for those poor bastards."

"We can all assume that you got the patron, Mr. Protégé," said Skylar, pouring another mimosa from a pitcher.

Zayn slipped a piece of bacon into his mouth, and it exploded across his tongue. After he swallowed, he said, "Yeah, I got Pri."

"Pri, he says, like he's one of the instructors," said Skylar, playfully poking him with an empty fork.

"It's going to be weird, not having every class together," said Keelan.

"Way weird," said Skylar.

"Does anyone know what their mentor is going to pick for their imbuement?" asked Portia.

"No idea," said Vin, who was paging through another booklet of novelty runic tattoos. It appeared he'd given a booklet to everyone on the team except Marley, and even that Zayn wasn't totally sure about.

"I'll find out first, I think," said Keelan. "Well, me and Skylar. We go on Thursday."

"Nice," said Zayn. "I wish I knew when I was going. I haven't heard anything from Priyanka. She's been out of the realm all summer."

"You're the one that picked her," said Skylar.

"I hope I don't regret it," said Zayn.

"You know you will," said Keelan, and everyone nodded with him.

Zayn couldn't help but let the shadow of a smile onto his lips. His reputation in the Academy for taking risks was well documented.

He grabbed a flute of mimosa and lifted it towards the center. The rest of the team matched him.

"To another year of learning, love, and hopefully living."

They clinked their glasses together and downed their drinks. Zayn coughed a little when the fizz hit the back of his throat, but otherwise, it felt good to be back with his teammates. Everyone looked equally optimistic about the upcoming year, with smiles at the ready. They stayed for the afternoon, drinking and talking about their first three years at the Academy, retelling stories that had grown a little in time, but no one seemed to mind. Zayn stayed out of the storytelling, as he was content to listen, add his laughter, and occasionally roll his eyes.

But beneath that good feeling was an emptiness, a cavern in his soul that he couldn't quite understand. When he searched his mind, he couldn't find a reason for this dissonance, but it remained. For now, he was content, but something didn't seem quite right, and he worried that whatever it was, was not going to end well for him.

Chapter Two
The Honeycomb, August 2016
The Art of not Death

The Honeycomb bustled with three years of students. Zayn dodged through the sitting area, catching whispers from a pair of second years, who were staring right at him. An elbow jabbed him in the ribs.

"I think they're about to ask for your autograph," said Keelan.

Zayn jabbed him right back. "I'll make a terrible spy if I become famous."

"Maybe you ought to try keeping a low profile this year," said Keelan, raising an eyebrow.

"How's your mom doing? I feel like I didn't get to see you this summer," said Zayn, changing the subject.

"She's joined a knitting club—the new arm is amazing. It's like she never lost it," said Keelan. "You know you could have stopped by. It's not like you didn't know where we live."

"And you know where the Stack is," said Zayn, and when

he realized how harsh it had sounded, he added, "I'm sorry, cuz. It was a weird summer for me."

"Me too," said Keelan, his gaze turning faraway. "You know, Watcher initiation stuff."

"I suppose that's all super-secret," said Zayn, running his fingers across his lips as if he were zipping them.

"Always," said Keelan. "It feels weird having a secret from you. Even if it's not as cool as you think it might be."

"I've never thought the Watchers were cool, so don't worry."

As they neared class, Keelan pulled him short. "Hey, I talked to Neveah a couple of weeks ago. The food truck came by the Gardens. Man, I swear she's enchanting those tacos. I could have eaten twenty of them."

"I have, trust me, and it ain't pretty," said Zayn, rubbing his stomach.

Keelan looked into the classroom, which was filling up. His lips had flattened. "Nev said you've been having migraines, like really bad. She said you almost fell off the Stack when you were running a wire up for Uncle Maceo."

Zayn glanced at his shoes. "It's nothing. I got some pills for it. I'm sure it's okay."

"You should go by Golden Willow. They have the best doctors, all Aura Healer trained," said Keelan.

Through the open door, he spied Instructor O'Keefe moving to the front of the class, so he tugged on Keelan's sleeve. "Class time."

Keelan gave him a look, letting him know he knew he was avoiding the question, but there was nothing he could do about it.

"Good morning, lads and lassies," said Instructor O'Keefe, who was dressed in a kilted skirt and white blouse. She stood in front of a table full of household items, including a remote control, bath squeegee, and a can of spray paint. "Today, we're going to discuss the arts of improvisation. And I don't mean that silly crap at the Laugh Out Loud. What I'm talkin' about eh using the tools around you to survive a sticky situation. You know, when it's gone tatties o'wer the side."

The last line received a room full of blank stares, but it didn't seem to slow Instructor O'Keefe, who looked like she was only winding up. Her accent seemed to come and go with her excitement which only made understanding her more difficult.

"Sometimes, you make all the plans in the world, only to have them go pear shaped on ya, and that's when you need to know how to improvise, you know, using whatcha got to get the job done," said Instructor O'Keefe.

From the back row, Eddie called out, "Like MacGyver."

Instructor O'Keefe screwed her face up as if she'd eaten a lemon. "Never heard of 'im. So as I was sayin', you need to learn how to use these pretties to get the job done." She ran her hand over the items on the table.

The instructor grabbed a paint pen from the table. "I think er'yone in this room knows the value of a good paint pen. Not a rune o' secret message that can't be written with this little bad boy. But yur not always gonna have the right tool for the job."

She threw the paint pen over her shoulder. "Sometimes, ya need something quick and dirty."

The instructor held up a paper clip, slowly unfolded it, and then, before anyone could cry out, jammed it into her forefinger.

To his left, Zayn heard Vin mumble, "I wish she would have warned us."

Instructor O'Keefe held up her finger with a drop of blood beading on it. "Best writing tool in the universe, and it never runs dry, or at least if it does, you got other problems."

She sucked the blood off her finger, tossed the paperclip onto the table, and picked up a colorful box of animal crackers.

"There was once a mage I knew who sacrificed a handful o' animal crackers to pacify a horrible curse. Of course, that could have been a tall tale, but I appreciate the creativeness.

"But this last one es the truth, as I knew the mage well. He was flying over the Pacific in a small plane when it crashed, killing everyone but him. He made it to a small island, and boiled seawater to make salt so he could summon an imp that could fly him back to the mainland."

"Does he live in Invictus?" asked Eddie.

"Eh, no," said Instructor O'Keefe. "Unfortunately, he was dehydrated and made a mistake with his enunciation. The imp turned on him and they battled to the death. He killed the imp, but only survived long enough to record the experience in his notebook."

A low groan went through the room, which brought a twinkle to the instructor's eye. She liked to tell them stories with horrible endings, which Keelan liked to argue was to help teach them the importance of crisp spell casting. Zayn thought she had a morbid sense of humor.

"For today's lesson, lads and lassies, you're going to be escaping from eh locked room, using nothing but yur wits and whatever you can scrounge up. To get through the door, you're going to have to be clever. Brute force won't work here." She glanced at Zayn, who held his hands up in faux outrage. "There's a camera in the room, so we can see how you did, and if ya screw it up extra special, we'll all watch it next week and have a go at ya. Everyone line up by the door, and we'll do this one by one."

Zayn's team was closest to the escape room, so he was

second in line. Vin was first to go, throwing his arms up as if he were on a roller coaster.

As soon as the door shut, Zayn turned to his cousin.

"If you talk to my parents, please tell them not to worry. It's not uncommon to get headaches in the Halls."

Keelan raised an eyebrow. "You can't believe that."

"It'll be okay."

They waited patiently for about twenty minutes until the door clicked open.

"Good luck," said Keelan, though Zayn didn't think he meant the locked room.

Zayn didn't go in right away, staying in the doorway to examine the new location. He figured the door closing would start the challenge, so he wanted to delay it as long as possible.

It looked like a college dormitory with a foldout couch, a desk, and an avocado green mini-refrigerator. There was a door on the opposite side of the room that he assumed he'd have to get through to escape, since he hadn't seen Vin come out his way.

When he had a good layout of the room in his head, Zayn stepped inside, and the door clicked shut behind him. Immediately, a hissing noise erupted from the radiator in the corner of the room. A quick sniff revealed the oily smell of propane.

"That's not good," said Zayn, craning his neck in all directions. "Definitely no fire."

He checked the opposite door, finding it locked, and the keyhole was pin-sized. He didn't think he could bypass the lock using manual methods, especially with no picks.

Zayn took a quick inventory of the refrigerator, finding a bowl of hardboiled eggs, a bottle of seltzer water, some mints, a loaf of bread, and a row of mustards and ketchups. The desk held the usual stuff like pens and pencils, but there were also packets of salt and soy sauce with a Chinese delivery logo on them.

Zayn took a moment to dig around in the couch, finding a piece of hard bread, some lint, and three pennies. Overall, it wasn't much of a haul, but it would have to do. He wracked his brain for spells that could use the available reagents, but his mind was blank.

"Come on, Zayn, think."

He dropped to his belly, searching under the couch for more resources, but there were only a few tufts of dust bunnies underneath.

Back at the open refrigerator, Zayn picked through the items while trying to breathe as shallowly as possible. The propane gas was making him dizzy.

When an idea came to him, he knew it was a bad one, but it was better to try something stupid than to do nothing at all. After testing the ketchup by squirting it on the front of the refrigerator, he scooped up the boiled eggs, packets of salt, and mustard containers.

Zayn quickly cracked open the hardboiled eggs, tossed away the white protein and shells, and dumped the greenish-yellow yolks into the bowl along with the pennies. Next he unscrewed the ketchup and dumped out the contents onto the floor. Then he opened up the mustard container and scooped it into the squeeze bottle. Once it was full, he squirted mustard on the wall, determined that it stuck more cleanly than the ketchup had, and then opened it back up and emptied the packets of salt into the mustard, mixing it with a long spoon from the mini-kitchen.

Then he collected the bowl of hard-boiled egg yolks with pennies mixed amongst them and the squeeze bottle of mustard and moved to the exit. He knew a spell that could turn sulfur and zinc from the pennies into a brutal acid, but it needed a little extra oomph from some runes. Zayn hoped the mustard would work well enough as a substrate to hold the salt.

After testing a few lines on the wall, Zayn got right to work, using both hands on the squeeze bottle to draw the runes on the wall around the lock. He kept the tip close to the surface so the lines were neat, keeping the pressure on the bottle constant so the line didn't have any breaks. He could always go back over any gaps, but that might create impurities in the lines, which would reduce the efficacy of the runes.

When he was finished, he surveyed his work. There were eight relatively neat runes drawn around the lock. He'd had to make them larger than he would have preferred, but the mustard wasn't the best writing material.

Zayn leaned down to grab the bowl of egg yolks, only to have a rush of vertigo pass through him. The propane gas was filling the room. He had little time before he passed out.

After moving to the opposite side of the room, he took a huge breath, using the imbuement technique to hold more air than otherwise was possible. Immediately, he could hear his heartbeat in his ears, but got right to work on the egg yolks, smashing them with his fist until the yolks were paste. Then he smeared it around the lock, sticking the pennies to the gunk and hoping that would satisfy the necessary zinc for the spell.

With everything in place, Zayn weaved the complex incantation, articulating carefully, using only the air in his lungs. His fingers danced, forming the cage of faez that he fed into the air like a spider spinning a web. As the spell neared completion, the gunky yellow paste began to smolder around the edges of the pennies.

Internally, he cheered, though he kept the incantation up, for to pause or mispronounce would cause the whole thing to fail. When the spell was complete, he let out the rest of his breath and watched the acid eat through the brass covering on the lock. As it melted away, the inner workings of the lock were revealed. Zayn was confused at first, expecting a mechanical system—cylinder and tumblers—only to find a host of wires behind the cover.

As the plastic on the wax began to smoke, Zayn realized his mistake almost too late. He threw up a protective enchantment the moment before a wire sparked, igniting the propane gas to explode.

The concussive force knocked him over, but his enchantment protected him from the worst of the effects. Lying on his side groaning, he watched as Instructor O'Keefe stuck her head into the room.

"Eh, laddie, it was a good attempt, but you made one major mistake," she said.

"I forgot to check to see how the lock worked," said Zayn.

"Right-o," she said with a wink. "You got so in a hurry to solve the problem, you didn't make sure you understood the whole situation. But don't beat yourself up there, laddie. Not many students pass this test."

She helped him to his feet while a couple of fifth years hurried in to clean up the room for the next attempt. Vin was sitting in the next room with a single black eye.

"Are you trying out a new cologne? You smell like rotten eggs and burnt hair," said Vin.

"It's a cologne for demons, I think. What happened to you?" asked Zayn.

"I tried punching my way through the lock, but the impact rebounded on me and knocked me out," said Vin.

While they waited, the rest of the class tested the escape room. Only three students passed: Portia, Sofia, and Eddie. The last was particularly disheartening, since the rest of them would have to hear about his victory for the next hundred years or so.

After class, Zayn went to Instructor O'Keefe and asked, "Is there any way I can try again? Just for my own peace of mind."

"No laddie, that's not how it works. Sometimes you fail, and you have to deal with that. Take the lesson learned and move on," she said.

He nodded even though he didn't feel like he'd learned anything except that he'd screwed up. He hated that he hadn't been given time to plan. While he knew he could improvise with the best of them, he worked best when he could formulate a good plan.

Outside class, Portia raised an eyebrow when she saw him. "Don't beat yourself up, Zayn. You can't always win."

"I know, I know," he said. "But I feel like I should have been able to figure it out. I'm not sure what's wrong with me."

By the time he got back to his room, the events in the locked room had swirled in his head long enough he'd come up with three more solutions to getting out.

"Next time, Zayn, next time," he told himself. He just hoped there'd be a next time when he screwed up again.

Chapter Three
The Honeycomb, September 2016
It should have been named Greenland

The next few weeks passed in a crawl as his classmates received their fourth imbuements and spent time with their mentors. Portia came home each night with bruises and face-splitting grins, Vin—with the aid of enchantment—morphed into a new persona each night, and Skylar and Keelan worked furiously in their rooms, which made it sound like a tinker's workshop. He was beginning to regret asking Priyanka to be his mentor when he received a text.

[Meet me at Empire Ink. Bring a travel bag and your best parka.]

The second part made him wonder about where they'd be going after getting his imbuement, but he knew better than to ask, responding only with an acknowledgement.

He reached Empire Ink within the hour, expecting to find Priyanka waiting for him, but it was only Percival in a three-piece tweed suit.

"Oh, hey Percival," he said disappointedly.

Percival adjusted his wire-rimmed glasses, the hint of a frown tugging at the corner of his lips. It was more emotion than Zayn had ever seen from the English tattooist.

"Well then," he said.

"Sorry, Percival. It's good to see you. I was just expecting to see Priyanka here. I have yet to meet with her, and she's my mentor."

Percival squeezed his lips together and sighed in a way that suggested Zayn shouldn't have been surprised by Priyanka's absence.

"And this is why I don't get attached to you students," said Percival. "You either get yourselves killed through bumbling stupidity, or ignore my contributions to your education."

"You're right," said Zayn, sitting on the table. "I'm a complete ass."

Percival raised an eyebrow. "But you'd like your imbuement now."

"I can chat for a while first, if you'd like," said Zayn.

"No, no. We're on a tight schedule," said Percival as he pulled blue rubber gloves on.

"Don't we need to wait for Priyanka?" he asked.

"She's delayed, but we decided on your imbuement months ago." Percival eyed his midsection. "Off with your shirt. This will hurt more than usual. It's best if the imbuement is under your arms."

"Okay," said Zayn, yanking off his black T-shirt.

Inking the tattoo and the imbuement took nearly three hours. Zayn had to hold his arms up, one at a time, while Percival worked his sides. Whenever the tattoo needle went over his ribs, it was a cross between a tickle and a bad sunburn, leaving him grimacing. When he was finished, sides bandaged with gauze and medical tape, Percival set down the gun.

"It's best if you don't use the imbuement for at least three days, to give your flesh time to heal and the connections time to, well, connect," said Percival.

"What does it do?" asked Zayn.

"It gives you the ability to influence non-humans by absorbing their particular pheromones and sending them back like a seductive cologne," said Percival.

"Wow," said Zayn, considering the ramifications. "That sounds complicated."

"It is. The right side of the imbuement absorbs," said Percival as he tapped on Zayn's ribs. "And the left side puts out the new pheromones."

"I feel like this imbuement has an intended immediate purpose," said Zayn.

Percival opened his mouth to speak, but his phone buzzed, interrupting him. After checking it, he said, "I'm sorry. If there is, Pri will have to tell you. She'll meet you at the airport. You'll have to hurry."

Zayn grabbed his bag and ran to the nearest station in the thirteenth ward. His sides hurt the whole time, but he kept going. He did *not* want to miss a chance to work with Priyanka. It seemed like his teammates had already met with their mentors a half dozen times.

When he reached the airport, Priyanka was waiting for him at security in jeans, a white V-neck, sunglasses, and a black leather jacket. The way she was standing on her back foot suggested she was exhausted but willing to push on.

"Hey Pri—"

He didn't get a chance to finish when she said, "Come on, we can't miss this flight."

Zayn moved towards the security line, but Priyanka headed towards a door marked Private. No one moved to stop them. They went through a maze of corridors, coming out on the tarmac. A 767 with the logo for Viking Airlines waited with a set of stairs.

The air steward gave them a strange look when they climbed into the plane, directing them towards two first-class seats. The other passengers craned their heads to see who they were, making Zayn feel like a rock star.

Priyanka slumped into the window seat. When the air steward came over to check on them with a look of awe, Priyanka muttered, "Crap."

The gesture was brief, only a riffling of the fingers as if Priyanka were playing a piano trill in midair and a whiff of faez, and the steward stood erect, the earlier expression wiped from her face.

Zayn took a tentative glance over the cushy seat to find the rest of the first-class passengers staring blankly ahead.

"What did you do?" he asked.

But Priyanka didn't answer. She was already lightly snoring, the dark sunglasses slipped from the bridge of her nose.

He wished he'd had a chance to ask where they were going, but he didn't have long to wonder, as the pilot welcomed them to Viking Airlines on their journey to Reykjavik, Iceland. His mind whirled with the possibilities of what they might be investigating, but since he knew nothing about the northern island country, he had to rely on speculation.

The flight at least was better than the one he'd taken last year to England with the rest of his team, though he declined the free champagne they kept offering him. As soon as the wheels touched down, Priyanka snapped awake, the dark bags around her eyes looking less pronounced than when she'd gotten on the plane.

As they neared customs, Zayn said, "I don't have a passport."

But Priyanka said nothing, and they were waved through

the booth, which seemed especially odd because there were magic detectors surrounding the station and nothing went off.

After a quick stop at a car rental place, they were in a dark gray Land Cruiser, speeding north. The brief summer was coming to an end, though the days were still abnormally long. At first, Zayn said nothing, entranced by the alien landscape of up-thrust volcanic rock covered in a thick blanket of light green moss. But the further north they went, the more pastoral the land became, with sheep and long-maned Icelandic ponies.

"Where are we headed?" asked Zayn.

Priyanka looked over as if she'd forgotten he was in the car, which made him feel like an afterthought.

"Dettifoss," she said, "about eight hours from here."

"And why didn't we take a portal?"

"There aren't any portals that connect to Iceland, but that's not unusual because there are few portals that reach outside of Invictus in our world. The energy required is too large. The portals that we use regularly are only possible because of the uniqueness of the city."

"What about the other realms?" he asked.

"Have we not taught this?" she asked, and when he shook his head, she added, "I guess I haven't been doing a good job as your patron. The portals to the other realms work because the city lies on a thin membrane, so reaching them takes less energy. It's the same reason we can move about the city easily, because both ends of the portal have ample background faez to facilitate the transfer. And the realms that we visit often, the Eternal City, the Fae, and others, are close, making it easier."

He was about to ask another question when she pulled onto a gravel side road.

"You're going to need to drive. I have to prepare," she said.

"Prepare for what?" he asked as he got out of the passenger side, moving around to the driver's door.

"We're going to talk to some powerful beings, and I need to be ready," she said.

"Powerful beings?" he asked as he settled into the driver's seat.

Priyanka pulled her sunglasses from her face and slipped them into an inside pocket.

"Dragons," she said with a wry smile. "Drive on, we don't want to be late for the party."

Zayn pulled onto the road as Priyanka pulled her legs into a crossed position, relaxed her hands against her bent knees, and let her eyes drift closed. She wasn't asleep like she was on the plane, and he detected low-level faez emanating from her.

Dragons, he thought. He had a million questions, but he wasn't going to get a chance to ask them. What he knew about them wasn't much: only that they were reclusive, each more powerful than dozens of mages, and they could take human form if they wanted.

He also thought they were solitary, but she'd said dragons rather than dragon, and mentioned a party. Multiple dragons were getting together? This seemed bad. But why would she come alone with only him as her companion? He knew it was best to trust Priyanka, but it felt like they were headed into the lion's den.

Of course, who was he to complain? He'd done the same to his teammates over and over again. It was probably why Priyanka was willing to be his mentor, because he understood the risks of leadership.

"Karma," he muttered to himself.

The drive, at least, was breathtaking. It seemed like every new bend in the road brought a different landscape. Fluffy white clouds against a clear blue sky sometimes brought spats of rain that in turn caught rays of sunshine. There was no shortage of rainbows on his trip.

The mountains, often in the conical volcanic shape, lumbered across the landscape, sometimes sheer and rocky, other times crowned with mist. Waterfalls sprinted down the mountainsides, tumbling off rocky cliffs, eventually gathering into sparkling streams.

Few cars navigated the narrow two-lane highway, but occasionally he had to veer around a tourist foolishly parked in the middle of the road, taking pictures of the glorious views. It might not have been a problem, but there was no side of the road on which to pull off.

By the late afternoon, the clouds had descended upon the valleys, bringing a cold rain. Zayn sped through the mist, keeping an eye out for sheep that might wander onto the road.

He made a brief stop at a gas station in Akureyri, grabbing sandwiches for the rest of the journey, wishing he had time to visit.

Later, they passed through a volcanic region filled with sulfurous mud pits with steam rising from the earth. The landscape turned to blasted rock, making Zayn feel like he was traveling across the surface of Mars. As the road turned to gravel, they were met with a Road Closed sign. Before Zayn could ask, Priyanka snapped awake.

"We walk from here," she said.

Zayn sensed an inward focus from Priyanka, so he kept his mouth shut, which earned him a quirk in her lips after a few minutes.

"You must be disappointed that you picked me," said Priyanka.

"What? No."

A little snort came out of her nose. "You haven't had a single class with me, and now I've dragged you to a desolate place and put you in terrible danger."

"I didn't come to the Academy to be coddled," said Zayn.

"I know."

The look she gave him said everything at once: Varna.

"We've got a ways to go," she said, glancing at the diminishing light and low clouds, masquerading as mist, that had returned. "I will allow some questions while we walk, though I can't promise I'll answer everything."

"You said we were headed to Dettifoss. What is that?"

"A waterfall," she said.

He motioned towards the nearly flat landscape of blasted rock. "Here? I haven't seen anything alive in the last hour. How can there be a waterfall out here?"

"You'll see," she said.

"Is that where the dragons are?" he asked.

She nodded. "The Circle of the Scale. When the dragons gather, it is a worrisome event. Normally they are far too individualistic, but from time to time, their interests align enough for them to come together."

Interests align. Zayn didn't like the sound of that.

"What are we doing here?"

Priyanka sighed. "Finding out what they intend."

"Just you?"

"And you." She smiled. "More mages might be considered an insult."

"When's the last time they met?"

"One hundred and forty-eight years ago," she said, "nearly to the day."

He sensed a familiarity to her comment. "You were here then."

"I was in your spot as a companion to Invictus." She looked away to the mist, her expression tightening. "But we are but a shade to him. I fear I'm not enough."

"Is Invictus dead?" he asked tentatively.

Her lips squeezed together. "I wish I knew. It's been thirteen years since we've seen him. There are signs that suggest he's dead, yet, the connection between the patrons remains, which suggests he's alive. Maybe it's best to say he's dead and not dead, but either way, it's left the Hundred Halls in a terrible state."

"Can't someone take over for him? Like you?" he asked.

"That would be a terrible burden," she said, shaking her head. "But better than the others. Not that we could ever agree on one person."

"The others? Do you mean the original patrons?" he asked.

Priyanka wore a pained smile. "Semyon. Malden. Celesse. Bannon. Once we were inseparable. Now we're strangers to each other. Invictus' absence has only made that worse. I fear their motives, as they likely fear mine. Invictus was smart to bind us together, but I don't know how long we can avoid the question of who should lead us in his absence."

"I think you'd make a good head patron," said Zayn.

"Thank you, that's very sweet. But I'm not so sure. The centuries have made me a little bitter. And I have certain complications that make things harder."

Varna, again, Zayn decided.

"But Invictus brought you with him on this important journey last time," he said. "He must have brought you for a reason."

"He brought me because it's my job to protect the Halls from the other realms, which includes the dragons'. Bannon is in charge of internal security, Semyon gathering knowledge, Celesse to make us stronger through alchemy, and Malden, well, his role is unique to our future struggles."

"Why not throw your support to one of the others? Semyon

has a good reputation," said Zayn.

"He's also insufferable with his righteousness. I would, truly, but the others wouldn't support him. And that's the problem. There's not one of us that we would all agree on, so we languish," said Priyanka.

A massive shape moved through the mist above them. At first, Zayn thought a 767 had flown too low, but then he realized what it'd been, even though he'd only gotten a glimpse of it.

One word slipped from Priyanka's lips, and it held a weight that punched a shiver through him.

"Dragon."

Chapter Four
Dettifoss, Iceland, September 2016
The Majesty of Earth and Dragons

Zayn wasn't cold, as the heavy coat he'd brought protected him, but he shoved his hands into his pockets as he walked. He kept wanting to crane his head in all directions, expecting a dragon to land at any moment. Before, he'd thought of dragons as majestic and awe-inspiring, but now that he'd gotten a glimpse of one, and how large it was, he felt like a wounded antelope on the Serengeti.

He wrestled with his fear until the land fell away. A deep canyon cut through the gray rock. To his right, the gap stretched into the distance, a river winding along the bottom, but to his left, a great mist rose, suggesting the furious pounding of water. He couldn't see the waterfall, but he could sense its power.

"We're here," said Priyanka, slipping a vial of sparkling blue liquid from the inside of her jacket.

It smelled like peppermint when she unstoppered it. Priyanka threw it down her throat, grimacing and shaking it off as if it were a bitter whiskey.

"Oh Merlin, she warned me it would taste bad," said Priyanka.

"She?"

Priyanka raised an eyebrow in his direction. "Celesse."

"What will it do?"

Priyanka put a fist over her mouth as she belched. "Hopefully keep me alive. It's something from her personal stash, and she doesn't give those up lightly. She can brew up a potion for damn near anything if she has enough time. There's some trick she has that makes her potions different from anyone else's. Significantly more powerful too."

"Could she make something for...you know," Zayn blurted out before his mind caught up.

Priyanka looked ready to admonish him, but sighed into a brief explanation. "Not that, unfortunately, as much as she tried."

Zayn hadn't meant to ask such a sensitive question, but as soon as she answered, he sensed his mistake and tried to cover it up with another question.

"Is she still mad about when I broke into her research facility?" he asked.

"Once she understood what you did and why, she wanted to hire you," said Priyanka, then she glanced askew. "Amongst other things." She glanced ahead. "This next part is going to be dangerous. I want to be very clear that you cannot get involved, no matter what happens. It's more than likely that I will die here."

"What? Wait, you can't," said Zayn.

"It's part of the job," said Priyanka. "I hope you'll come to understand this."

"What will happen to the Academy? The students?" he

asked.

"Some will die, others will go mad. The hearty ones, like yourself, will go on with their lives," said Priyanka.

"Is it fair to make a decision like that that will affect their lives?" he asked, a little rougher than he planned.

Priyanka didn't answer, but tilted her head at him as if he should know better.

"Fine," he said.

They made their way to the waterfall over broken rocks. The churning cacophony grew louder as they approached, along with the mist that kissed their faces. When they made it to the river's edge, right at the point the water dropped into the canyon, Zayn felt a primal emotion surge up through him, sending his heart rate soaring and making him feel like he'd run a marathon.

"I felt the same way the first time I came here," said Priyanka. "This place gets in your soul."

Zayn sensed Priyanka's tension before he saw the man on the other side of the river. He had broad shoulders and ice-blond hair pulled back into a braid. His grim expression marred his Viking good looks, and to Zayn's surprise, he stepped into the river.

"No," slipped from Zayn's lips, but beside him, Priyanka crossed her arms as if she had expected this display of power. The man strode through the water, right at the edge, the water cascading around him as if he were made of granite. When he reached their side, he was dry as a bone.

"Jörm," said Priyanka.

"Where's your keeper?" Jörm asked derisively, with an Icelandic accent.

"You'll have to deal with me this time," said Priyanka, pulling her shoulders back.

Jörm towered over his patron. Zayn hadn't realized the

scope of her challenge, but seeing the display of power, walking through the falling edge of a river, had convinced him that her battle was unwinnable.

"Do you seek an audience at the Circle of the Scale?" asked Jörm.

"I do," said Priyanka, slipping off her leather jacket and handing it to Zayn. She wore a gray tank top underneath. When she flexed her arms, ripples of tattoos appeared on her skin momentarily. She was covered from head to toe with imbuements, which spoke to her inherent power, since the human body could only handle so many.

Jörm's eyes grew wide in anticipation. He seemed to be relishing the upcoming fight.

"Then let us—"

Priyanka didn't give him a chance to finish. She blurred forward, the impact knocking them both off the edge of the waterfall.

"No!" said Zayn, stepping forward, but the mist and darkness hid their descent.

His breath caught in his chest. He held it in solidarity with his patron, as if that might help her in her battle. It was a good twenty seconds before he caught sight of them and allowed himself to breathe.

A blur flew up the waterfall, landing on the rocky cliff above the canyon. Even with his imbuement maxed out, Zayn could only see Jörm, because Priyanka was staying on the move, dancing around him as he swung his powerful arms.

Zayn was so focused on their fight, he didn't realize anyone had snuck up on him until he heard the voice behind him.

"She moves like a snake, doesn't she?"

Zayn spun around to find a short stocky man with a bald head and deep bronze skin. His smoky dark eyes held mirth, and the fine cut of his clothes and his darkwood cane made him look like either an entertainment lawyer or a high-priced pimp.

"I am Akhekh, and you are Zayn Carter, a boy out of his depth."

Zayn bowed deeply, bringing his head almost to the rocks. "It's an honor to meet you, Akhekh."

Akhekh snapped his ring-covered fingers. "I like you, Zayn. It will be a shame if I have to kill you."

Zayn sensed that Akhekh wasn't being serious, so he turned partially to face the battle, which had moved into the middle of the river. Priyanka's form appeared like a flash in a strobe light, always at Jörm's back.

"She's quick, but when he gets hold of her, this fight is done," said Akhekh.

"*If* he gets hold of her," said Zayn.

Akhekh clucked his tongue. "My dear boy, I was here when Invictus fought Jörm for an audience with the circle. *There's* a man who had power. They battled for three days before Jörm called it, and afterwards, the river had been changed forever by their blows. As much as Priyanka has learned in the time between, she's no Invictus."

As if on cue, Jörm guessed where Priyanka was going to be next and slammed into her chest with his fist, throwing her across the river to land on top of the cliff. He ran after her, and the battle moved out of sight.

Zayn felt in his gut that it was true. Even Priyanka knew she wasn't at Invictus' level, but why would she come and challenge a fight she couldn't win? Maybe there were other reasons.

Though his imbuement was fresh, not even a day old, Zayn tentatively slipped faez into it, trying to absorb what he could from Akhekh. It felt like inhaling, and the imbuement stretched against his side, aching as an insubstantial membrane took in Akhekh's essence. The pheromone was heady and sulphuric, and made Zayn break out in a thick sweat. It was as if he'd inhaled a volcanic gust. He shifted the sensation to the opposite side of the imbuement, letting the tattoo circuit board modify the essence before spitting it towards Akhekh.

"Is there something we can do to help her?" asked Zayn.

"The challenge must go unabated, but if..."

The words trailed off as Akhekh turned towards Zayn, a look of admiration in his gaze. "Well done. I almost didn't notice that. A worthy attempt, and such a light question that it slipped beneath my expectations. You are a formidable whelp. A whelp, but one with promise. I can see why she brought you."

Akhekh gestured to the battle. "But know that I am the least of my kind here, and the most generous. The others would crush you beneath their claws or swallow you whole for such a transgression. That trick might work on lesser beings, but do not dare attempt again on dragonfolk. It will not serve you well."

The battle, which had moved out of sight, came crashing into the cliffside like a meteor strike. An explosion of rocks and dust rolled away from the nearby stone wall, making Zayn duck to avoid the rocky spray.

When the dust cleared, Jörm stood over a fallen Priyanka, trapped beneath his boot. He held his fist above her head, ready to strike.

Zayn's face went numb with fear. He moved to support her, but Akhekh held him back easily.

"Just wait," whispered Akhekh.

The moment stretched until Zayn wanted to jump out of his skin.

Then Jörm stepped off Priyanka and walked towards the edge of the cliff, where he dove off into the mist.

When Akhekh released him, Zayn ran to Priyanka, who was pulling herself up into a sitting position. She looked like she'd been packed in a concrete truck full of boulders and shoved off a mountainside to roll to the bottom.

Priyanka grimaced when he helped her to her feet. Zayn suspected she had multiple ribs broken.

"Why did he stop?" asked Zayn.

Priyanka shook her head, her dark hair dancing in her face. "I don't know."

Akhekh stepped up behind them. "Greetings, Priyanka."

"Hello, Akhekh," she said with a faint smile. "It's good to see you. How's the casino business?"

"Lucrative," said Akhekh. "It never ceases to amaze me that humans can knowingly throw their money away playing games of statistics, thinking that luck will save them from the long arm of math."

"We are creatures of hope," said Priyanka, rubbing her jaw. "Even when we have no reason for it."

"As you just demonstrated," said Akhekh.

"You run a casino?" asked Zayn, incredulous.

When Akhekh shot Priyanka a look, he quickly added, "Sorry, I didn't know dragons bothered with the affairs of humankind."

Akhekh chuckled. "What better way to build my hoard than to run a casino? Especially given the loose rules around magic. Back when we had to hide it, it was hard to keep anything more modest than you could fit in a castle vault."

"Castle? Not a pyramid?" asked Zayn.

"I'm not that old, my boy," said Akhekh with a smile. "And I prefer the mountains of the Alps to the deserts of Egypt."

"Then why Vegas?" asked Zayn.

"When the price is right," he said with a shrug.

Priyanka flattened her lips. "More like that Vegas has a

nice wizard scene in addition to the casinos. Some call it Little Invictus."

Akhekh clasped them both on the shoulders. "Come now, I need to take you to the council." He looked over the edge. "Since you're still walking, sort of, follow me. I'll take you by the back way, since you don't look well enough to go through the waterfall."

Not far from their position, a tunnel opened in the earth. Akhekh led the way, followed by Priyanka after he'd handed over her jacket. As Zayn made his way down the stone steps, the tunnel closed behind him, entombing him in darkness.

Chapter Five
Circle of the Scale, September 2016
A dangerous selfie

Zayn waited to get his bearings, but then Priyanka touched his forehead and his vision bloomed into existence. The world was outlined in shades of gray.

"I'll teach you that spell on the way back," she said.

They followed Akhekh into the earth. The stairway went down for a couple of hundred feet or so before opening up in a massive cavern.

Zayn's breath caught in his throat when he saw the dragon at the back of the cave. His scales had an oily luminance, a blackish green that reminded Zayn of the deep swamp. Judging by the human figures standing nearby, the dragon was at least a couple of hundred feet long, much larger than the dragon that had flown over them earlier. Seeing the creature put a pause in every step.

"That is Vaximarillion," said Priyanka over her shoulder as she limped downward. "He is one of the oldest of their race."

"Merlin," exclaimed Zayn.

He could barely keep his eyes off the dragon as he made his way down the narrow staircase. When they reached the rocky floor of the cavern and started off towards the others, Zayn felt an overwhelming urge to flee.

Why am I walking towards that? he asked himself.

Priyanka slowed, putting her hand on his arm. "Use your imbuement to mute your senses. It won't make the fear go away, but it'll help."

"You feel it too?" he whispered.

Wide-eyed, she nodded, before continuing after Akhekh. Once Zayn adjusted his imbuement he found the presence of the dragon bearable.

There were seven men and women standing in a circle upon their approach. Jörm stood on the left, followed by a young Korean woman wearing bright red glasses, a frilly black skirt, and impossibly tall heels, a lanky gentleman with a hollow stare, a beautiful woman with jet-black skin wearing a floral dress, a woman with broad shoulders who looked like she was a soldier, a man with a big belly and a bushy face-swallowing beard, and lastly, an androgynous person wearing a long trench coat, black boots, and braids.

Akhekh paused before the group, motioning towards Priyanka as he said, "I present to you Priyanka Sai, representative of the Hundred Halls from the City of Invictus, and her assistant, Zayn Carter, of the Academy of the Subtle Arts."

"It's been one hundred and forty-eight years since we've had a visitor," said the dark-skinned woman. "And rarely have we received the same visitor twice."

Priyanka bowed her head reverently. "Thank you for seeing me, Faetellaxeleia."

The dragon-woman let a smile curl her lips. "Fate will do, I know how our names can be difficult."

The soldier-woman stomped her foot against the stone, and though she was only his size, the cavern shook slightly.

"Enough chitchat with the *skeel*. Let it speak so we can get rid of it."

Fate glowered at the woman. "She honored us with the proper rituals, Sphyianna. Do not bring shame upon us with your haste."

The animosity between the two brought tension to the circle. A few of the dragon-humans stepped back as if they expected a fight, but then Vaximarillion growled out a few words that sounded like thunder trapped in a canyon. Fate and Sphyianna each took a step back and bowed their heads in reverence to the elder dragon.

Fate glanced around the circle before speaking again. "Apologies for our rudeness. We are solitary creatures, so coming together in such large numbers makes us irritable."

"No need to apologize on our account," said Priyanka.

"Speak then, so we might resume our discussion," said Fate.

As the eight sets of human eyes and one enormous set of dragon eyes fell upon Priyanka, Zayn took the opportunity to step back, away from the attention thrust upon his patron. He moved to a location away from the circle, but towards the ancient dragon Vaximarillion.

Priyanka reached into her leather jacket, pulling out a smooth round stone. It was so black it seemed to absorb the light. She tossed it into the center of the circle and it landed without bouncing. For a moment, Zayn almost expected it to explode. The dragons stared at the stone with suspicion.

"This was given to me by Atticus Salinger, Patron of Oculus Hall. It is the direst warning the seers can give, portending dangers that threaten the city of sorcery and the multiverse itself. This prophecy was made by none other than Atticus, so

I trust that it is of the highest probability."

Sphyianna sneered at the stone. "Why do we care about *skeel* visions? Do I bring you *my* problems?"

Zayn was standing far enough away that he caught the others glancing at each other. They knew what it meant, even if Sphyianna tried to hide it.

"The last time I was here, I stood with Head Patron Invictus. At that time, the Circle of the Scale contemplated taking over the city of Invictus. The head patron came here to warn you that it would be a mistake, and as a credit to your wisdom, you listened.

"But time has passed, and the head patron is no longer with us. And how interesting it is to me that another Circle has formed at the same time I am delivered this prophecy," said Priyanka.

Sphyianna stepped forward again. "How dare you come here and accuse us?"

Before Priyanka could respond, Vaximarillion erupted with a forceful word that momentarily deafened Zayn. Had his senses not been muted, he thought he might have lost his hearing. Sphyianna paled, returning back to the circle, looking like she'd tucked her tail between her legs.

The young Korean woman chuckled lightly, "Our apologies again. Sphyianna is a young dragon, only a few centuries old. She speaks before she thinks."

"Thank you, Ne Yong," said Priyanka. "But I must confess, I *am* accusing the Circle of plotting against the Halls. I've spoken to the majority of patrons. We are prepared to fight if that's what it takes."

A low grumble, like thunder rolling across the plains, emanated from Vaximarillion. Ne Yong nodded along with the dragon speak, then responded in that same language, though it sounded strange coming from a human throat. The two spoke back and forth as the others glanced amongst themselves. Zayn could sense they each wanted to speak, but they seemed deferential to the gargantuan dragon.

When the conversation was finished, Ne Yong turned to them. Whatever had been decided brought an angry snarl to Sphyianna's lips, which was only slightly different from her resting expression.

"Vax honors your seer's vision. He sees well and true," said Ne Yong.

A crackle of nervous energy went through Zayn. Their admission that they were plotting against the Halls put him and Priyanka in terrible danger. He half expected her to run from the room, but she stayed at the edge of the circle, defiant in her acknowledgement.

"This is not a decision we take lightly," said Ne Yong. "For we recognize the importance of your school in keeping the peace in the multi-realm. But without a head patron, you are rudderless, and open to interference."

Priyanka's previously reverent tone cracked with sarcasm. "Let me guess, you'd be happy to help set us straight, with one of your own taking control of the Halls."

Ne Yong's eyes flashed with anger. Zayn could almost imagine smoke coming out of her nose.

"It was not we who built the Halls in such a precarious place. Vax warned Invictus not to place the school there, but he refused to listen, and now it could endanger us all," said Ne Yong.

Zayn had been edging towards Vaximarillion because he wanted to get a closer look at the gargantuan dragon, but her words stopped him in his tracks. This was news to him about a greater danger.

"The wells of power are holding fine without Invictus," said Priyanka. "They do not require tending."

"Yet, the membrane between this world and the demonic one thins," said Ne Yong. "The Halls needs a head patron to help focus your efforts. Right now you squabble like children fighting over toys while the house burns down."

Priyanka held her tongue, squeezing her lips together in acknowledgement. It wasn't news to Zayn that the patrons, especially the originals, weren't getting along. Even before Priyanka had mentioned it, the conflict was speculated about in the *Herald of the Halls*, though until this moment, Zayn had thought it petty gossip.

"It's our problem alone to solve," said Priyanka.

"Not if it destroys the world in which we live," said Fate. "While half of us hail from other realms, the other half live here. And make no mistake, that demonic horde wouldn't stop with this realm. Before long, they'd overrun the rest."

Priyanka nodded slowly. "I acknowledge that the danger is real, but I assure you that the wells are intact. We may not have Invictus anymore, but we're not letting our responsibilities slip."

Vaximarillion rumbled, the echoes dancing around the massive cavern. Standing so close, the vibration rattled Zayn's teeth. He used the distraction to snap a few photos with his phone behind his back. As crazy as their last few years had been, he didn't think the others would believe how large Vaximarillion was unless he had proof.

"Vax says that while he agrees the wells are intact, they haven't been maintained as well as you claim," said Ne Yong.

Priyanka's silence seemed damning. Ne Yong continued in the absence of a response.

"The question of the Hundred Halls is not one that dragonkind take lightly. Especially when it is not us alone involved in the discussion. What we will discuss here will have to be relayed back to the others, which will take time. So we're giving you exactly two hundred and forty-one days, which is a lucky prime, to decide if you will hand over ownership of the Halls to one of ours, or if we will need to take it forcibly," said Ne Yong.

"This will not end well," said Priyanka. "The Halls will not accept a head patron that is not one of our own, and a war would be catastrophic. If you're worried about the wells, then do not make this threat, because attacking us, bringing forth that much faez into the city, would surely tear them asunder, releasing that horde that you so fear."

Ne Yong adjusted her ruby-rimmed glasses. "Still, that is our demand. In two hundred and forty-one days we will require an answer."

Without another word, Priyanka gestured towards Zayn, and together they marched from the room. He held his tongue until they'd climbed up the stairs, stepping into the misty air above the Dettifoss waterfall.

"Can they really do that? Can they take control of the Halls?" he asked.

"Unfortunately yes, but the bigger question is why? They damn well know we'd never allow it, which means they're practically announcing a war in nine months," said Priyanka, shaking her head.

"Could we win that war?" asked Zayn, hopefully.

Priyanka looked into his eyes, her lips thinned with seriousness. "No."

Chapter Six
Thirteenth Ward, September 2016
The parable of the scorpion and the frog

A few weeks later, Zayn was in the middle of a sparring session with Keelan. Since most of their classes were with their mentors, they hadn't been getting enough physical work-outs, especially Zayn, since Priyanka was absent again, so they'd been getting up before dawn to train on their own.

They fought at an abandoned skate park. The obstacles and oddly shaped surfaces created more challenging footwork than the Honeycomb dojo.

After Keelan threw a Broken Tree maneuver, landing with his foot next to Zayn's head along the curved wall of quarter pipe, he asked, "Heard any more about the dragons?"

Zayn brought Headlong Zipper, forcing his cousin, who'd let his balance get shifted forward, into a retreating scuttle.

"Haven't even heard from Priyanka," grunted Zayn. "Said we'd check out the wells when she gets back."

As Keelan backed into the vert wall, he threw a Singing

Rocket—a complicated maneuver that used a forcebolt blasted downward to provide extra lift in a flipping jump—reversing the advantage and trapping Zayn against the wall. The move was named as such because a mistake left male mages singing nothing but high notes.

"You should have picked Allgood," said Keelan as he brought a Cascading Frog.

Zayn faked the Singing Rocket, and when his cousin bit, he twirled away, blocking with Gorilla Shield.

"Nice," said Keelan as they shifted into a freeform throw down. "You never do the same thing twice, not even if I do it."

"Got to keep it unpredictable," said Zayn with a grin.

Keelan feinted Bomb Run, following it up with a Towering Triple, but Zayn countered with Flying Rickshaw.

"Do you really think the dragons could take the city?" asked Keelan.

Zayn threw a series of force-blocks. "Pri said they could. She barely held her own against one dragon. In human form. Even Invictus only fought Jörm to a draw after three days. Sure we have superior numbers, but at what cost?"

Dodging around a Flowering Beaver, Zayn stepped on a walnut that had rolled into the skate pool. He recovered quickly, but Keelan used the momentary stagger to bring Headlong Zipper, forcing him backwards towards the vert wall again. Zayn caught a smirk at the corner of Keelan's lips right as he had to throw a counter or be trapped against the wall. He knew what his cousin was thinking, so he did the last thing that Keelan would expect: he did the exact same move as before—fake Singing Rocket into Gorilla Shield...right into Keelan's Broken Tree.

The ball of Keelan's foot caught Zayn right under the jaw, spinning him around. His legs went to liquid, and he collapsed on the ground.

"Augh, my jaw," said Zayn, rubbing it as he sat on the concrete. "That was a nice setup. You put it in my head with that comment of yours."

Keelan had his lips pursed to one side as he held his hand out. "You okay, cuz? I normally don't get you with traps like that, even good ones. You usually sniff them out like a dog after peanut butter."

"I'm fine," said Zayn as he let himself be pulled to standing. "You just got me good. That was some next-level stuff, planting a seed and then a double fake."

Keelan grabbed a towel from the edge of the half-pipe and wiped the glistening sweat from his face and chest.

"You know you ain't been right," said Keelan, eyeing him carefully. "What with the migraines and other mistakes, like O'Keefe's class. You normally ace that stuff."

"Oh, I know I'm in for it if you're falling back into an Alabama accent," said Zayn with a smile.

"Zayn," said Keelan with his head tilted, the corners of his eyes creased.

Zayn held his hands up. "I'm fine. I swear."

Keelan suddenly checked the time. "Crap. I'm going to be late for my session with O'Keefe. Later." He went jogging off towards the portal at the back of Empire Ink.

Zayn grabbed his water bottle and poured half of it down his throat while he contemplated his cousin's words. Keelan was right, he hadn't been feeling himself lately, and the migraines had been hitting him far too often to ignore. If one got him during an important moment, like when he'd been driving his motorcycle at two hundred plus, he might not survive. He was so busy thinking about taking a trip to Golden Willow that he didn't notice the figure standing on the edge of the skate pool until he'd turned completely around.

Zayn fell into a combat stance, relaxing only after recognizing the Watcher.

"Watcher Sabrina," said Zayn. "I almost didn't recognize you in your disguise."

Watcher Sabrina's lips crinkled and then she touched her fingertips to her temple where her sunglasses normally resided.

"It's too dark for them," said Sabrina, though Zayn knew it for a lie. They wore their sunglasses day or night in Varna. He guessed that whatever psychic link the Lady had on her Watchers, it didn't work at this distance.

Zayn sprinted up the side of the pool, grabbed the edge, and swung himself onto the upper portion, landing right next to her. Sabrina was in her early thirties, with long dark hair and a pale complexion. She was one of the youngest Watchers allowed to have a public face for the Lady. Zayn guessed it was due to her lanky attractiveness.

"What's in the box?" he asked, nodding towards the steel cage at her feet.

"I'll get to that in a moment," said Sabrina, her eyes searching around as if she were uncomfortable standing in a public place.

"You haven't been outside Varna in a long time, have you?" he asked.

She blinked hard. "No. First time since I graduated."

"Feel good to be back?" he asked.

A frown tugged on the corners of her lips as she glanced around. "The city is different now. More run-down, more tourists, more trash on the street. I remember this skate park. It overflowed with skaters in the evening, but now it doesn't look like it's been used in years."

"You were here before Invictus died?" he asked.

She nodded. "I graduated...well, I graduated before."

He took the hint that maybe she was older than he'd first

thought.

"So, to what do I owe the pleasure of your visit?" he asked with a smile.

Sabrina's lips thinned. "Her Ladyship sent me to collect what information you have for her."

"Oh, yes," he said, feeling a little hollow around the middle. He'd known this moment was coming, but he hadn't expected a surprise early morning visit. He supposed that was the best way to ensure his cooperation.

"What information do you have about your...target?" asked Sabrina.

The hesitation suggested that Sabrina still had respect for her former patron, but Zayn wasn't fooled that she wasn't beholden to her new master.

"I haven't really seen her much," said Zayn, leaving Priyanka's name out of it in case she had magical censors listening for her name.

"That's not how this works," said Sabrina, her dark eyes surveying him keenly.

"There's a group of dragons threatening the school. They claim they could take it over," said Zayn.

"She doesn't care about external threats. She only cares about herself," said Sabrina. "Now, do you have any information in that regard?"

"I don't know..."

"Remember, you're the one that asked for this," said Sabrina sternly.

He knew. He hated the idea of having freedom for himself, but not for his family, but now that he was presented with the idea that he had to betray Priyanka for that privilege, an oily regret coiled around his midsection.

There was also the fear that this was a setup by Priyanka and the Lady. He'd never quite determined their relationship, but he knew it was possible that Priyanka was fully on board with the arrangement, due to the regular flow of students she received. In either case, spying on her felt problematic. Maybe this whole thing was a test.

"There is one thing that she let slip..."

"Wait," said Sabrina, leaning down to grab the metal box. "I need to make sure you're telling the truth."

When she lifted off the metal shield, Zayn's heart leapt into his throat. Inside a wire cage was a scorpion the size of his hand with a vicious stinger held above its segmented body.

"This is a—"

"Deathhead scorpion," finished Zayn.

She wrinkled her forehead. "You've seen one before?"

"Unfortunately, yes. I was with Priyanka on a job a few years ago," said Zayn.

Sabrina gave him a second glance, as if she hadn't been expecting that news. She hesitated before shaking her head momentarily.

"Well, then you know the severity of its sting. One hit from that tail and you'll be in agonizing pain for decades."

Sabrina pulled out a steel ring and placed it on her finger. She whispered a command word and runes glowed on the back of the deathhead scorpion.

"This particular deathhead has been enchanted to detect lies," she said.

"How specific do I have to be?" he asked.

She skewed her mouth to one side. "Are you planning on lying?"

"No. No. But what if I don't explain the exact color of wallpaper, or something trivial like that?" said Zayn.

She took a breath as she considered his words. "It doesn't work like that. It detects if you believe the words or not. Much like a polygraph, but more accurate."

Sabrina opened the cage, which made Zayn take a step back.

"It's okay. I'm controlling the deathhead with this ring," said Sabrina.

"That doesn't make me feel any better," said Zayn.

"Put your hand in the cage, rest it right in front of the deathhead," said Sabrina. "It won't move a bit."

A light sweat broke out on his forehead. If he hadn't seen what the creature could do, he might not have been so nervous. As slowly as he could, he moved his hand into the cage, readying to yank it out at the slightest twitch, but true to her word, the scorpion stayed immobile. Once his hand rested before the creature, he took his eyes off it and looked at Sabrina.

"What now?"

"The information," said Sabrina. "No lies."

It was hard to think with his hand in the cage, but he didn't know what he wanted to do. He hated the idea of double-crossing his patron, even though he'd given up his quest to kill the Lady. He'd thought that once he'd done that he was free from these kinds of decisions.

It didn't help that he liked Priyanka. He saw what she was trying to do, and supported that goal. What if this factoid led the Lady to turn against his patron? And at this delicate time with the Circle of the Scale, that could be catastrophic.

"What's with the delay?" asked Sabrina, frowning.

"Just want to make sure I get my facts right," said Zayn.

"Just tell the truth," said Sabrina.

He looked her in the eye. "What if this information isn't important enough?"

"Things can get worse for your family as easily as they can get better," she said, delivering the threat as if she'd done it a thousand times before. "It's entirely up to you."

"Yes, right," he said.

Pray this deal doesn't get any worse, he thought to himself, chuckling.

"Something funny?"

"Not particularly," he said, and took a breath.

"The information?"

"Right," he said. "When we were in Iceland, traveling to where the dragons were laired, she let something slip."

As he said the words, he thought, *Does she ever let something slip?*

He looked at his hand, and the proximity of the deathhead scorpion. Even at faez speed, he wouldn't be able to remove his hand before he got stung. Truth or pain? Should he tell the Watcher about Priyanka trying to copy the Lady's poison? Or something in between?

"Priyanka mentioned that she had been working with someone on a special project, something to do with the Lady's poison," said Zayn.

Both their gazes stayed trained on the scorpion. When the stinger didn't so much as twitch, he breathed a sigh of relief.

"Do you know any more about it?" she asked.

He looked Sabrina in the eye. "I'll try to learn more at our next meeting."

Sabrina paused. He'd purposely not answered her question, since he knew he couldn't do it truthfully. He worried that she'd guessed his game and he'd have to come clean, but then she nodded.

"Fair enough," she said. "You may take your hand out of the cage."

As soon as he was done, she closed the cage, locked it, and placed the metal shield around it.

Zayn was expecting Sabrina to say something, but she merely lifted the cage and started walking away.

"What now? What happens?"

"You passed your first test," said Sabrina. "Your family will receive some additional privileges, to be determined by the Lady. But next time I come back, you'd better have more information, detailed and significant."

"When will you come back?" he asked.

Sabrina let the hint of a grin curl the corners of her lips. "Soon."

Chapter Seven
Seventh Ward, October 2016
Tacowitch

Finding a parking spot for "Sojourner," Neveah's beloved food truck, took over two hours due to the fact that every time she found a good location in the second ward, a police officer told her that she couldn't park there before she could even get set up. Finally she asked the last one and he told her, "Not in the second ward unless you have a permit."

"What about the third?" she'd asked, but he told her not there either.

"Which one can I set up in?"

"None without a permit, but you can spend a few days in the seventh until you get one."

"Thanks," she said, but that was on the other side of the city, and by the time she made it there, she was running on fumes.

Neveah parked the food truck up the street from a section of apartment buildings. There weren't as many tourists as in the other areas of the ward, but she didn't think she could make it another block without running out of gas.

She climbed out of the driver's seat and took stock of her location. She'd been so busy trying to find a spot, she hadn't really registered that she was in the city of sorcery.

"Don't look like much," she said, though her skin tingled with a burgeoning excitement. The feeling doubled the moment she laid her eyes on the Spire, towering over the center of the city. It looked like a jewel punching through the clouds.

"Zayn was right, it really takes your breath away," she said.

But then she glanced at the food truck. Her father had painted a mural across the surface depicting Neveah as a mage in the kitchen using telekinetic powers to move the pots and pans around while starry-eyed customers stood outside stuffing overflowing tacos into their hungry mouths. Above her smiling face, the name of the business, "Kitchen Witch," was painted in stylized lettering.

"I'd better get to work, or this is gonna be a short trip."

Neveah threw on a backpack and went in search of the nearest grocery store. She bypassed three bodegas before she found a proper produce section. She only had a handful of bills left—the food truck had required a new transmission last month, draining her of funds—so she had to make it count.

She would have preferred to wow the locals with something they'd never eaten before, like her lamb tikki masala bowls, but she needed a cheap dish that would bring customers, and that dish was carnitas tacos.

When Neveah realized she could buy everything but the pork rump, she went to the butcher, a greasy-looking guy with a red-smudged apron.

"Do you have any cheaper cuts of pork shoulder?" she asked with her hands on the counter.

"You see what you get," he said in an Eastern European accent, gesturing towards the glass cases full of meat.

"Any way to get one on loan?" she asked, knowing how ridiculous it sounded.

"Loan? What kinda place you think we're running here? Whoever heard of a meat bank?" he said.

"I just got to town and I own a food truck," she said. "I just need a few days to get my feet under me. You sure you don't have anything?"

The butcher stared back blankly, and Neveah suddenly wished she had powers of persuasion like Zayn and Keelan. They could have snapped their fingers and the butcher would have handed over the meat.

"I might be able to help you out," he said, lowering his voice. "I got a piece that I was getting ready to throw out. If you cut the bad parts out, it should be fine. I'll sell it for next to nothing."

"Great," she said. "I can work with that."

He wrapped up the meat and priced it accordingly, and Neveah walked out of the grocery store with less than two dollars left to her name.

Back in the food truck, she set out the food she'd bought at the grocery store and put her hands on her head while she looked up at the photos she'd stuck above the steel window. Each picture showed her standing with her family, usually with their arms around each other. The one in the middle was her and Zayn sitting on top of the food truck with paint all over their clothes and smiles plastered on their faces.

When she opened up the package, a sour smell hit her nose. The pork shoulder roast had gone rancid, the whole side gray. The butcher should have never sold her the meat. She grabbed her cleaver and started hacking the bad parts off, hoping there was enough left to cook. When she was done, there was a great piece of pork shoulder with fatty marbling that would make for great flavor, but the problem was there wasn't enough left for even a dozen tacos.

"Great. What a waste of money," she said, shoving the cleaver back into its station.

Neveah wiped her forehead with the back of her hand. It was already getting hot inside the truck. She had air conditioning, but not enough gas to run it, so she opened up the customer window.

"Better think of something fast," she said, rummaging through her ingredients.

Neveah got to work right away—making something from nothing was a tried and true skill for those that grew up poor in the south. While her parents sometimes splurged and bought her the ingredients she needed for a full gourmet meal, most of the time she was operating on a tiny budget.

She chopped up onions and started cooking them down in a pan. She didn't have much meat, but caramelized onions would go a long way, plus they smelled great and would do half her advertising for her.

Then she placed the remaining pork shoulder into a saucepan, spicing it liberally to hide the lingering smell from the bad part. She preferred to smoke the meat, but she didn't have that option in the food truck like she did at home.

Next, she needed a way to stretch the pork. The cheapest way was to add oats or another grain, but that reduced the flavor, watering down the taco experience. Thankfully, she'd bought some potatoes with the idea that she'd make fresh chips, but that would have to be tabled for another day. After washing and scrubbing them, Neveah cut the potatoes into little squares, brushed them with butter, and flash cooked them in a hot skillet. Once they were cooked on each side, she set them on a tray to bake in the oven until they were soft, adding a little tarragon for color.

In between chopping up the cabbage for a sweet slaw, Neveah stood over the pork pan with a handful of salt. She'd never had the access to faez that her brother or cousin had, but she had enough to make a difference. Neveah concentrated, focusing deep inside herself, and blew the salt from her palm into the food, along with a hint of faez. She didn't remember when she'd first come up with this technique, it seemed like she'd always known about it, but it amplified the flavors in the food, especially for mages. There was a danger with an old piece of meat, but she was sure she'd cut away the bad parts. The salt-faez infusion would overcome the lingering smell and bring out the true flavor of the fatty meat.

Neveah was so deep into cooking, she didn't realize there were customers gathering in front of her food truck until she looked up to find a line of five people.

The man in front, a young businessman in a suit fidgeting with his tie, said when she caught his notice, "I'm sorry to bother you, but I have to get to work real soon and I don't know what you're cooking, but I'd like an order of it."

Neveah was aware that while she was in the middle of working, she could be a terror, so she made sure to let a smile bloom onto her lips. She'd learned from Zayn how to dial back her accent, but she left enough of it to color her words, to help with the image of her food truck.

"Gourmet Pork and Potato Tacos," she said, wishing she'd thought of a better name.

"How much?" he asked.

Neveah did quick math in her head, determining what kind of profit she needed to stay afloat, and gave him a price.

"I'll take three," he said right away, making her wonder if she could have asked for more.

She handed over a plate full of pork and potato tacos,

then dealt with the next customer, bouncing between the window and the grill. Before the businessman left, he shoved a ten-spot in her tip jar and gave her the thumbs-up.

After that, Neveah fell into a routine, ignoring the sweat rolling down her back in the hot truck. She didn't have an imbuement like Zayn, but she knew how to draw on the faez to give herself a little extra energy. It helped knowing that she wouldn't go mad from the faez, which was the only good thing about the Lady's poison.

The food truck had customers until the tacos ran out in the afternoon. There was a groan of disappointment from those in line that hadn't gotten any, so she promised them a discount if they came back the next day.

After chugging three glasses of water, Neveah cleaned up the kitchen, scrubbing every crack and crevasse. The worst thing about living in your kitchen was that everything ended up with a layer of grease on it, so she had to take extra time to clean up.

When she finished, she counted a decent profit. She'd have enough to buy groceries for the next day, plus extra she would save towards a permit. She wished she'd made enough to run the air conditioning, but that would have to wait. At least it was cooler in the north than in Alabama.

Neveah waited until the grocery store was about to close, making an offer on the cabbage and other vegetables that they were going to throw out. Nothing bad, just the stuff that needed a little trimming. She also bought a real pork shoulder, which she could let sit in spices overnight, and have enough to make tacos all day without running out.

By the time she got back to the food truck, she was bone-tired. After spicing the meat and placing it in the little refrigerator, she checked the propane. It was half full, which should be good for another week. But that was another expense she had to factor in.

Making the food truck work in the city was harder than she'd thought it'd be. She'd forgotten about all the little expenses she didn't have to worry about when living at home.

Neveah pulled out the cot that attached to the back wall, stripped down to her underclothes, and lay on her back. She'd slept in the food truck before, once on the way up, and another time when she'd first gotten it, but it seemed different, and not just because of why she'd come to the city of Invictus.

Once she finished planning out the next day's cooking, her thoughts turned to Zayn. Under normal circumstances, she could reach out to him and ask for help. The same was true of her parents.

She'd told them she was headed to Atlanta to prove herself, which was true, sort of. She did have the aching urge to leave Varna, not just for the obvious reasons, but to know the wilder world, and if she could survive in it. The size and scope of the city reminded her that she was a small-town girl who only felt comfortable in a kitchen, preferably the one at the Stack.

But that wasn't the only reason she'd come to the Hundred Halls. She wanted to figure out what was going on with Zayn. Something had happened to him last year. While he was the same brother she'd always known, there was something different going on underneath, as if he were unconsciously hiding something. When he nearly fell off the Stack on account of a piercing migraine, she'd known she had to get to the bottom of it.

Once she'd been given the okay to leave Varna, along with the extra doses of poison, she knew exactly where she was going—the city of sorcery.

Neveah was so busy thinking about her brother, and all the strange things from the summer, that she didn't register the click of the back door opening, thinking it was a random noise from the street. It wasn't until she heard the clacking of claws along the wall that she realized the noises were coming from inside the food truck.

She sat up quickly, catching a group of small creatures in the act of looting her kitchen. They were shiny black with feathers and a beak like a raven, but a body like a squirrel with a big bushy tail. One of them had the pork shoulder in its paws, while the others had handfuls of cabbage or tomatoes. A host of clicking erupted from their beaks, a signal for retreat.

The gestures for a Five Elements wind spear came to her fingers, but she was out of practice, and the spell fizzled into a light breeze, giving the creatures the opportunity to flee out the back door.

Neveah burst onto the street in her underclothes. The creatures scattered in all directions, scampering away in bounding motions with her foodstuffs in their possession.

The one with the pork shoulder was having a harder time escaping, so Neveah attempted the wind spear again, firing it successfully the second time.

She knocked the pork shoulder from its grasp.

The spiced meat tumbled towards the sewer. She tried to ignore the fact she was in her underclothes as she ran forward.

Neveah stumbled to her knees, right as the hunk of meat disappeared into the hole.

She stared into the darkness. Even if she could somehow rescue it, there was no way she would ever consider cooking it.

A frothing rage filled her chest. Neveah slammed her fist onto the curb.

She was glad she didn't know any destructive magic, because she would have blown up a few cars at that point. When the fury subsided, she was left with a teary hollowness.

A car turned onto the street, forcing Neveah to jump back

into her food truck. Once inside, she took stock of her remaining supplies, only to find the raven-like creatures had devastated her stock.

Neveah sat in silence with her head in her hands for a good portion of the night. Once she realized she needed to sleep, she found a chain inside her toolbox, and barred the back door from the inside. Only after she checked the locks on the other entry points did she try to sleep. When at last she felt the weight of slumber upon her, the sky lightened and a nimbus of morning stretched across the eastern horizon. She put on a fresh pair of clothes and climbed onto the roof of the food truck, watching the sunlight turn the Spire into a sparkling jewel. When the sun had passed above the three-story apartment buildings to the east, Neveah climbed back into the food truck. It was a new day to work.

Chapter Eight
Undercity, November 2016
Not a mood ring

"Wake up."

Zayn rubbed his eyes, knocking away the sleep.

"Are you awake?" asked Priyanka, standing at the end of his bed with one hand on her hip. She was wearing her black leather jacket.

He was suddenly aware that he wasn't wearing anything and the thin blanket barely covered him.

"Uhm, yeah."

"Good, we have work to do," said Priyanka, looking annoyed. "Grab your stuff and meet me at the portal."

"Stuff? Where are we going? What do I need? And isn't it three in the morning?" he asked as he pulled the blanket over his midsection.

Her gaze danced downward, resulting in a frown. "It wasn't three where I was, and if you're looking for a nine-to-five job, you shouldn't have joined the Academy."

The brisk tone surprised Zayn. He nodded and climbed out of bed as she left the room. He threw on his clothes and grabbed a travel pack he kept by the bed in case of emergencies. Last year's class with Instructor Minoan had taught him to be prepared.

When he reached the portal room, the corners of her eyes creased as she noticed the travel pack. He *hoped* it was a good sign, but her sour mood didn't change.

Priyanka handed him a list. "Memorize these. They're the passwords for the Garden Network. Since you're going to be working with me, I want you to be able to move around the city without me needing to hold your hand."

"What about the Academy portals?"

"They won't give you the access that the patron portals have," said Priyanka.

He looked at the list of dozens of passwords, then back up at her. "Now?"

She blinked, before nodding. "Here's a trick. Let a little faez flow through the paper, as if you were preparing it for an enchantment, then as the ink catches the golden glow fix the paper in your mind. You can memorize lists and other sorted information easily that way."

The flow of faez tingled as it went through his hand into the paper. When the ink lines glistened gold, he locked it in his mind. Afterwards, he found the information at the tip of his tongue.

"Don't try that with a spellbook, or the spell might think you're trying to cast it." She nodded towards the obsidian arch. "Take this into the sixth ward, and then to the Museum of Magical Artifacts. There's a Garden Network node behind it, use the password to get you past the gate. Take it to the Undercity portal near the earth well." She tapped on the paper near a password halfway down the list. "I'll meet you there. I have to pick up something along the way."

Zayn didn't know if she was testing him, or if she really had to grab something, but he left right away. He assumed it was the latter, since she'd been gone so much lately. It seemed like she'd only just returned this evening.

"Remember, you asked for this," he said as he made his way through the glistening streets towards the restaurant. It'd rained earlier in the day after a long dry spell, so the streets looked oily in the neon-lit darkness.

The Garden Network archway was surrounded by manicured lavender bushes as if the patrons sat around and drank tea before going through the portals. It was quite a bit different than the maintenance tunnels and janitor closets that the Academy students used.

Vertigo hit him a little harder than usual on the trip into the Undercity. Using portals in quick succession only made the nausea worse. He'd heard stories of upperclassman holding races, the winner making it through all the Academy portals in a specific order. The hard part wasn't the speed, but staying upright after a few trips.

The air had a musty smell, almost claustrophobic. He didn't get to see the reason why until he used the darkvision spell that Priyanka had taught him in Iceland. The underground cavern bloomed into grays and white and blacks, revealing a field of chest-high mushrooms surrounding a circular wall in which the Garden Network resided. The giant fungi looked like squat huts only large enough for a child.

Zayn waited for ten minutes before curiosity tugged him into the mushroom field. He pulled a knife from a hidden sheath along his ankle and placed the tip against the spongy flesh of a giant mushroom.

"I wouldn't do that if I were you," said Priyanka from behind him. "If you disturb them, they'll spray you with itchy spores. You'll think you've had the worst case of poison ivy that you've ever had in your life."

Warmth grew in his cheeks. Zayn was glad the darkvision hid his blushing. He slipped the knife back into the sheath.

"Follow me. Be careful not to jostle the mushrooms, or you'll trigger the spores," she said.

After contorting their way through the fungus field, they cut through a large cavern. Priyanka seemed to know which way she wanted to go even though there was no visible path. Within ten minutes, Zayn was sure there was no way he'd be able to find his way back to the Garden Network portal.

He had questions, but her pace gave him no opportunity to ask them. Their path kept them going deeper into the Undercity. Priyanka never once looked conflicted, taking turns and passageways confidently as if she'd done it a thousand times.

The whole way he kept looking for opportunities to talk to his patron. He needed more information for the Lady, or things would get worse for his family.

Finally, Zayn couldn't take it any longer, and moved beside her as the cavern opened up.

"I have a few questions," he said.

"Contrary to popular belief, sometimes it does hurt to ask," she said, increasing their pace.

Realizing there wasn't going to be a good time on the journey, he pressed his question. "In Iceland you told me that Celesse had once tried to copy the Lady's poison. Why couldn't she do it? It seems like someone of her skill should be able to copy a simple liquid."

"Which suggests it's not simple," said Priyanka. "I'm not sure I like this line of questioning."

"I know you've warned me away from questions about Varna, but don't you think I might want to know more about something as important as that?" he asked.

She stopped cold, her eyes narrowing to a point. "The only thing that matters is that it didn't work and that was a long time ago."

"But technology has improved," said Zayn. "Couldn't she try again?"

Priyanka's jaw pulsed with thought. When she spoke, it came out as sharp as a razor. "If you had access to this substitute poison, what would you do with it?"

He suddenly felt like he'd wandered onto a frozen lake and realized the ice wasn't as thick as he'd thought. Once again, he tendered the thought that the Lady was testing his loyalty, and Priyanka was in on it.

"Nothing," he said and realizing that wouldn't satisfy her added, "but maybe it could help the Lady by not having to produce so much."

Instead of answering him, she marched into the darkness, forcing Zayn to hurry to keep up.

Another two hours passed before Priyanka paused. The air had grown warmer even though they were much deeper below ground.

"Something wrong?" he asked, relishing the chance to speak again.

"There are two ways to the earth well," said Priyanka, frowning. "One of them is safer but it takes longer. The other is shorter but adds a level of danger."

"I'm sure whatever lies on that path can't be that bad," said Zayn. "I saw you take on a dragon."

Priyanka raised an eyebrow at him, acknowledging his naked attempt at flattery.

"In human form, and technically I lost, but I think they wanted to talk to me regardless of the result." Priyanka sighed. "I'm not worried about myself, but you. It would hardly be good form if I let my only mentee in years perish in the Under-city on an errand."

"I'm up for the challenge," he said eagerly.

"Truthfully, I would normally go the other way but I'm exhausted. I haven't slept in a week and I'd like nothing more than to curl into a ball on my bed and forget about my endless responsibilities."

Zayn had always seen Priyanka in a different light, as if she were a demigod or supernatural being beyond the realms of mortals, but the hint of frustration mixed with exhaustion and loneliness reminded him that she was flesh and blood like him.

"Are you sure you're up to it?" she asked.

"Absolutely."

"Okay, but no complaining if you're dead," she said with a wink, before forging ahead into the darkness.

The passage led them to an oblong cavern filled with sta-lactites. Somewhere inside, he heard the dripping of water.

Priyanka motioned toward her ear, indicating he should imbue his senses. When he did, he heard the patient clicking of claws on stone, even though he couldn't see anything. After a few minutes of watching but seeing nothing, she pulled him out of the cavern.

"What was in there?" he asked quietly.

"Modrats," she said. "They use psychic camouflage to project a false image into your mind, rendering them invisible, at least until they swarm you and pick your body clean while you are calmed. Then you can see them, but you won't care."

"That's nasty," he said.

"Wishing we'd gone the other way yet?"

Zayn glanced back the way they'd come. "No, not yet."

"Good," she said, looking more awake than she had the whole journey. "So what's your plan for getting us through this?"

He opened his mouth to complain, but realized she was testing him.

"How many are there and how do their abilities work?" he asked.

"Hundreds. Each one is no bigger than a normal rat," said Priyanka. "They project their psychic camouflage passively, but calm emotions actively. If they don't notice you, they won't try to subdue you and eat you."

"Do we use the Veil?" he asked.

"It's an option, but not a good one. It's a large cavern, and the modrats are spread out. You'd have to faez-sprint to get through it, and that would likely draw their attention," she said. "Plus the Veil wouldn't protect you from their psychic ability."

"Burn them out with flame spells?" he asked, squinting regretfully because he already knew the answer. "How about...?"

"Remember to use everything you've got. You should have had O'Keefe's improvisation class already. Expand your thinking," she said.

Zayn kept it to himself that he'd failed that class. He looked around, considering the items he had in his travel pack. Nothing came to mind that would help until he was scratching the back of his head, thinking while staring at the ceiling. He was marveling at the craggy nature of the cavern when he had an idea.

"Can we go over them? Climb up that wall and use those stalactites to make our way to the other side?" he asked.

With her hands on her hips, Priyanka looked up only using her eyes. She nodded. "Sounds like a good workout. You go first. I'll follow."

The rocky wall had enough handholds that he could climb to the space where the ceiling began. He reached out, placing a sneaker against a stalactite, making sure it was solid, before using it to spring towards a protrusion in the wall.

With Priyanka behind him, Zayn patiently made his way across the cavern, testing each spot before relying on it to hold his weight. One slip and either the fall or the modrats would kill him.

Halfway across, he found a ledge that could fit the both of them to rest. Zayn shook out his forearms, which trembled with the effort of vertical climbing for a hundred feet.

Zayn wasn't ready to move, but Priyanka tapped on his shoulder. He nodded, leaned out to the next stalactite, and kept moving.

Nearing the exit of the cave, he reached out to grab a rocky edge only to have the stone crumble away beneath his fingers, cascading down the wall, sounding like a mini-avalanche. Off-balance, Zayn threw himself to the next handhold. The limestone shifted under his weight but held him.

As he clung to the wall, a host of squeaking erupted beneath him. He felt their minds searching, pinging off his consciousness like they were echolocating for him. The pressure on his thoughts triggered the beginnings of a migraine. The tightening of his mind, like a giant vise was squeezing his head, turned his magic-aided vision to darkness.

He felt his fingers slip from the rock, his weight sag towards the ground. As the pain pummeled his consciousness, Zayn fought through it, focusing what little thought he could muster into his fingers to convince them to hold on.

Tap.

Tap.

Tap. Tap.

Zayn looked up, realizing he still clung to the wall. Priyanka was beside him, tapping him on the shoulder, eyes wide with worry. Her forehead wrinkled with questions, but he shook her off.

The modrats hadn't given up trying to find him, but their psychic echolocating had moved elsewhere in the cavern.

Zayn reached out, grabbed a new handhold, and made his way the rest of the way across the ceiling. Outside the cavern, he made his way to the floor, relishing the stability of his own two feet.

"What was that back there?" she asked.

He hesitated, but knew he couldn't lie to her. "A migraine. I've been getting them lately. Pushing myself too hard I think."

Her eyes searched him as if she were trying to figure out if he were obfuscating, but eventually she nodded, patted him on the shoulder, and said, "Come on, only a little bit further."

The passage sloped downward at an ever-increasing angle. His nose itched with the presence of faez, the source of which he couldn't determine, but it seemed to be increasing the deeper they went. During the final part of the descent, Zayn thought he was going to have to slide in on his rear, but the passage opened up, revealing a vast cavern.

His breath caught in his throat, not because there was too much faez in the cavern—although there was—but because he couldn't believe what he was seeing. When Priyanka had told him they were going to visit the earth well, he'd been expecting a hole in the ground.

But this wasn't a hole, and technically, it wasn't really in the ground. What it was, was one of the most impressive and frightening things he'd ever laid eyes upon.

Chapter Nine
Well of Power, November 2016
Man can dig a well, but they can't make magic

The wells of power weren't in any pamphlets about the Hundred Halls, nor were they studied in any classes. Before Zayn had gone to Iceland, he'd heard of them, but only as a rumor, a conspiracy—a place one could go and tap into a font of faez so large it would tear one apart—and he hadn't believed in them then. Even after the visit to the dragons, Zayn had thought them simple holes in the earth, places where faez collected, not fortresses of steel and runes.

"This is the earth well," said Priyanka with uncharacteristic awe in her voice. "It's always impressive no matter how many times I lay my eyes upon it."

"Well," said Zayn. "You keep using the word *well*, but I don't think that word fits."

Priyanka chuckled. "A fair point, but these places had humble beginnings when the term *well* did apply."

It was hard for Zayn to even really look at it. The runes glowing on the massive steel cylinder burned so bright they were like looking at the sun. The whole structure sat in a depression at the center of the cavern. He assumed the cylinder was capped at the top because runes glowed against the ceiling.

He was craning his neck when a flare billowed from the side, licking off the stone, turning the air to a prism of colors before dissipating, as if magic itself warped the air. Moments later, his skin prickled, and the overwhelming scent of faez made him want to choke. It was a few seconds before he could breathe again.

"Few people have seen these besides patrons and those we trust," said Priyanka, raising an eyebrow.

"Why do I sense you're going to ask me to do something incredibly dangerous?" said Zayn.

Priyanka quirked a smile. "I knew I picked you for a reason—your instincts are impeccable."

"The rest of the team told me I would regret picking you as a mentor," said Zayn, chuckling. "So what is this place? A 'well of power' sounds properly ominous, but what is it?"

"As I've explained before, the membrane between our realm and others is thin in Invictus. No place is thinner than down here, and unfortunately, the realm it borders is not a pleasant one."

"The demonic horde," said Zayn, remembering Ne Yong's comment.

"Invictus picked this location for the city because it naturally improved the power of its mages. It was the best place to master our fates. Unfortunately, the more we use magic, the weaker the barrier becomes. Invictus was working on fixing the barrier before he died," said Priyanka, gaze flitting to the cylinder as if she were looking for something.

"Which is why the dragons want to take control of the city," said Zayn, slowly understanding. "They want to keep us from weakening it any further."

The reality hit him in the gut. They wouldn't want to just run the school, they'd probably shut it down, or put restrictions on it, to keep them from breaking the barrier. And did they have a point?

"Exactly," said Priyanka, pulling a brass vial from an inside pocket. "There are four wells. Earth, water, fire, and air. This is the earth well."

"Earth, water, fire, air," repeated Zayn. "Just like the Five Elements, minus force."

Priyanka's right eye twitched momentarily as if he'd said something important. "We need to check the runes to see how the capstone is holding up."

"The royal 'we,'" said Zayn, making air quotes with his fingers.

Priyanka shoved the brass vial into his midsection, before looking back to the cylinder.

"Yes, you're going to get a sample of the off gas," she said.

Another flare rolled off the runed cylinder, scorching the ceiling.

"Don't worry," she added, "those are like fumes being burnt off at an oil well."

"You sound like my doctor when he told me my tetanus shot wouldn't hurt, but I was bruised for three days," said Zayn.

"Don't worry. I'll be protecting you from the off-faez. While you take the sample, I'll be standing back here keeping you safe with a linked enchantment," she said, but her glance towards the cylinder told him she wasn't finished explaining the dangers.

When he turned to look, he saw what appeared to be a

giant rainbow snake with a sloth-like face, scales occasionally sparking with electricity. It pulled itself around the runed cylinder on tiny stunted legs.

"Is that a kwalic?" he asked in horror.

"It is."

"How did it get to be so big?" asked Zayn with his mouth hanging open.

"They grow bigger in the ocean, and this one is much larger than its brethren due to its proximity to so much faez. It's the guardian Invictus placed here to protect the well from mischief," said Priyanka.

His breath caught in his throat again. The last time he'd tangled with a kwalic, it'd nearly killed him. And this one was fifty times its size. Zayn marshalled his courage, looking back to Priyanka with grim determination.

"So how do we do this?" he asked.

Priyanka stared him straight in the eyes. "The giant kwalic can easily sense human clothing, so you're going to have to do this naked."

"Wha—"

Zayn imagined himself creeping over the rocks towards the giant electricity-emitting snake guarding a massive runed cylinder that protected the city from falling into the demonic realm. Somehow this last bit of news seemed worse than everything else.

"I have to be naked?" he asked, incredulous.

"Of course not," said Priyanka, patting him on the arm. "But you looked as tight as a drum. If you tried to go up there like that, the kwalic would toast you like a marshmallow."

"Oh, thank Merlin," said Zayn. "I'm not sure why, but the dying *naked* part seemed much worse than the dying part."

"Naked is always preferable to dying," said Priyanka. "Embarrassment is something you can get over. Death is not."

"Says the centuries-old woman," said Zayn.

"One never talks about a lady's age." She wrinkled her nose as she stared intently at him. "You know, I've had many mentees over the years, but they've always treated me with a mix of deference and horror. You're not afraid of me."

He made a face that she must have interpreted as concern, so she added, "Please, this is not a bad thing. I enjoy having a human conversation from time to time. My peers are not what they used to be."

Zayn searched his thoughts. "I don't know. I guess I never thought about it. My mom and dad, Maceo and Sela, always encouraged us to engage. All my childhood, we had important conversations around the dinner table. They cared what we thought, made us feel like we had a voice. I guess I see you like I do my parents."

Priyanka's eyes widened with a glassy sheen. She looked away. "I think that's the nicest thing anyone has said to me in a long time. Thank you, Zayn."

"You're welcome."

Priyanka focused her attention on the runed cylinder. "Let's get this over with."

Preparation took about ten minutes. A mixture of gold dust and black walnut hull powder created an ink that she used to draw on both their arms. The matching runes were of a style that seemed vaguely familiar though he had no specific knowledge about its origin.

While she drew the runes on them, Zayn felt his connection with his patron grow deeper. It made him feel more content with his decision to give up his quest to kill Lady Arcadia. He would do his best to make good with his time in the Academy of the Subtle Arts, and the task ahead was a good example of why he was needed.

When she was finished, he asked, "Why can't I slip into

the Veil to reach the cylinder?"

"You could, but you'd have to come out to take the sample, and the kwalic would kill you before you could get back into the Veil," she explained.

"Gotcha. Good to know. What about my fourth imbuement?" he asked.

"Keep that as a backup plan for now. You won't be able to get near enough to absorb its pheromone before it would attack you," she said.

"Then what will I do?"

"You know the trick with the kwalic, right? Create a fiction in your mind that matches what you want to do," she said.

He lifted one shoulder in a throwaway shrug. "I'm just on a stroll, no big deal. I'm just moseying around to get a cup of water from that large fountain over there."

"Good," she said, patting him on the arm. "I'll be protecting you from the well from back here. Let's get this and get back to the surface. I'll buy breakfast, or whatever meal it is up there."

"Breakfast it is, though I should warn you I can eat enough bacon and pancakes to put a dent in your bank account," he said.

"Try me."

Zayn readied himself to approach the well of power. He took a minute to set the fiction in his mind. He imagined a pristine park filled with towering oaks and happy picnickers on the lawn, surrounding a gorgeous fountain.

Once the idea was fixed firmly in his thoughts, and the kwalic had moved to the far side of the well, he strolled forward, keeping his chest light and his arms swinging as if he didn't have a care in the world. He resisted the urge to whistle, but let a meandering tune circulate through his mind.

The runed steel cylinder was further away than he had

originally thought, the whole structure growing larger upon approach. The air thickened like an Alabama summer day, heat rolling from it in waves. When he was closer than a hundred feet, the air around him spit sparks, as if the energies from the well were impacting with an invisible shield around him.

Even with Priyanka's linked enchantment, sweat beaded onto his forehead and spilled into his eyes. He dared not wipe it away, imagining instead the cool spring day in his mind.

When he reached the well, the air vibrated with power and gagged him with potency. He couldn't wait to get away, but he had a job to do first. Calmly, he produced the brass vial, pressed the opening against the cylinder, and let the collection device do its thing. When he felt a click in the palm of his hand, he removed it from the surface and placed it back into his pocket.

When he turned, he checked to see if the kwalic was near, but the massive cylinder hid the location of the guardian, which was the best possible sign. Putting the well at his back brought a sense of relief that he would survive his dangerous task. Keeping the fiction of the sunlit park firmly in his mind, he strode back towards Priyanka on the far side of the cavern, looking forward to the moment when he was out of the oppressive heat.

Zayn was only a few steps away when he heard a light squeaking from somewhere ahead, along with a pinging against his consciousness.

Oh no, he thought.

Some of the modrats had followed him into the cavern. He didn't think it was enough to directly harm him, but their presence endangered him.

Even without looking over his shoulder, he sensed the kwalic nearing by the hairs on the back of his neck standing at attention.

Zayn froze.

He heard a throaty reverberation from the direction of the kwalic, like a strange growl. The creature had spotted him.

He was trapped with nowhere to run.

Chapter Ten
Well of Power, November 2016
The strands of the future

Zayn took stock of his situation. Priyanka was still too far away to help, and he was close enough to the well that she couldn't stop protecting him. Even now he could see her arms moving as she kept up the linked enchantment.

The modrats, maybe a dozen he guessed by the strength of their mental signature, were between him and Priyanka. The heat and presence of the kwalic was keeping them from getting closer, but he couldn't get past them without getting calmed. He thought about the Veil, but the modrats could affect him there, so he marked that option off.

But the kwalic, immune to the effects of the well, stalked him from his back right. The only thing saving him so far was that it was distracted by the presence of the modrats. Without turning his head too much, he could see the kwalic's sloth-like head looking at him, then back to the place where the modrats were located.

He was stuck.

Hoping that he could avoid the kwalic's final attention, Zayn kept up the fiction of the park in his mind, but it was hard with the crackles of electricity emanating from the scaly creature.

He tried using his imbuement, but as soon as he thought about absorbing the essence of the kwalic, it growled, suggesting that its prophetic protection extended to his magic.

Deciding that doing nothing was worse than doing something, he decided to try moving away.

I'm on a stroll, he reminded himself. *A stroll.*

Since the kwalic was coming up on his right, he moved to the left, angling away from the cylinder and the modrats towards the cavern wall, which was nearer on that side. The modrats psychic pinging grew frenzied.

He couldn't see them directly, but figured out generally where they were based on a hazy area of the rocky cavern floor. Their psychic ability hid their location, but it couldn't falsify what he was seeing perfectly.

If he could get far enough away from the cylinder, then Priyanka could help him, but the modrats seemed to sense his intent and moved to cut him off.

When a host of prickles rose against Zayn's back, he knew the kwalic had decided that he should be its next meal. Electricity crackled around him as he broke into a faez-imbued run.

With the well on his left, the modrats on his right, and the kwalic in pursuit, he had no choice but to sprint forward. Zayn spied a gap in the wall ahead, and hoped it went somewhere, because if it didn't he was going to have to turn and fight.

He flew into the space ahead of the modrats, who easily followed him into the passage. The kwalic, enraged by his escape, flew in after him.

He heard the wide body slam against the tight walls, felt the electricity against his skin. A few psychic signatures popped like soap bubbles. Zayn assumed the kwalic had pulverized a few modrats with its girth as it overtook them.

When the walls opened back up, he knew he was in trouble. The kwalic was much faster than he expected. Glancing back he saw that it had abandoned its forearms and slithered ahead on its hardened scales.

He was running nearly blind, as his eyes hadn't adjusted back to his black-and-white vision. He tried to use his sensing imbuement, but his faez was focused on escape, so he had to use his normal senses to guess at the twists and turns of the passage, praying he didn't hit a low-hanging stalactite and knock himself out.

He'd put a little distance between himself and the kwalic when he felt the floor fall away.

"No!"

His arms and legs pinwheeled as he fell.

Uhmph.

Fears that he would fall forever quickly silenced when he slammed onto a hard slope. He barely kept conscious as he tumbled downward, sliding in a rocky scree for what felt like ten minutes.

When at last he tumbled to rest, he didn't move, mostly because every part of his body ached, and to protect himself from the kwalic's psychic ability, Zayn let his mind blank out as much as he could.

Zayn sensed the snake-like creature somewhere far above, but none of the soft pings from the modrats. They must have been crushed or shocked into oblivion by the kwalic.

After a time, the presence disappeared, and Zayn was left alone. He didn't quite want to get up, but he knew the Undercity was too dangerous to just lie around, especially in the deep sections, so he renewed his darkvision spell.

As the world bloomed in around him, he suddenly realized how lucky he'd been. Zayn lay next to a deep cliff. During his fall, he'd crossed a crevasse, landing on the far side and sliding to the edge. A few feet more and he would have been lost to the depths.

Zayn took a few moments to check for wounds, and realized he'd lost his travel pack. He was beat up and bloody, but no bones were broken, and he'd miraculously not knocked himself out.

He figured out pretty quickly that Priyanka, even if she could find him, wasn't going to be able to help. And it was doubtful that she would tangle with the kwalic. He'd have to get out of the Undercity on his own.

The upward slope was difficult to traverse due to the slippery scree, but there were enough handholds that Zayn kept himself from sliding back down. He made it to a cliff face, and carefully climbed up until he could stand.

The cavern he stood in had multiple exits, none of them heading back the way he'd come, so Zayn picked one at random and started walking.

Keeping his sensing imbuement on high, Zayn made his way through passages and tunnels, avoiding any presences he detected. He chose the ways that led upward, but sometimes he had to backtrack.

After a few hours, he felt like he was no closer to finding his way out, his belly was rumbling, and his mouth was dry. He'd heard distant water a few times, but never came anywhere near it.

Zayn stopped frequently, especially at any junction, to listen for signs of other creatures or water. This practice saved him.

He hadn't heard the spider, because it moved on eight silent feet, but he recognized it right away when it meandered into view, perched on an outcropping like a scout. He'd been about to walk into the cavern that the spider had come from.

Zayn leaned back into the shadows, hoping the spider wouldn't notice him.

He was rewarded for his caution when another half dozen spiders ambled into view. It looked like the pack was on a hunting mission.

As the scout approached his hiding position, Zayn recognized the spider.

Achaeranea Magicaencia.

Magic Eaters.

It was the same genus of spider that had trapped him and Keelan in the cave where they'd found Jesse's body.

He'd had no idea that any of the spiders lived outside of Varna.

The spider, about five inches in diameter, scurried past him with the others following. Zayn squeezed himself as far into the cubby as he could.

Before long, they disappeared the way he'd come, but Zayn didn't let himself relax. Magicaencia lived in large colonies. Where there were a few, there were many.

And the scouting party had gone the way he'd come from, which meant going backwards was out of the question. Which was probably for the best, since he'd traveled that passage for a good ways. He hated the idea of having to go back and find a new way to the surface.

Zayn crept ahead carefully, stopping at each corner to check for magic-eating spiders before continuing. He crossed a small cavern with stagnant water, which only made his thirst worse.

At the next turn, a passage opened up into a larger cavern. What he saw inside made his heart skip a beat. In the far corner, a massive web covered the wall, shimmering in an unseen breeze. It looked like the sail of an ancient pirate ship.

Crawling over it were hundreds of the spiders. A pit opened up in his stomach. This was the only way forward. But there was no way he wanted to go in.

Shaking his head, Zayn backtracked. He didn't want to add another couple of hours onto his journey, but he also didn't want to go through a cavern full of spiders that his magic would only make worse.

But when he neared the corner, he caught sight of the scout returning. Which meant the others were right behind.

Not good, he thought.

He considered using the Veil to slip past them, but he didn't know if their ability to eat magic might extend into the otherworldly realm, especially when he had to activate the imbuement with faez.

Zayn backed up into the larger cavern, checking his immediate location for spiders. The web was far enough away that they didn't see him. He quickly surveyed the room, looking for other exits, spotting a ledge on the far wall, high above the floor.

Thankfully, it was on the opposite side of the web, so Zayn crept that direction, being extra careful at each step not to dislodge a rock and draw the attention of the spider. He moved with slow-motion surety until he reached a rocky wall.

This would be the most dangerous part of the escape. When he'd first come into the room, the web was mostly blocked by the curvature of the wall, but once he started climbing, he'd be exposed. He had no idea what kind of vision the critters had, and he really didn't want to find out, but he wasn't going to have a choice if he wanted to leave.

Zayn climbed the cliff, moving at sloth-like speed, which

strained his muscles since he couldn't use his imbuement for strength. But the years of training had hardened his muscles and he made it to the top without incident, though afterwards his limbs quivered with exhaustion.

All those times Instructor Allgood had cracked them in the head during sparring sessions, reminding them that not every problem could be solved with magic, came back to him. He planned on giving the grouchy instructor a kiss on the forehead next time he saw him.

The ledge led out of the cavern, but Zayn took a moment to catch his breath and let his muscles loosen up. He was a little dehydrated, and he didn't want to cramp. He was also curious about the spiders since they were connected to his hometown.

He watched in absolute silence, picking up the way the spiders interacted with each other. The colony operated like a small city. Scouting parties left through small tunnels in the back of the cavern, returning with small prey like ordinary rats. Other spiders repaired the massive web, which acted not as a trap for unsuspecting creatures, but as a home. The web had hundreds of grooves, like the funnel of a trap spider, which the critters disappeared into, as if they were ants in an ant farm.

He was impressed at their community, which seemed unlike anything he'd ever seen before. He'd thought most spiders were solitary hunters, but these *achaeranea magicaencia* seemed to be one big family.

Eventually Zayn's muscles relaxed enough for him to leave. He made note of his location, hoping to find his way back at a later date, bringing Keelan if he could, as he'd enjoy seeing the colony.

Ten minutes later, as he worked his way through a ravine, he heard a voice calling his name. He replied, and then saw

Priyanka's smiling face peering over the edge.

"I see you survived well enough," said Priyanka.

"You wouldn't happen to have any water up there, I think my tongue is sticking to the roof of my mouth," he said.

"Hurry up and it's all yours."

Zayn made leaping jumps up the side of the ravine, utilizing his imbuement to make it over the edge easily. When the cool water hit his lips, he thought it was the best thing he'd ever tasted. He chugged half the bottle before he heard Priyanka clear her throat.

"Uhm, sorry."

"No worries, but don't get a cramp." Her forehead wrinkled. "Did you get the sample?"

Zayn handed it to her. "Thankfully. I wouldn't want to have to do that again."

Priyanka cupped her hands around the brass vial. She looked visibly relieved that it had survived.

"So do I get that pancake and bacon reward you promised?" he asked, cocking a grin.

He was looking forward to sitting down and talking with his patron, maybe learning a few things from her, rather than running from one task to the next, but the way she bit her lower lip and the corners of her eyes creased told him that wasn't going to happen today.

"I'm sorry, Zayn. I really am. This trip has taken longer than planned. I have a meeting I can't avoid." Her expression of contrition suggested the meeting was with the other patrons. "I'm a terrible mentor. If you decide you'd rather have one of the instructors, I won't feel bad."

"About the dragons?" he asked.

Her nodding sigh suggested it wasn't going as planned.

"No, no. It's okay," he said. "I learn more on our short visits than I would in a regular class. Nothing like having to run for your life from a giant rainbow snake with static electricity problems to teach you the importance of improvising."

"You sure?"

"I'm positive."

She squeezed his shoulder. "Good. At the very least, I can show you the way back to the Garden Network."

The portal wasn't far from their location. Before Zayn went through, Priyanka shoved a roll of bills into his midsection and told him to have all the bacon and pancakes he could eat on her.

By the time he made it back to his room, he collapsed on his bed, falling asleep instantly. He didn't sleep long, because he had class with Instructor O'Keefe that evening, but while he did, he dreamt of huge spiders in a cavern the size of the Glitterdome. In the dream, he kept wondering why they were so big, and more importantly, why the spiders weren't attacking him. He didn't remember the dream when he woke up.

Chapter Eleven
Seventh Ward, November 2016
Two kinds of jerk

The line to the food truck, which earlier in the day had gone around the corner, was down to twenty or so. Neveah leaned her head into her shoulder to wipe the sweat from her cheek as she tossed chopped cabbage into the tacos with an artful twist. The weather had turned cool, but she had a furnace in her chest from constantly moving.

She handed over the last plate and said in a loud voice so the people in back would hear, "Sorry, folks, I'm all out. Come again tomorrow. I open at eleven in the morning, the line usually starts around ten."

A collective groan filled the air. A mousy looking guy with a thin mustache hung on the counter in desperation.

"I'll give you thirty bucks for a plate. I'm leaving the city tomorrow," he said.

"Sorry, sweetie," said Neveah as she was counting the

bills in her register. "I'm all out of carnitas and salsa and half the fixings. There just ain't nothing left to make."

The customer left with his head down while a few other customers hung around as if they were hoping she might have been mistaken.

Neveah counted her earnings twice to make sure she had the number right. It was enough to finally get ahead. The last few weeks, she'd barely been making enough to pay for the propane, and then the permit, or all the other little expenses that had snuck up on her. Today was the first day the profit could be locked away in the mini-safe she'd purchased (another expense she hadn't planned on).

She checked the time, seeing there was enough daylight left to make a few non-taco related errands before she'd have to prepare the next day's meals, and was pulling down the window when a woman strolled up.

Neveah's hackles went up even before she laid her eyes upon the visitor. Something about the way she walked as if she were a queen without a throne, or maybe it was the expensive perfume she wore, the kind of stuff sold in boutiques, not the corner mall, warned Neveah to be careful.

"I ain't got no more food," said Neveah, laying into her accent real thick. She'd found that a lot of the city folk treated her accent like an insult, so she'd learned to use it to her advantage.

The woman, a golden blonde with an agelessly young face, held her clutch purse like a scepter. She was vaguely familiar to Neveah, but she couldn't place why. Maybe a famous mage, or something.

"I don't appreciate being stolen from," said the blonde mage in effortless diction.

Neveah gave the woman her best "back off" expression, the one that usually scared her siblings out of the kitchen, and said, "Excuse me?"

Undeterred, the blonde mage tapped her perfectly manicured fingernail on the stainless-steel counter. "I know when
someone is violating my IPs. You have been warned."

The woman strode away, leaving Neveah mired in confusion. She stared at the back of the woman for a good minute
before resuming her counting.

"That was weird," she said.

When she was finished putting the money in the safe,
Neveah gathered up the extra corn tortillas, the ones she'd
already cooked, and rolled them in a paper towel to keep her
hands clean before locking up the food truck.

The park wasn't too far out of her way. The afternoon
stroller crowd had headed back home to collect their kids from
the bus, or get dinner ready for their spouses. But that's not
why Neveah had come.

She walked under the canopy of oaks, shoes crunching
the fallen leaves, checking the nearly barren limbs for her
thieves. She heard their clicking speech before she saw them,
congregated in a pine tree at the edge of the park.

From what she'd found on the internet, they were called
ravelles and they were only found in the city of Invictus. No
one knew their origins, though some suspected a mage had
found a way to breed ravens and squirrels, never once asking
if just because something *can* be done, *should* it be done. Especially because ravelles were as smart as ravens and had the
fearlessness of squirrels.

When she got near, after making sure no one was close
enough to hear, she unwrapped the towel and threw the extra
tortillas on the ground near the pine tree.

"I brought you some food," she said. "I hope ya'll take this
as an offering. No more trying to sneak into my truck at night,
rattling the door, keeping me awake. I need my sleep."

A particularly large ravelle climbed to the edge of a branch and made a bright caw at her.

"I'll take that as a yes," she said with a curt nod. "I gotta go. Ya'll be good."

During her first month, she hadn't had much time to experience the city except for the few blocks between the grocery store and the food truck, so when she climbed onto the packed Green Line station platform, a wave of anxiety passed through her.

A businessman carrying a briefcase covered in runes slammed into her from behind when she stopped to figure out where she was going.

"Out of the way, girl," said the man gruffly.

Neveah fought her way to the side, suddenly feeling out of place. Clinging to the wall, she stayed out of the flow until forging back in didn't give her the panics. Once she knew she was ready she studied the color-coded maps before purchasing a ticket from a kiosk and hurrying onto the train.

When the doors closed, she was stuck against a heavyset girl carrying a stand-up bass case. The musician didn't seem to care that she was taking up a big part of the car with her instrument.

The train rattled away from the station and Neveah was beset with scents and smells. She'd always had an excellent nose, a boon in the kitchen, but packed into a rush-hour train car that ability seemed like a curse. The guy standing behind the bassist had a bad case of halitosis, and he was breathing in her direction.

She was relieved when she reached her destination and stumbled out of the car, adjusting the red handkerchief holding her hair back before continuing on. Once she was on the street, she had to check the map she'd scribbled onto the back of a piece of paper from when she was back in Varna.

The walk only took a few minutes. She felt like she was finally seeing the city, even though the tenth ward was similar to the seventh. Along the way she passed a line of kids in front of a purple kiosk purchasing novelty rub-on runes. The side of the machine read Rocky's Rockin' Runes. She'd heard some of the people in her food truck lines complaining about the trash everywhere and the runes being etched onto everything. She saw signs of them on trash cans and traffic light poles.

As soon as she heard the Jamaican music rolling out the front door of the corner bodega like a lazy Saturday afternoon, she knew she was in the right place. The bodega sported a Jamaican flag behind the counter. An old man with graying dreads was scrolling through his phone while nodding his head to the music. She had no doubt it was Uncle Larice based on the stories that Zayn had told her.

"Hey girl, how can I help ya?" he asked in his lyrical way, kind eyes flitting up from whatever he was reading on his phone.

"You're Uncle Larice," she said.

At the word "uncle," his easy manner disappeared and he put his phone into his lap.

"I ain't your uncle, so what you getting at, girl?" he said.

Neveah checked the bodega to make sure no one else was inside before speaking.

"My brother worked here a few years ago," she said. "I wanted to ask you a few questions about that."

His frown deepened the wrinkles in his face. "The only person to have worked here was my nephew Zayn, and he moved back to Kingston already. That's it."

"Look, I know the deal," she said. "I just have to ask some questions, please. Something's wrong with Zayn, and I have to understand why."

His gaze softened, and he opened his mouth to speak, but

a customer came through the door, ringing the bell, and his lips squeezed tight. His eyes flitted to the woman, who was at the drink cooler in back.

"I'm sorry about whatever's going on with your brother, but I tell you I don't know him. But good luck to you, girl," he said, turning his attention back to the phone.

"My name is Neveah," she said, and the creasing around the eyes told her that he knew her name from when Zayn had worked in the bodega.

She lowered her voice. "My brother spoke highly of you. Said you was good people. I'm not asking you to betray the Academy. I just want to know what's going on with my brother."

"Then maybe you should ask the Academy," he said briskly, then pointed to the door. "Unless you're gonna buy something, you need to go."

She gripped the counter, imploring him with her eyes. "Please."

When he looked over her shoulder, indicating the woman had come up to the counter, Neveah left the bodega, wishing she could slam the door on the way out. The little bell tinkling almost felt like an insult.

Neveah glanced back at the bodega one more time before she headed back to her food truck to prepare the next day's meals.

"I know something's wrong with Zayn."

Chapter Twelve
Invictus Menagerie and Cryptozoo, December 2016
We'd make great pets

The wrought iron fence around the Invictus Menagerie and Cryptozoo did little to stop Instructor O'Keefe's class from leaping onto the grounds and making their way to the domed enclosures scattered across the park.

Zayn felt like he was ten years old again, trespassing on Farmer Johnson's strawberry farm. The night sky with the moon behind thin clouds cast the same light as it did back then. Keelan wagged his eyebrows at him, suggesting he was having the same thoughts.

The class of twenty-one students stopped outside a stone wall. The enclosure was about eight feet in diameter with a pond at the center, around which mounds of fur rose and fell in slumber.

In a hushed tone, completely at odds with the normally boisterous instructor, O'Keefe said, "This evening's lesson is another chance to demonstrate yur improvisation skills. Let's hope eh lot of you do better than the last, it was eh poor showing, through and through."

True to form, Eddie interrupted without getting the instructor's attention first.

"Are we really trespassing in the zoo? Or are you just messing with us like you always do?" asked Eddie, who clearly hadn't forgiven her for making him think she'd blown him up during their first year.

"Aye, laddie, in years past, Patron Adele let us on the grounds with her blessing, but der was an incident with a griffon and she never forgave me." The instructor looked repentant for a moment with her head hung, before she seemed to remember she had a class of students waiting for her next instruction. "Truth be told, if it were closer, I'd rather take you to the Portland Magical Zoo, deh have proper supernatural creatures like a two-headed hydra, basilisks, a Cthulhu beast, and others. Oh, let me tell you, they're magnificent, deadly, too. This place is eh bit pastoral, but that has to do with Adele."

Eddie, who had stepped closer for his question, looked bewildered and uncomfortable. He faded back into the group as if he were looking for protection from Instructor O'Keefe.

Keelan leaned over and whispered, "I get the feeling she'd throw us in a pen with hellhounds for training."

The wind died for a moment and the noise from a distant helicopter became ascendant. Instructor O'Keefe paused, checking the night sky before resuming her lesson.

"Anyone know what we have in this enclosure?" she asked.

No one answered. Zayn craned his head to get a better view. Using his sensing imbuement, he listened to their breathing, which sounded like a thrumming furnace.

A voice from the back sounded over the others.

"Ur-bears," said Portia.

"Aye, very good. Now how did ya know that? Are they common in Mexico?" asked Instructor O'Keefe.

A puzzled expression took over Portia's face. "No, there's a sign on that wall that says 'Do not feed the Ur-Bears.'"

Portia pointed to the gift shop building next to the enclosure. The lettering from a sign on the wall glistened in the moonlight.

Instructor O'Keefe cleared her throat. "Well then. Ur-bears. What can I tell you about them? As the name suggests, they aren't bears at all, but they look similar. They're closer to birds, owls even, and they have a particularly cruel poison in their claws. Nothing that would kill you, but it'd give you cramps and diarrhea for weeks."

At that moment, one of the sleeping ur-bears rolled onto its side, revealing a flat face and wide owl-like eyes over a black beak.

As Instructor O'Keefe spoke, her hands danced in front of her like a football coach explaining a play. "The challenge is going to go like this. There's a safe at the bottom of the pond. You have to sneak into the enclosure without disturbing the ur-bears, dive into the pond, break into the safe, and remove an item from inside and bring it back to me. There's one for each group, you'll know it when you see it, no messing with the others or I'll put you over me knee and give you a good whoopin'. And no hurting the ur-bears, not even a scratch."

Zayn shared glances with his teammates. Everyone seemed confident about the challenge, though the instructor was known for adding surprises. They'd have to be wary.

"Alright, Charla's team will go first. You have fifteen minutes to bring me the item," said Instructor O'Keefe, forgetting to be quiet and using her announcer voice.

Like all of them, Charla had changed in her three and a

half years in the Academy. The sculpted bottle-blonde coif had been replaced with a short, almost military bob in her natural auburn tones. The failed trip to the Eternal City had changed her. Zayn remembered the cocky Southern rich girl at the beginning of their first year, but after Chen and Elana had died, all that bluster had been knocked away.

While Charla huddled her team near the enclosure, speaking in hushed tones about their plan, Zayn moved his team to the other side of the souvenir hut.

"What's the plan?" asked Skylar, rubbing her hands together impatiently.

Vin flashed his hand over his face like a magician, morphing it into an exact copy of Instructor O'Keefe. Little lines sparked with faez, indicating where his fourth-year imbuement tattoo had been given. When he spoke, he managed to mostly sound like her.

"Lads and lassies, we got to get in there like a wee scunner and wipe the dish-cloot with our bums oot the windea," he said, receiving a round of chuckles from the team.

"Do you even know what you said?" asked Portia.

"Not a clue, which is like eighty percent of the time with her. It's a miracle I've learned anything," said Vin as he waved his hand over his face to change it back into his own.

"Don't worry," said Keelan, shaking his head. "Me and Skylar have regular classes with her and I maybe understand sixty percent. I learned Mandarin Chinese easier."

Skylar nodded along with Keelan.

"Anyway, this should be easy, right?" asked Vin. "Zayn will just do his thing and the ur-bears will let us stroll into the pond and take the safe."

"It doesn't work exactly like that," said Zayn, biting his lower lip. He didn't want to tell them that he hadn't used it but a few times, and never successfully. He'd been hoping to have a lesson with Priyanka, but she'd been away on business again. "But I'm sure I can keep them distracted."

"I can get us into the safe," said Portia.

"I think the safe is supposed to be intact after we're done," said Vin.

Portia blinked innocently. "Why, I don't know what you mean, Vincent."

"Okay, Portia's got the safe, I'll keep the ur-bears docile," said Zayn. *I hope.*

After rummaging through the inner pockets of his jacket, Keelan produced two small pipes and handed one to Portia. "This should let you breathe underwater for a few minutes. I haven't tested it yet, but it should work. I'll go down with you in case there are surprises."

Portia nodded confidently. When Keelan made a trinket, it almost always worked. Skylar had mentioned more than once that Keelan was Instructor O'Keefe's favorite student.

"I guess me and Vin will be on standby in case something else happens," said Skylar.

"In case? More like 'when,'" said Vin.

True to form, Charla's team was victorious in bringing back their item from the safe in the pond. Zayn didn't get to see what it was, but Charla looked relieved to get rid of it.

"Yur up next," said Instructor O'Keefe with her hands on her hips, her kilt swaying in the breeze.

Her mirthful expression left Zayn worried about what surprises she had hidden in the challenge.

The five of them easily hopped over the stone enclosure. The uneven ground was a mixture of dirt and tufts of weeds, leading to the pond at the center. There were seven ur-bears, lying around the edge of the water in various states of repose. The nearest was on its back, legs spread wide like an old man passed out on the couch after a day drunk.

As Zayn and his team walked up, a few stirred, wide eyes blinking awake with a clarity that made him more than a little nervous.

Keelan elbowed him in the ribs. "This is all you, cuz."

Zayn took a deep breath and focused on the imbuement under his right arm. It wasn't easy channeling the pheromones from the ur-bears rather than his teammates, since they were surrounding him, so he took a few steps away and tried again. The second time, he caught the scents of the ur-bears. It was like pulling them in with a huge vacuum. Their earthy aroma caught in his throat, like the smell of damp straw and pine needles.

His chest swelled as if it were full, the ache of his imbuement trickling from the right to the left, crossing over his heart. Converting their essence brought images to his mind: tromping through the trees after prey, lumbering beneath the earth in shallow caves, ripping gooey entrails from small mammals before swallowing them like noodles.

He was so entranced, he almost forgot what he was doing, until Skylar whispered, "Come on, Zayn."

Zayn opened his eyes to find four of the ur-bears had woken and were stumbling towards them in an awkward upright march. Their wide eyes made them appear surprised.

Pushing the pheromone back at them stung, like hot water over a sunburn, but the effect was immediate. The creatures stopped, eyes blinking, beaks opening and closing mutely. It felt like having a tether connected to the ur-bears, and though he felt he could get them to wander back and fall asleep, he let them stand in place.

When Zayn gave them the go sign, Keelan and Portia stripped down to their underwear, placed the pipes in their mouths, and dove into the water.

Even though he knew they had ways of breathing beneath

the surface, Zayn kept willing them to appear again. He didn't have a watch, but it felt like they were underwater for far too long. Vin and Skylar had similar expressions of unease, glancing to the pond and then back to Zayn, waiting for his signal to go in after them.

He was so focused on the pond, he almost forgot the ur-bears. They started to stir, rocking back and forth on their huge paws, but Zayn sent out a new flow of pheromone, mentally willing them to stay put.

Right as the surface of the water broke, a stab of migraine caught him at the temple. He relaxed his mind, and the headache faded into the background, but he felt like it could come back at any time.

Keelan and Portia crawled out of the pond with something carried between them. As soon as they tried to pull it from the water, it fell into the mud. They collapsed onto their knees beside it looking like they'd just completed a marathon.

"What is it?" whispered Skylar, not wanting to disturb the sleeping ur-bears on the opposite side of the pond.

Keelan and Portia looked to him with mirth in their eyes. Even with the moon partially covered, soft silvery light fell upon them, and Zayn could see them holding back laughter.

"She put an enchantment on it to make it heavy. We need to decode the runes to disable it," said Keelan.

While Zayn kept the ur-bears at bay, his four teammates worked on the runes. After a minute, they cast a few spells and lifted the item from the mud.

As soon as Zayn saw the oblong shape, he knew what it was. Somehow, Instructor O'Keefe had rescued one of the pink vibrators from the sex-geist.

"I hope to Merlin that's not one of hers," said Vin, smirking.

Zayn breathed a sigh of relief that they were finished. He

prepared to release the ur-bears, but a spike of migraine hit him like a thunderbolt. He was brought to his knees, and as the white light faded from his vision he realized his imbuement burned as if his side had been rubbed with a cheese grater and dosed in hot sauce.

The ur-bears, all seven of them, now completely awake, had every eye focused on him. Between the ache in his imbuement and the attention the ur-bears were giving him, he knew he'd forced a wad of faez through the imbuement.

"What did you do, Zayn?" asked Vin, walking backward as the ur-bears stumbled forward like zombies.

"I...I don't know," said Zayn. "I think, maybe, I overdid it."

"Turn it off then," said Vin.

"I'm not controlling them anymore. I think I overclocked my imbuement," said Zayn, grimacing.

"Let's just get out of here," said Keelan.

The other three jogged towards the concrete wall, while Vin helped Zayn to his feet. Every shift and step felt like a thousand suns burned in his side.

"Come on, Zayn, they're gaining on us," said Vin.

Through gritted teeth Zayn said, "Sorry, it hurts."

Vin grabbed him around the legs to pick him up like a baby, and the ur-bears surged forward, moving much faster than anyone expected. There was an anxiousness to their headlong rush, as if they were trying to stop their child from being kidnapped.

The ur-bears surrounded them, reaching with their four-inch claws. Zayn sensed that they were trying to protect him. He'd laid the enchantment on too thick.

"They think you're stealing me," said Zayn with tears in his eyes from the pain, but it was too late.

Vin took one look at the pack of ur-bears, and without dropping Zayn, waved his hand over his face, turning it to a misshapen ur-bear. The eyes were oblong, and the beak wasn't in the right place, but if Zayn squinted then Vin looked like one.

The face changing seemed to do the trick as the ur-bears slowed their aggression. It helped that Vin was the size of a small ur-bear. Looking over Vin's shoulder, Zayn saw that his teammates had escaped the enclosure.

With surprising gentleness, the ur-bears took him from Vin's arms as they made soft chirps that could have been a version of cooing.

The largest ur-bear, one that stood around eight feet tall and had a white patch in the shape of a star on its chest, took sudden interest in the new Vin ur-bear. One of the others moved towards Vin, and the big one, Star Bear, pushed it away, making a violent clacking sound in the back of its throat.

While the other ur-bears crowded around Zayn, touching him gently as if he were a swaddled baby, Star Bear lifted Vin into his arms, cradling him like the world's largest baby. One false move and Star Bear's poisoned claws would pierce Vin's flesh. Though Vin's ur-bear face was misshapen, Zayn had no problem interpreting his look of horror as Star Bear began to rock him.

The situation got worse when an ur-bear with light brown fur leaned over and tried to shove a piece of bloody meat that it had sequestered on its body somewhere into Zayn's mouth. The raw, bloody meat could have been a squirrel or mouse, but it was hard to tell because it had been mauled to a pulp. The ur-bear shoved the bloody meat against his clenched mouth, knocking his hand away when he tried to block.

"What do we do?" asked Vin from the arms of Star Bear.

The massive ur-bear was making clacking noises in his throat, as if he were singing to Vin.

"I think you've been adopted," said Zayn, still fending off the raw meat from the insistent ur-bears.

"And they think you're malnourished," said Vin. "This might be funny if it wasn't us."

"Do you see the—"

His question was interrupted by a brownish ur-bear who grabbed his right hand and slammed the bloody meat into his open mouth. A quick attempt to spit it out was stymied by a massive clawed paw that nudged him in the back of the head. Zayn reflexively swallowed, feeling the slimy hunk slip down his throat.

"Augh," he said, wishing for a drink to wash away the sour taste.

Zayn remembered helping his mom feed the twins when they were babies, and how he would force the spoon past their defiant arms. He felt terrible and planned on apologizing to the twins next time he saw them.

A snort of laughter erupted from Vin. "They need to give you a bib and high chair."

Zayn opened his mouth for a retort when another piece of bloody meat was slipped past his defenses. This one was gritty, as if it'd been dropped into the dirt a few times. The same head nudge trick forced a second swallow, and made him a little queasy.

Vin's laughter turned to a muffle as Star Bear pressed him against his chest in a hug. As Star Bear squeezed, Vin started choking.

When he was allowed up for air, Vin said, "Oh Merlin, his fur stinks. I think he's been rolling in dung for about...*his whole fricking life.*"

"Where are the others?" asked Zayn, fighting off more meat.

It was at that moment he noticed the rising chorus of

laughter from the edge of the enclosure.

Through the legs of an ur-bear, Zayn saw the rest of his class, Instructor O'Keefe included, bent over and holding their sides.

To Zayn's immense relief, the cacophony was broken by a sharp whistle from the other side of the enclosure. Portia, standing on the concrete wall, dumped a bucket of bloody meat and entrails into the enclosure. The smell of fresh blood distracted the ur-bears, and both he and Vin were forgotten. The ur-bears ambled away, moaning in hunger.

Even though his side burned, Zayn forced himself to stumble to the wall, and with Keelan's help, let himself be pulled to safety. Vin joined him a moment later, blushing so hard his face looked like it might explode.

Skylar had tears in her eyes when she handed him a towel to wipe the blood off his face.

"I swear if one of them had tried to breastfeed you I would have peed my pants," she said, in that quivering voice of post-laughter exhaustion.

"I eh nev'er seen a more arsed-up job in mae life," said Instructor O'Keefe, who looked like she'd just run a marathon by her blotchy red complexion.

"At least Portia was looking out for us, while you'all were havin' a good laugh," said Vin.

Portia, who had returned from the other side of the enclosure, said, "Oh, don't think I wasn't laughing. It was hard carrying that bucket of fresh meat with my gut hurting."

Vin scraped mud from his cheek. "I think that ur-bear must have been sleeping in a bed of squirrel carcasses. I can't get that smell out of my nose."

Zayn held his stomach. "I'm going to need some shots or something. Old raw meat can't be good for you."

Instructor O'Keefe slapped him on the arm. "I'll fix ya up

after class."

"Alright, alright," said Instructor O'Keefe, shooing the other teams away. "We've had some fun at Zayn and Vin's expense. Eh next team should get ready."

Once the other teams moved away, Instructor O'Keefe leaned in, suddenly serious. "What happened? Ain't like you to arse up a job like that, Zayn."

Zayn grimaced as he held his side. "A little malfunction in my imbuement I think."

"Ya sure? Percival ain't never made a mistake in all the years he's worked for Pri," said Instructor O'Keefe.

"No, not sure. It might have been me. Maybe I put too much faez into it," he said.

Instructor O'Keefe's lips were sealed flat. "Ya might want to figure that out. Out on a job ain't no time for a screw up like that. You're lucky the ur-bears only wanted to hold ya like a baby, not tear you limb from limb."

He nodded. "Yeah, I know. It was my fault all the way."

"Fault or not, get it fixed, eh?"

She left without waiting for his answer. He decided he needed to take a trip to Golden Willow. He couldn't wait to see if his migraines would work themselves out. They might kill him before that happened.

Then he wiped a piece of warm gut from his neck. But first he needed a shower: for about three days.

Chapter Thirteen
Tenth ward, December 2016
A comic interlude

On a chilly morning when the city had been buried in a foot of early snow, Neveah decided not to open the food truck for business. Besides, she wanted a day off after working straight through the fall—the exact number of days lost to the Groundhog Day–like existence.

With Sojourner locked up tight to protect against thieves and ravelles, Neveah headed into the city carrying a thermal cooler. She immediately regretted not purchasing a pair of heavy boots a few days before when she saw the forecast, as the snow was wet and went right through her canvas high-tops. By the time she'd made it to the train station, her feet felt like blocks of ice.

"I wish I knew some weather enchantments," she mumbled as she bought a ticket for the Green Line, envious of her older brother and cousin, who had a thousand spells memorized for every occasion.

But while she envied their magical knowledge, she hadn't wanted to join the Hundred Halls herself. She preferred cooking. But she did make a note to have Zayn teach her a few personal spells next summer.

The train car was surprisingly empty, which meant she got a seat for once. Usually, on her few trips around the city, the car had been packed so tight that she was constantly worrying she was being pickpocketed.

Neveah placed the thermal cooler between her knees, warming her hands against the side. She was enjoying the view of the Glitterdome and the soft rocking of the train as it sped around a curve, when something she glanced out of the corner of her eye put a shock of recognition right through her gut.

A kid in a green "Wizards Do It With Magic" hoodie was reading a comic book. The image on the cover made her nearly come out of her seat to snatch the book from his hands.

KILL THE SPIDER QUEEN!

The title of the comic book was written in a drippy purple font that suggested it was either humorous or completely over-the-top bonkers, but it wasn't the title that made her go cold, it was an exact replica of the Lady's plantation, complete with canopy oaks and white columns.

When the train car jerked, she nearly fell out of her seat. The kid glanced over the edge of the comic book, his pale face twitching with a cautious smile at her attention.

"Where did you get that?" she asked.

He closed the comic book and looked at the cover as if he were seeing it for the first time.

"J.J.'s Comics & Collectibles." His smile grew with confidence. "You read it? It's pretty wicked, from the point of view of the villain. She like, murders people regularly."

Her hand went right to her pocket. "I'll give you twenty

bucks for it."

The kid pulled the comic towards his chest possessively. "What? Is it worth something? It's new, just came out."

Neveah steeled her face. "I remembered I didn't get my brother a birthday present. He loves comics. I'm headed to the party right now."

The kid seemed to be working through if she were lying to him or not. "How about twenty bucks and your number?"

"I'm way older than you," she said.

"I'm seventeen," he said.

"Thirty bucks, no number."

He squinted at her. "Come on."

"Sorry, I don't have time for dating," she said.

"Fine."

She pulled the bills from the wallet in her front pocket. He cautiously made the trade as if he were expecting a trick. Almost as soon as she had the comic book, the train car squealed to a stop. She slipped out the door, back into the wintery air before he could ask for her number again.

Not wanting to stand around on the platform and get frostbite, Neveah shoved it into the inside pocket of her coat and headed towards the Jamaican bodega.

An older black woman in a maroon business dress was buying cold medicine when Neveah came in. The woman pushed out the front door, leaving her alone with the owner Larice.

His eyes creased with recognition. "I told ya I don't have no information for ya."

"I didn't come for information," she said.

The creases deepened until they were shadowy valleys. "I seriously doubt it, girl."

"I wanted to thank you," said Neveah as she unzipped the thermal cooler. "For looking after Zayn during his first year.

He told me you looked out for him, beyond what the Academy expected."

Larice stayed suspicious as she maneuvered the stacked containers from the cooler, releasing hints of paprika and coriander into the air. As the aromas hit his nose, he straightened, suddenly interested in what she had in her hands.

"That smells like..."

"Goat curry with rice and beans," she finished. "I made some extra and thought you could use a little. You're far too skinny for your age."

"Eh, girl," he said, absently, licking his lips. "That smells good. Real good."

Neveah set the two containers onto the counter next to each other, then broke the seal on the goat curry, letting the warm steam escape.

"Dat smells like Kingston," he said. "How you do that?"

"I'm a chef. I make food. After my brother came home and told me about you, I made Jamaican-style meals for the family, including this dish. I found a few recipes, but they didn't taste right to me, so I made some adjustments."

Larice stared at the bowl of brown broth with chunks of seared goat as if it were a million dollars about to be given to him.

Neveah pulled out a plastic plate and scooped a generous portion of goat curry and rice and beans onto it. As he took the plate, he said, "What's the catch? Is it poisoned? Or is it alchemy?"

"Just home cooking," she said matter-of-factly. "And no catch."

"There's always a catch."

"Not this time," she said.

As suspicious as he was, he couldn't help but place his plastic spoon into the broth and taste it. A faraway gaze overcame him as he savored it.

"It's like what my baba used to make," he said, before eating a chunk of seared goat.

"You like it?" she asked.

"You're an angel in disguise," he said, shaking his head as he ladled another spoonful into his mouth.

"If you want, I'll leave the rest with you," she said. "I have another container for myself at home. I'm used to cooking for more people. I could bring you my extras from time to time."

Larice looked like she'd offered him a reprieve from the headsman. She figured he was sick of cooking his own meals, living on his own like he was. While he had the bodega, Zayn had said he hadn't any family in the city. Something had happened back in Kingston when he was younger that had driven him away.

"I would like that, respect," he said.

"Great," she replied. "I have to get back to work. Enjoy the curry goat. I'll stop by another time."

Larice nodded absently, looking like someone had stepped on his soul. She left him behind the counter with his bowl of goat curry, and was almost out the door, when he told her to hold up.

"What do you want to know?" he asked.

Neveah fought back the urge to smile, keeping her face as unreadable as possible. "Anything that might have happened to him last year."

"I don't know anything. Only saw him once," he said.

"Did he seem the same?"

He nodded.

"What about the Academy? Did anyone come by asking about him? Anyone else I can talk to?" she asked.

He thought for a moment. "There was a place he talked about once. Madwoman's Spells, or something like that." He gave her an address. "Maybe she can help."

"Great," she said, "I'll check it out on my way home."

It wasn't too far to the location he'd told her. She was disappointed as soon as she saw the "Out of Business" sign on the glass door. Neveah placed her face against the window to see an empty store before deciding to head back to the food truck.

The train was more crowded than the earlier ride, so she didn't get a seat, but she cradled the pole with one arm while she paged through the comic book with the other. It was exactly as the kid had said, about a half-woman half-spider who defended her home against assassins hell-bent on killing her. The brief comic did a good job of humanizing her, and Neveah found herself rooting for the Spider Queen whenever she was attacked, but she couldn't shake the overwhelming idea that this story was based on the Lady of Varna.

Neveah read it a half dozen times that evening trying to decipher it for clues to its existence. Suspiciously, there was no author, and the publisher, Hilltop Comics, had no address listed.

By the time she was ready to turn in for the night, Neveah was convinced that it was a coincidence of cosmic proportions. But she also thought she was wrong.

Chapter Fourteen
Golden Willow Hospital, December 2016
A path nearly crossed

The fluorescent lights from inside the waiting room spilled outside onto the crunchy snow. It was the third time he'd visited the hospital, but he'd never gone in. Each time he'd gotten as far as he was standing now, but just couldn't get his feet to move forward.

The sirens from an ambulance grew louder, until the flashing reds and blues danced across the cars, making Zayn squint away the bright lights. He shoved his hands in his pockets, looking back towards the city. The top of the Spire was hidden by a layer of clouds, making him feel like the city was a giant dome.

"Why don't I want to go in?" he asked himself.

Under any other circumstances his last big migraine, the one he'd had at the Cryptozoo, would have gotten him killed. He had to take care of whatever was ailing him, but every time he tried to get help he went back home instead.

He was thinking about calling Keelan to drag him inside when he sensed a presence lurking in the shadows to his left. Zayn spun around, alert and ready to fight, only to find Watcher Sabrina.

"You shouldn't sneak up on me like that," he said.

Watcher Sabrina looked unenthused to be in the city. She wasn't wearing her sunglasses, but the darkness cloaked her eyes.

"I wouldn't have to be here if you were doing your job," she said.

"I am," he said, "but she hasn't been here."

"That's not our problem. You need to try harder."

His gaze fell on the empty spot near her boots. "You didn't bring your pet."

"You don't have any information," she said.

"Which suggests you already knew. Why ask if you're spying on me?" he asked, throwing the words into her face.

His amped senses caught the increase of her heartbeat, a sure sign he was right.

"We have to make sure," she said.

"Sure of what?" he asked, though he knew the answer.

"Of your loyalty."

Behind him, the automatic doors to the hospital opened, releasing the sounds of a busy emergency room.

"Why are you here?" she asked.

"Headaches."

She frowned. "You've been standing here for a half hour."

"I hate hospitals, I guess."

"You don't seem very convinced by your words," she said, pursing her lips to one side.

"If I knew the answer I'd go inside," he said.

"You're no good to anyone if you're damaged," said Watcher Sabrina. "If working for the Lady is causing problems, maybe she needs to reconsider the deal."

He tried to get angry, to bark back at her, but the way she coldly delivered the threat put him on his heels.

"I'll be fine," he said. "It's just an imbuement issue, I think. Nothing I can't fix."

"What is your fourth-year imbuement?" she asked, tilting her head slightly.

"None of your business," said Zayn.

"I think it *is* our business," she replied.

"Not this time. It's my imbuement. Priyanka said we should keep our abilities secret, even from our friends," he said.

"The Lady is not your friend, she's your employer," she said.

Zayn wasn't sure how far he could push it, but he had to try. "Still."

"You're not going to tell me?"

"Nope."

Her lips thinned. "Then I will have to report this back to her."

"I wouldn't expect anything less," he said.

Watcher Sabrina lifted her chin slightly. "Remember, this deal exists for as long as you are useful and not a threat. As soon as either of those disappear, then so do you, and your family."

"I understand."

"Clearly you don't since you have no new information for the Lady. Try harder. The next time I show up you won't like what has happened."

Without waiting for him to respond, Watcher Sabrina disappeared into the darkness, but her threat hung in the air long after she was gone.

Chapter Fifteen
Harmony, December 2016
Dodge and weave

Zayn didn't have long to wait to see Priyanka again. He was sitting on the couch at his place in the tenth ward with Marley in his lap while he was studying when she came through the door. The security enchantments had notified him of her approach, so he got to greet her without looking up from his tome.

"Good evening, Patron Priyanka Sai," he said.

Despite the chilly weather outside, she wore jeans and a dark V-neck. Snowflakes melted in her hair. Her smoky brown skin looked healthier than when he'd seen her last.

"If I didn't want you to know I was coming, you wouldn't have known." Priyanka chuckled. "So is this the famous Marley? I'm sorry I didn't get to greet you in the warehouse."

Much to his surprise, Marley leapt out of his lap and into Priyanka's arms. She cooed over the callolo while Marley buried his face in her neck.

Zayn set the tome, *Infiltration & Deception: A Study of the Animal Kingdom*, on the table.

"So where are we headed? Back to the Undercity?" he asked, standing up.

"Not this time," she said.

"Iceland?"

She tossed him a vial of pale blue liquid. "No, the dragons aren't a problem right now." Her flat gaze said that it weighed on her mind. "Drink this, you're going to need it where we're going."

"Which is?"

Priyanka motioned impatiently with her hand. "Drink."

The liquid tasted like minty cough syrup with a bitter aftertaste that made him want to scrape his tongue with a comb.

"What was that for?" he asked.

"Inoculation," she said. "It's best if you don't bring any diseases back from where we're going."

"Diseases? Where are we going? Boston?"

Priyanka smirked. "You're headed to class."

"Class? You mean there's actually going to be a lesson?" he asked.

Priyanka's chin sunk toward her chest as her right eyebrow arched. "Since it's dreadfully true, I will ignore your lack of respect. This time."

They went to the nearby Blackest Cup Coffee shop, where an Academy portal was hidden in the back next to the break area. The illusionary wall let them through, revealing a small room with an obsidian arch.

Priyanka grabbed his hand. Her grip was calloused and firm. She pulled the obsidian key from beneath her shirt and together they stepped through the portal. The vertigo put water in his knees, but he held his ground, receiving a nod of approval from his patron.

The lingering vertigo was quickly replaced with awe. They stood in a stone circle, much like the one in the Ice Hold, except they were surrounded by lush jungle. Purple-green leaves formed a wall around the circle. Priyanka stepped through them, the jungle swallowing her in an instant.

Zayn hurried to catch up. An insect with a fat, black body and gossamer wings buzzed past his head. He resisted the urge to knock it away, since he didn't know how dangerous it was.

"Is this Harmony?" he asked, remembering the visit to her office his first year.

"You have a good memory," she said.

The trees were rarely straight, bending and twisting as they fought for space in the crowded jungle. Priyanka made her way along a path that seemed to open up for her as she took long strides.

Priyanka stepped through another wall of purple-green leaves, and when Zayn followed her through his breath caught in his throat. He stood at the back of a sprawling house built into the side of the mountain. A stream meandered through the center, presumably dropping from the heights on the far, unseen side.

But it wasn't the house that took his breath away, but the view beyond it. They stood at the upper portion of a mountain. The jungle had hid their elevation.

Beyond, a valley lay nestled between two mountains with mist rolling off them, collecting in the depths, swirling languidly like a great maelstrom. The aliveness of Harmony gave him chills, even without his imbuement.

"It's quite a sight, isn't it?" she said, resting her foot on a rock near the stream. "This is the Aerie. Here you're safe enough, though never let your guard completely down. When we leave the Aerie, consider yourself in enemy territory."

Zayn glanced around at the lush valley. "Enemy territory? Who's the enemy?"

"Harmony."

They went into the house after she taught him the passwords. She explained the Aerie was protected by powerful magics. The place looked like it could comfortably hold twenty people. She showed him a small furnished room, and explained that it would be his whenever he came to the Aerie.

"The rest of the house is open except for my office on the west side. Feel free to use the facilities while you're here, though you won't have much time in the Aerie." She nodded towards the front window. "Mostly you'll be down there."

"What will we be doing?"

"Imbuement weaving."

She led him through the front door to a stone staircase cut into the side of the mountain. The angle was steep enough that he kept one hand on the wall while they descended, and he noted the runes carved into the stairs, presumably to keep whatever dangers lay below out.

It took about ten minutes to reach the bottom of the stone staircase, but when they did, he realized the air had changed. The mist was light enough to see through but breathing felt claustrophobic.

Not far from the stone stairs was a series of posts in the earth, each one successively higher, leading into the jungle at the canopy level.

"How many imbuements can you use at the same time? Be honest," she said.

"One, maybe two."

Her forehead tightened. "There are no maybes here. One or two."

"One then," he said, receiving a slight nod of approval.

"And what's the most important skill of an Academy student?" she asked.

Zayn thought about his classes, from Instructor Allgood's to Minoan's and O'Keefe's. A central thread ran through them all.

"Adaptability."

"Good," she said. "You've been paying attention. The best agents are the most flexible, adaptable on the fly. A successful mission is often like a jazz piece. The pieces are there, but they've been cut up and rearranged, deconstructed into their fundamental forms to create something new and unique."

"Will I be playing jazz today?" he asked.

"No," she said. "You have raw talent, and a knack for coming out of difficult situations, but you've also been lucky. Today you're going to learn to play scales."

"Scales?"

She lifted one shoulder. "The Academy version of scales. You need to be able to use more than one imbuement at a time. This will give you more flexibility. Like when you were taking the sample at the earth well. Had you been able to use more than one imbuement at a time, you might have been able to calm the kwalic while speeding away from the modrats."

The disappointment in her voice burned at his pride, but he nodded, accepting his limitation. Maceo had always taught them to be humble in the face of feedback, though it was difficult every time.

"Stand on that first pole," she said.

It was only five feet high. She leapt onto the pole next to him and produced a metal staff from an inside pocket. The weapon seemed to jump into existence.

"Arms up," she said, mimicking the gruff tone of Instructor Allgood.

He lifted his arms and grimaced as he pushed faez into his ribs, strengthening them against what was about to happen.

The first strike nearly knocked the wind out of Zayn, forcing him to concentrate harder. Without his imbuement, the blows with the staff would have broken his ribs, but he had to concentrate.

"Now, use your sensing imbuement to tell me what's going on behind you," she said as she swung the staff into his ribs, back and forth, like a pendulum.

The flow of faez was centered into his strength imbuement. Each time he tried diverting some to the sensing one, the staff smacked into his side, forcing him to maintain the first.

"You're not sensing," she said.

"I...can't," he said.

"You're not trying then," she said, swinging harder.

"How...do...I...do...both?" he asked between the blows.

The corners of her eyes creased. "Faez is like water, it can be diverted into multiple flows. Think about putting your finger over the end of a hose to get two separate sprays."

He tried to imagine the faez as she described but each time he wanted to split it, he got nervous and sucked it back in.

"You need to lean into it," she said. "Forget your fear, forget the staff. Think of the two streams, the two imbuements. Draw more faez and divert the flow."

After taking a cleansing breath, Zayn let more faez into his mind. He had a twinge of worry that he might trigger a migraine, but pushed that fear away, concentrating on splitting the streams.

He imagined it like she'd said, putting a thumb over the hose. At first, it was only a trickle, wetting the pathways, but then he adjusted the flow until an equal amount balanced between them.

As the metal staff struck his hardened ribs, Zayn reached

out with his senses, listening to the insects buzzing around the jungle, feeling the sunlight on his back.

"Now tell me what you sense," she said.

"There's a big fat bug flying around, maybe about ten feet back. It's hovering over a flower? Yes, a flower. It smells like lavender, but grittier, as if someone dumped dirt into it. There's a...there's a creature, something larger in the trees, back and to my right, I can hear it grinding its teeth as it watches us."

"Good, good," she said. "The creature is a maulapine. It's like a cross between a monkey and a porcupine with the disposition of an angry badger."

"Wonderful."

"What else do you sense?" she asked.

He focused, drawing on faez until it made him a little dizzy. "I...more of the same. Bugs, wind, trees."

"Do you sense the centipede crawling up your leg?" she asked.

"What...?"

His faez faltered as he looked down at his leg, right when the staff hit, knocking him off the pole to land in a thorny bush.

"Augh," he said, tangled in the branches, as jagged thorns sawed at his skin in multiple locations. "You lied."

"Which you should have detected with your sensing imbuement," she said sternly. "How are your ribs?"

He tentatively probed. "Not broken."

"Good, or that would have made your next task more difficult," she said.

Zayn dislodged himself from the thorn bush, knocking away little crawling bugs that had decided that he was their new home.

When at last he was back on the pole, he asked, "Why is

this lesson only for me? Shouldn't imbuement weaving be a skill everyone is taught?"

"Not everyone is capable," she said, squinting into the valley. "It takes a high level of faez to accomplish, and very few mages have it. The Lady's poison helps you in this regard. But the most important thing is that you have to be willing to push past the limits of what you think your ability is."

"How many can you weave?"

A sly smile took residence on her lips. "Twenty."

Zayn let out a low whistle. He understood a little more how she was able to survive her fight with Jörm. Priyanka motioned for him to raise his arms. The lesson in imbuement weaving continued. Priyanka slammed the staff into his ribs while asking him questions about the environment behind him.

After an hour, she shook her hand and the staff disappeared as if it'd teleported away.

Sweat rolled from his forehead, dripping into his eyes. He used what little dry area on his shirt remained to wipe his face. Though he was exhausted, he was feeling good about his progress.

"Are we done?" he asked.

"Do you want to be done?"

He shook his head. "I can go all day."

"Good, because your weaving sucks. You're still working too hard to maintain the two flows. It needs to come naturally. If you have to think about it, you won't be able to do it. I was hoping you'd be further along than you are," she said, looking at him severely.

Though they'd both been standing in the humid air for an hour, she looked like she'd been having drinks under a cabana, while he felt like he was swimming in a pool of sweat. But if he had to keep going he would. Zayn raised his arms for the next round.

A twitch of a smile formed at the corner of her lips before disappearing.

"That's enough of that drill. You aren't going to be able to move tomorrow if I keep it up." Priyanka checked the sky for the sun's location. "It's a few more hours until sunset. You don't want to be out here after dark. The mystdrakons that live in the valley sometimes climb to the higher elevations at night as it cools."

"Mystdrakons?"

"Like a larger Komodo dragon if you gave it perfect natural camouflage and the speed of a drag racer. If you see one, which you won't, you're probably already dead. Which is why we're staying up here near the Aerie."

Zayn stared into the mist at the center of the valley. It had a more ominous feel now that he knew one of the creatures that lived in it.

"I'm going to head up. I have a few things to do. But you're going to stay. I want you to practice your weaving. This time, you'll be hopping from pole to pole, but don't go into the jungle, as our friend over there would object. As you're moving you want to be keeping your sensing imbuement flowing. If you're feeling like that's too easy, try slipping into the Veil for a few seconds occasionally."

Priyanka left him at the training grounds. He got to work as soon as she started up the stone stairs. The poles were between five and ten feet apart, requiring a mix of strength and balance to make each leap. While he jumped, he kept his senses circulating around him like a lighthouse.

After an hour, he noticed that the single maulapine that had been watching him had been joined by three others. The pack sat on a long branch.

Zayn decided to try his influence imbuement on them as

he continued through his pole circuit. It was harder to use his fourth imbuement, since his ribs were already tightening with soreness from the earlier impacts, but he pushed himself regardless.

When he caught their pheromone, the quiet rage within it surprised him. The singular maulapine had watched him without much indication of its intention, but as he sampled their auras, he realized they were dangerous beings. He assumed they were territorial, which was why Priyanka had warned him not to stray.

Zayn reached out with his imbuement, pressing a soothing blanket around them. The compact furry bodies seemed to deflate, as if their rage was keeping them expanded, but he kept going, sending out a wave of relaxation.

When the first maulapine fell from its perch, Zayn almost missed his landing. The creature hit the soft ground beneath it, and quickly hopped up unhurt, but Zayn withdrew the imbuement, feeling guilty about what had happened.

The maulapines, freed from his influence, bristled, their spiny backs raising in defiance. Growling barks called into the jungle, quickly answered by other nearby maulapines. One of the critters on the branch jumped down onto a pole, testing Zayn's response. When the others followed, Zayn decided that his lesson for the day was over.

As the pack leapt from the trees, Zayn sped back to the stone staircase, climbing a ways before looking back down. The maulapines, maybe twenty in number, milled about the bottom without getting near the stairs.

When he reached the Aerie, Priyanka was nowhere to be found, but he wasn't worried. Mostly he was hungry and sore. After devouring a bowl of bananas and half a block of cheese, followed by a couple mugs of water, he searched the place, wondering if he'd missed her.

His investigation proved what he'd first thought. She was gone. Either into Harmony, or back through the portal. He had a momentary flash of worry that if something happened to her, he was stuck in this place forever.

Then he remembered Watcher Sabrina's warning. He didn't know if he'd get another chance like this to take a peek into her office. He wished he would have thought about it when he first came back to the Aerie, but he'd assumed she was somewhere near, and he was hungry.

Zayn did a quick loop again, pushing his sensing imbuement for any sign of her, before returning to the door to her office. He cast what spells he knew for detecting traps, knowing they were probably futile, since she would be unlikely to use protections that her students were aware of, and came away empty.

Either she wasn't using any protections on her office, or he didn't have the ability or knowledge to detect them. He almost turned away, but he remembered his siblings. He had to protect them from the Lady, even if it meant betraying his patron.

As he opened the door, he promised himself he wouldn't use any information that would put Priyanka's position with the Lady at risk. But as he looked around, he wondered if that was a promise he could keep.

The office was as neat and organized as an obsessive librarian. He wouldn't have been surprised to see labels on everything. The tomes on the shelves were meticulously placed, the few knickknacks fit with the décor of the room, the leather-backed chair was in its position behind the desk—not a millimeter out of place.

The only thing that seemed odd was a mirror on the end table by the couch. The reflective surface was surrounded by thick, twisted metal. It looked like a hunk of molten iron had fallen from a crucible, been stepped on by a giant, and then fitted with a mirror.

As soon as he positioned himself in front of the mirror, he felt vertigo, a dislocation as if he'd been shot out of a cannon without moving.

The mirror did not show his reflection, only swirling mist within which shapes moved. Enthralled by what it was showing, Zayn leaned closer. He was surprised by what he saw.

In the distance was the outline of the Lady's plantation, the mist hiding most of its features, but for Zayn, the shape was unmistakable. Between the plantation and the front gate stood two figures. The first was Watcher Sabrina wearing her dark sunglasses, the steel cage at her feet. The second was his sister Neveah with her red handkerchief holding back her braids. He was shocked to see his sister alongside Watcher Sabrina. He didn't know what it meant, but it felt ominous.

It was like he was looking through a window rather than a mirror. The two figures stood back a ways, but as he studied the scene, either his sister or the Watcher faded from view, almost as if they were balanced on scales. But each time he looked at the disappearing one, they would reform.

Prickles of worry formed on his back. He spun around, expecting to see Priyanka standing behind him, relieved when he only saw the open door.

Zayn quickly left her office, checking the door twice to make sure it was closed, and removed all traces of his presence with a trio of spells. He was just sitting down at the kitchen counter to peel an orange when she came strolling into the Aerie.

Night had fallen on Harmony. She came out of the shadows as if she were made of them.

Priyanka's gaze flitted over him, her forehead knotting with questions that she left unsaid. His heart thundered in his chest, knowing that he'd disobeyed her orders. She looked like she was about to make an accusation, so he quickly asked a question.

"Whatever happened with the earth well? Did the sample tell you anything?"

Her face rippled with annoyance, before a mien of calmness overtook it.

"Yes," she said, shaking off a previous thought. "There are concerns, but we already knew that. Nothing to the level that Ne Yong suggested."

"Then they're making the wells a pretense," said Zayn.

"Not necessarily. That was only one well. If we're doing our due diligence, we need to check the others," she said.

"When are we going?"

Her earlier tenseness softened. "So eager after last time?"

"Another chance to prove myself."

She glanced away. "Another chance to die. But yes, we're going. Soon." She looked him in the eye. "But for now, I need to take you back. Lesson's over."

Priyanka took him back to the Honeycomb. Before she left, she looked like she wanted to say something, like that she knew he'd snuck into her office. But she disappeared like smoke into the portal, leaving Zayn wondering where his loyalties lay.

Chapter Sixteen
Herald of the Halls, January 2017
An interview for a job she doesn't want

The magelight sign for the Herald of the Halls office building, shining like a beacon into the second ward, fit with the rest of the gaudy architecture. The whole area screamed "look at me," which on principle gave Neveah a firm dislike. It wasn't that she didn't mind a little razzle-dazzle—she spent hours worrying about how to plate her food—but she hated when there wasn't any substance beneath.

She hadn't read the *Herald of the Halls* but a few times, as her time in the city had been spent mostly in her food truck, but it seemed like far too many stories were focused on the scandal of the day, or scaring people rather than offering solutions to any of those problems.

Her mother's advice about drama, *if someone's trying to get you excited, it means they're trying to get you to do something you don't want to, or shouldn't, be doing*, seemed to fit the paper in her estimation. But Neveah hadn't been reading for her own enjoyment, but to study up for a job interview.

The publisher of *The Spider Queen Must Die!* was Hilltop Comics. She'd found no traces of the company on the internet and the comic bookstores that she'd called only had a P.O. Box to send returns to. Only when she checked the Invictus City Hall business licensing department did she find proof that the company existed. There were no names anywhere on the forms, but when she'd pulled up the ownership group, she found an address that led to the Herald. Her phone inquiries had gone nowhere, so she decided to try a roundabout way to get the information.

Neveah strode into the office building in a turquoise blouse and black pants with her beads tamed beneath a colorful headband. It felt weird to be wearing makeup since she'd been living in her food truck and taking nightly sponge baths, but she'd spent the night in a hotel room to have access to a real shower and bathroom. After sleeping on a hard cot, the bed had felt too squishy, but she'd managed a decent night's sleep.

The man at the desk smiled at her approach. "Can I help you?"

"I'm here for a nine o'clock interview. Neveah Carter."

"Wonderful." He gestured towards the waiting area. "Wait over there. I'll let Melissa know that you've arrived."

A few minutes later, a woman in a floral dress who looked like she was a weight lifter in her spare time marched into the waiting area.

"Hello, Neveah?"

Neveah joined her. They shook hands. Melissa took her to a small conference room with a small table and two chairs on opposite sides.

Neveah placed a small leather notebook open in front of her. It'd cost too much, but she knew little accouterments like that would help make a good impression, just as an edible garnish on a plated steak signaled to the customer that they were about to enjoy a great meal.

Melissa clasped her hands in front of her on the table. "So tell me about yourself and why you want to join the Herald team."

Neveah let a practiced smile rise to her lips. She didn't really want to join the team at the Herald, but she needed information and this was one way to get it.

"It's my dream to be a food critic. While I know that you currently have one on staff, I'm looking for an opportunity anywhere within the paper to get my start, and eventually work my way towards that position should an opening arise.

"As for myself, I'm a self-starter. I had top grades in high school, was on the school newspaper team, and have owned my own business for the last two years. I sent along samples of my writing with my resume, so you can see the quality of my work is professional level."

Melissa unclasped her hands. "The quality of your work was exceptional. Honestly, we don't normally take applicants without a degree in journalism, but your work stood out enough that I wanted to hear more. You must have had an impressive high school English teacher."

"My father was a high school teacher, so class never really ended around our house," she said.

"That makes sense," said Melissa. "I'm sure that was annoying."

Neveah sensed the trap and let a smile rise to her lips. "Not at all. If you enjoy doing it, it's not work."

Truthfully, it was annoying at times, since she preferred to be in the kitchen, but she knew it was better not to say it.

"If you were to work at the Herald, since as you said the position of your choice is unavailable, what would you like to do? Is there a particular department? Crime beat? Fashion? Hall politics?" asked Melissa.

"I'm open to anything really," said Neveah. "But if I had to pick, I was wondering if there were any openings in Hilltop Comics?"

Melissa's nose wrinkled. "Hilltop Comics. Never heard of it."

"It's a subsidiary of the Herald," said Neveah.

The interviewer blinked as if she hadn't understood a word that Neveah had said.

"I'm a manager in human resources. I would know if we had a comic book store in this building," said Melissa.

"Publisher, not store," said Neveah. "I've been seeing Hilltop Comics everywhere, so I thought it'd be good to position myself within an up-and-coming division."

Melissa squeezed her lips together. She bristled with annoyance. "But there *is* no Hilltop Comics. I would know."

Neveah knew the next part would be tenuous. She had to be careful not to insult Melissa any further, so she pulled out the sheet she'd printed off at the library and slid it across the table. It was the business license with the City of Invictus. Melissa's eyes widened as she read the address listed and the connection to the Herald.

"This company was started six months ago," said Melissa, who looked offended by what she was reading. "I don't understand why I don't know about it."

"So you don't know if there are any positions available?" asked Neveah.

Melissa's voice rose as she spoke. "I didn't even know this place existed before now." She sighed, staring at the paper as if it were proof that the world was really a giant radish. "Excuse me a moment, I want to make a few calls. I'm sure I can clear this up. This can't be real."

Neveah was left alone in the room for ten minutes. When Melissa returned, she shoved the paper across the table and slumped into the chair.

"Yep, it exists," said Melissa, exasperated. "Though nobody knows much about it. Supposedly, it was hatched by Ms. Cardwell herself, or maybe it's a vanity project of her spoiled daughter."

"Is there an office in the city?"

Melissa rubbed her temple absently. "No office. No name."

"Then how do the comics get printed?" asked Neveah.

Melissa shrugged one shoulder. "Probably sent from the artist directly to the printer. Not here, obviously—we only print the paper in this building—but we have other printers in the city."

A warm glow filled Neveah's midsection. She'd proved that the publisher existed, and maybe a little more about where she might find it. She decided she'd thrown poor Melissa's view of her importance in the company into question enough. Neveah could find the printers easily enough on her own.

"So do I get the job?" asked Neveah.

"Job? Oh yeah," said Melissa. "I'll get back to you. I need to consider where we might put you, but I know talent when I see it. I'd like to find a place for you."

"Great," said Neveah, extending her hand.

Melissa led her out of the building. Neveah was marching towards the train station when she saw her cousin Keelan. He was staring right at her.

"Oh shit."

Keelan crossed the distance quickly. He looked like he'd been looking for her.

"Hey, Kee," she said, putting on a bright smile.

"You're not in Atlanta," said Keelan.

"No, I'm not. Do they know?" she asked.

He nodded. "Uncle Maceo called me a few weeks ago. Told me they thought you might be here. I tracked down your food truck this morning, and then followed you here."

"Does Zayn?" she asked.

"No," said Keelan. "They didn't want to add more stress. They're already worried enough about him."

"I'm worried too."

"We all are," said Keelan, though the way he said it made it seem like he knew something. "Is that why you're here?"

She was going to lie and tell Keelan that she was in the city because of the food truck, but decided against it.

"Something's wrong with him. What with the headaches, the time he fell off the Stack, everything. He's not the same as he was before the third year," she said.

"Maybe," said Keelan. "Or maybe he's just pushing himself too hard. He goes days without sleep, is always throwing himself off cliffs before knowing where he's going to land. It could just be stress. You can't help him with that."

"I don't think it's just that," said Neveah. "And I don't think you believe that either. Will you help me?"

Keelan glanced at his shoes before answering. "I think it's best that I don't."

"Oh, yeah," she said, remembering that he was slated to become a Watcher. "I forget that sometimes."

"I don't."

Neveah caught the hook of responsibility in his tone. It was like someone who had signed up for war knowing that they probably wouldn't return. She remembered what a brat he'd been growing up and wondered how he'd changed so much.

"Don't tell Zayn I'm in the city."

A little frown tugged at Keelan's lips. "You should go back home, or at least to Atlanta."

"Promise you won't tell him," she said.

"I wasn't planning on it." He glanced at the sky as if that told him something. "I have to go. Be careful. Don't go messing in things you don't understand."

"Just like you did when you signed up for the Watchers," she replied.

He winced, but nodded.

"A hug before you go," said Neveah, opening her arms. They embraced. "Love you, Kee."

"Love you, Nev. Be good."

"Only if you will," she smirked, which brought a smile to her cousin's lips.

Before he left, he hesitated. "Any chance you're making tacos in the food truck?"

"You know it."

"Then don't leave for a week at least."

Neveah snorted. "You can't have it both ways, Kee!"

He raised his hand as he walked away. Seeing her cousin only tugged at her heart, reminding her of the stakes. Though he'd said otherwise, she knew he was lying when it came to Zayn. Something was wrong, they both knew it. It was up to her to find out what it was.

Chapter Seventeen
Seventh ward, January 2017
A waking nightmare

The cave angled downward like a throat through the earth, forcing Zayn to half-climb, half-jump to make progress. The whole time he felt his back prickle with worry.

Each time he turned his head, he though he heard something behind him. But it was nothing.

Beneath him, a light formed like an eye. Voices followed, too distant to make out. Had they found him? Had it all been for naught? All his plans and deceptions ruined?

The voices were coming up towards him, or he was still moving down, it was hard to tell. They were familiar, filling him with a sense of foreboding.

When he recognized the main one, his heart dropped ten feet. How had it all unraveled? All his threads clipped and burned, the web revealed...

Zayn woke in his underwear, standing on the edge of his roof in the seventh ward covered in a sheen of sweat. He tottered towards the abyss before slamming his foot forward to stop his momentum.

"Wha...?"

His legs collapsed beneath him, supports knocked out by the sudden shock of waking up in a place he hadn't gone to sleep.

"Why am I up here?" he muttered to himself, checking his limbs and flesh for wounds or signs of trauma.

The dream, which had been so vivid moments ago, faded quickly, leaving him with only the impression of the fear of discovery, and the adrenaline of escape.

Though it was nearly freezing, his skin was hot to the touch, but the wintery breeze and the exposure quickly cooled him and he was shivering in moments.

Zayn scooted to the edge of the roof, dangling over to see that the window to his room was open. He must have climbed out. But was he asleep?

Getting back inside was easy, but he still slammed the window shut emphatically, as if it'd had something to do with his existence on the roof. Marley, who'd been asleep on top of his pile of covers, looked up with a sleepy matted face, clearly annoyed by the loud noise.

"If you're here, that means no one did this to me, or at least if they did, they did it from afar," said Zayn, plopping on the bed and rubbing the back of Marley's neck with his fingers.

The callolo purred, arching into massaging fingers, clearly forgiving Zayn for the loud noise. Zayn scratched Marley's back while he thought about the implications of sleepwalking onto the roof.

"I'm not going to be able to sleep now," he decided after a few minutes, throwing on a pair of gym shorts before heading to the kitchen.

After rummaging through the refrigerator, Zayn dumped

his leftover kung pao chicken into a bowl. Chopsticks in hand, he was about to take his first bite when he heard a knock on the door.

A glance at the microwave told him it was far too late for visitors, so he set the bowl down, grabbed the throwing knife from behind the bookshelf in the living room, and approached the window by the door.

A woman stood on the front porch with her arms crossed. It was Watcher Sabrina.

"Dammit."

Zayn threw the door open.

"You picked a strange time for a visit," he said, wondering if she'd had something to do with his sleepwalking.

"I know my contacts," she said.

"That's all I am? A contact?"

Watcher Sabrina shut the door behind her. "You should know better than to ask me that." She glanced at the stairs. "Is anyone home?"

"Just Vin, but he sleeps like a hibernating bear. The others are staying at the Honeycomb." Zayn nodded towards her empty hand. "No deathhead cage? Is this a social visit?"

Her lips flattened. "I left it in the car. I didn't want any house protections to confuse my intent." She crossed her arms. "Have you performed as requested?"

As Zayn stared at Sabrina, he knew there was a secondary reason for her to show up in the middle of the night. It made it harder for him to deceive her. Never give your enemy favorable terrain in a battle.

"I have, though I don't know the value of the information." When she didn't move he added, "Don't want to get your little friend to verify my truthfulness?"

"You wouldn't be planning to lie if you requested the cage," said Sabrina.

"Or I'm playing a subtle game to make you think I am."

She tilted her head. "Stop stalling, Zayn."

He was about to refute her when he realized she was right. He didn't want to betray Priyanka, but he also wanted to keep his family safe. Delaying what he had to do wasn't going to make it any easier.

"Like I said before, I don't know if this is helpful, but Priyanka uses a scrying device," said Zayn.

Sabrina frowned. "Every good mage worth their salt uses a scrying device."

"This didn't seem like an everyday, run-of-the-mill kind. Something special, unique perhaps," said Zayn, remembering the visions it'd shown him.

"Describe it."

"It looked like a hunk of metal with a mirror slapped into the middle of it," said Zayn.

Sabrina scrunched up her forehead. "What kind of metal?"

"I don't know. It had an oily quality. The mirror didn't show my reflection, but a vision of other places and people, though it was hard to see them through the mist."

Sabrina's eyes slowly widened at his explanation. "The Starwood Mirror. That was supposedly lost two hundred years ago."

The excitement in her eyes twisted his stomach, making him suddenly not hungry. He'd hoped the information was useful enough to get the Lady off his back, but not so useful as to endanger Priyanka.

"What did you see in it?" she asked, studying him intently.

He answered right away to allay suspicion, even though part of him wondered what she would say if he'd told her that he saw her in the mirror.

"Nothing that signified anything," said Zayn. "I wanted to

see what it would show me, but Priyanka came back and I had to get out of her room."

Sabrina made a noise under her breath and looked away.

"Is this good?" he asked.

Sabrina Watcher folded her excitement behind a calm façade. "It's good enough, for now." She looked around as if she'd forgotten something. "I should go. It's a long drive back to Varna."

"You just got here," he said. "You could crash here. We have a spare room."

"No, no. I need to get back." She licked her lips. "I will report your findings to the Lady when I return."

"Well, drive safe," he said. "I suppose I'll see you in Varna after the school year is over."

Sabrina was halfway out the door when she turned back. "After? Oh, no. You'll be seeing me again. This was good information, but the Lady expects you to continue your surveillance. Remember, it is through her good graces that you and your family still live."

Zayn flipped off the closed door after she was gone. Alone in the living room, standing in his shorts, Zayn wondered how this was all going to end. But he knew for certain that next time he wasn't going to give her any new information. He hated that he'd betrayed Priyanka even one iota. There was no way he would do it again. Next time, he'd be more prepared, even if it meant chancing a sting from the deathhead scorpion.

Chapter Eighteen
Twelfth Ward, February 2017
By ink and page

It took a few weeks for Neveah to find the right printing house in the city. None of them were labeled with signs that said Printing Hilltop Comics Here. She'd had to call around, narrowing it down to a few locations, before setting aside a morning to check them out.

With a crockpot of carnitas cooking in the food truck, Neveah made her way to Poorhouse Printing. The location was a little sketchy. She had to step over two bums asleep on a heated grate when she left the train platform.

On the way, she felt the gaze of every passerby as if it were a branding iron, wishing she'd brought a weapon since she'd never really been that great at the Five Elements. She remembered being able to keep up with Zayn and Keelan as kids, but then they grew up and left her behind, while she focused herself in the kitchen.

A block away from her destination, a couple of older guys

crossed the street, headed in her direction. Suddenly, the business attire she was wearing felt like a target on her back. Her stomach rose into her throat, and her palms became sweaty.

As soon as the first guy's foot touched the curb, Neveah spun around, speared them with her gaze, and said, "I'm a Hall mage, so don't mess with me."

The first guy raised up his hands. "We're just headed to play basketball. Sorry."

They scurried the other way, tails tucked between their legs. Neveah almost felt bad, but decided that it was better to be on the safe side.

The printing house had no sign out front, just a small bronze nameplate next to the door covered with bars. Neveah glanced around before hitting the buzzer.

The motion from a camera above the door caught her notice. She gave it a little wave, feeling exposed. After a minute, a beefy guy with a bushy beard opened the door with a revolver in his hand.

"Whoa," said Neveah, "I'm just here to ask questions, no need for that."

His eyes were rounded with worry and his hands shook slightly.

"Who are you?" asked the beefy guy with a gun.

"My name is Neveah. I work in HR at the Herald." The guy's eyes didn't budge, nor did the gun move away from her, so she added, "I work for Camille."

It was a total lie—they hadn't contacted her yet—but as soon as she said Camille's name, the beefy guy's shoulders relaxed and he shoved the gun in the front of his pants.

He quickly unlatched the iron gate and ushered her inside, before returning the front door to its previously barricaded state.

"Is everything okay...?" she asked, pausing.

"Frank, and not really. Ever since we started printing this stupid comic, weird shit has been happening," he said, looking around as if he expected ghosts to come flying out of the walls at any moment.

This news both frightened and comforted Neveah. She was excited to know she was on the right track, but worried what it meant.

"Like what kind of things?" asked Neveah.

"We've been broken into twice, totally ransacked, looking for what I don't know. Then there's the weird buzzing noise that happens over the building, but only on rainy days, or when it's dark," he said.

"What does it sound like?" she asked.

Frank looked like he didn't want to answer. He kept smacking his lips and looking away.

"I don't know, like a freaking giant insect or something, but that's crazy talk," he said while blotched red spots formed on his face.

"It's okay, this *is* the city of sorcery. Weird shit happens," she said.

"Yeah, well it's never happened to me before." He lowered his voice. "Sometimes, when I'm busy at the press, or deep into my work, I glance away and catch one of 'em spying on me."

"One of them?"

Frank swallowed. "A spider. Big one. Would fit in the palm of your hand. And then it runs away before I can kill it. I've seen the damn thing four times."

As Frank spoke, her face went numb.

"You okay?" he asked, squinting. "You've seen one of these spiders before?"

"No," she said, trying to will some emotion back into her face. "I just don't like spiders. Can you describe the spider and show me where you saw it?"

"Yeah, purple striations, fit in the palm of my hand. Never seen one like it before. One of them crazy mages probably made it from scratch," he said, looking like he wished he had a cigarette.

As he led her into the printing area of the warehouse, she thought about all the times she and her brother had argued about whether or not the Lady could see through the spiders. This confirmed it for her.

Headed through the greasy equipment towards the back, Neveah worried what might happen if the spider returned and saw her. The Lady would surely recognize her from Varna. What would she think? Or maybe the Lady was trying to track down who was making the comic just like she was.

A pit in her stomach opened as she realized the comic probably had nothing to do with her brother, or why he was having his migraines. Maybe she'd gotten into something more dangerous than she first thought.

"Neveah, you there?" asked Frank, leaning into her field of vision.

"Oh, sorry, long day," she mumbled.

"Well, the last time I saw the spider, I was working the hydraulic lines. The pressure was high, and no matter how I fiddled...well, you don't give a lick about that. But I saw it over there," he said, pointing to a desk along the wall.

The old 1950s-era steel desk looked like it'd been left there because they couldn't move it. A barred window was right above it, cracked open a smidge, a gap large enough for a spider to slip through.

"I've seen it in this general area every time," said Frank.

"Is there an alleyway behind this wall?"

He tilted his head. "How'd you know that?"

"A guess." She sighed. "And you don't know what the

people who broke in were looking for?"

"Not a clue."

Frank didn't know, but Neveah had a good idea. A Watcher, she assumed, had broken into the warehouse looking for the address of the artist. It'd probably sent the spider to scout, or to overhear any relevant information. It was the same thing she was looking for.

"Can we head back to the front? It's cold," she said, rubbing her arms.

When they were back at the office, Neveah wrote something on a piece of paper and handed it to Frank. Puzzled, he read the paper and then nodded slowly.

"An internet dropbox," he said, handing back the paper. She'd asked him how they received the art files for the comics, but hadn't wanted to be overheard, so she'd written it down.

"So you know where?"

He shook his head. "But why? Seems like a lot of trouble over a comic."

"Maybe it's more than a comic," she said.

His forehead wrinkled. "Shouldn't you know this already?"

"I do," said Neveah, remembering Melissa's frustration when she learned about the comics. "That's why I'm here. We've had some strange things happen at the Herald too, and we wanted to make sure printing was going okay."

Frank shook his head. "Whoever wrote 'em, they're a genius. We're on the third printing for issue number two, and they've doubled the plan for the next one 'cause they were getting orders from all over the country. I guess some people love a villain."

"Or maybe they want to see her die," she mumbled under her breath.

"Sorry I haven't been much help," said Frank.

"No, you've been a ton of help. I'm sorry things aren't going well here. I'll make sure and tell Camille about the problems. She can authorize extra security," said Neveah.

"You know, that'd be mighty nice of you. I take back all those things I ever said about HR," said Frank with a wink.

"Don't take 'em back until we've followed through," said Neveah.

The whole way back to the food truck, Neveah tried to figure out what the connection between the Lady, the comic, and her brother might be. Sometimes as she thought about it, the connections seemed obvious, other times they seemed ridiculous. Maybe something could be cleared up if she could find the artist, but she wasn't the only one looking for him.

She was so focused on the problem with the comic she didn't notice the two guys in suits and briefcases until she reached the truck.

"Neveah Carter?" asked the shorter balder one.

"You already knew the answer to that," she said.

The two men shared a glance, before the taller bald one opened his briefcase and handed her a folder filled with papers. As she peeked into the manila folder, the short bald one started speaking.

"Neveah Carter, you are being served a Cease and Desist order in regards to the manufacture and production of the food products made in the truck parked at Allanon and Sepia. The current food products, also known as tacos, have been deemed in violation of the intellectual property rights of Celesse D'Agastine by the Fourth Federal District here in the city of Invictus. If you do not cease and desist, you will be held in contempt and will forfeit all equipment used to manufacture said food products, including the mobile equipment. You have been served."

The two men turned on their heels and left her with the folder, head swimming. Her knees wobbled before she crashed to the curb, barely getting her hand down to slow her fall. The world spun around her and she felt the air flee from her lungs.

"Why?" she muttered, but no answer came.

Chapter Nineteen
The Undercity, March 2017
Once a fire lizard...

The note reached him right before class with Instructor O'Keefe, so Zayn told his teammates to go on without him, and he ran to his room in the Honeycomb to collect his gear. A surge of excitement kept him checking the note repeatedly. He'd been waiting for the day they'd go back into the Undercity to check another well of power.

Water well. Meet at GN behind Olympias. –P

The whole way he wondered what kind of guardian might be at the water well. A kraken or slime beast? Maybe a seadragon. Any of them could possibly kill him, but that didn't tamp his excitement.

What he didn't expect was to find a tall woman with ebony skin so dark it seemed to absorb the light waiting for him rather than Priyanka. She stood as still as a tree, hands clasped in front, while her eyes had a luminous all-seeing quality that unnerved him. Her bald head seemed a choice made for efficiency rather than beauty, though the style suited her.

"Mr. Carter," she said in an English accent so proper it sounded like it'd been chiseled from marble and set in a museum.

"Yes?"

"It wasn't a question but a greeting," she said, her eyes blinking owl-like.

"Hello." He glanced around the small circle of hedges and the obsidian archway. "Is Priyanka coming?"

After an extended pause, the woman said, "No."

Her gaze seemed to judge him for his fidgeting, which only made him more self-conscious about every movement. Zayn had never felt as much like a bug under a magnifying glass as he did at that moment.

"Are...you going to the...?" he asked, hoping she might fill in the rest.

The awkward silence drew on for what seemed like five minutes, but was probably only thirty seconds, but it was the longest thirty seconds of his life.

"Adele," she said. "You are wishing my name.   Adele Montgomery."

The name rang true in his head. "Adele Montgomery. Patron Adele Montgomery? Animalians?"

Her nose wrinkled. "The proper name is the Society for the Understanding of Animals, not Animalians. The former is a search for knowledge, the latter is a fetish."

Zayn swallowed. "I'm very sorry. I didn't know. I'll do better next time."

She seemed to accept his apology, or at least he thought she did when her chin lifted slightly.

After another long pause, she said, "My apologies. I spend little time with other humans. I forget the social rituals."

"It's okay. I grew up in a small town. I regularly look like an ass in the big city with my small-town habits," he said.

Though her lips didn't move, her eyes creased with what he hoped was mirth.

"I have spent the last six months as a fire-tongue lizard in the lava baths of Hythia. I may need some time to adjust. But we should continue into the Undercity to the water well. We can converse along the way. This usually helps me return to the living," she said.

Adele took the lead once they traveled through the portal. After a few minutes, Zayn realized that he would need to initiate conversation.

"What...how much do you, uhm, know about what's going on?" he asked.

Her eyes rotated towards him in an inhuman manner. "I thought Academy students were more eloquent."

Zayn groaned internally. She really *had* forgotten the social niceties of humanity.

"The dragons and the wells. Do you know everything about that?"

"Of course, or why would I be here?" said Adele. "Pri briefed me in Hythia."

"As a fire lizard or a human?" asked Zayn.

She blinked twice before a short chuckle slipped from her lips. "A joke. I am amused."

Zayn wondered if she'd always been this wooden, or if it was just a side effect of her transformations.

"What do you think about the dragons?" he asked as they cut through a large cavern filled with stalactites.

"They are not the purview of my hall, if that's what you're asking. Dragons are majestic and highly intelligent, and have no need for my protections. On the contrary, they can be quite vicious, a predator just like the human race," she said.

Zayn swallowed, pondering her answer, which was not his

intended question. He knew the Animalians had odd views, but this was his first time interacting with someone from the hall.

"The Circle of Scale's accusations, that the wells of power have thinned, and the city is due for a breach from the demonic realm," he said.

"Oh that," she replied, looking down upon him with a slightly amused expression. "Always business, just like your patron. But I do agree with the dragons. The wells are thinning, and the absence of our head patron makes the breach inevitable."

"Inevitable? If that's what you think, why haven't you done anything before?" he asked.

"The problem lies within the originals. They're the only ones that can choose a new head patron, but they'll never agree on anyone. Personally, I think Invictus is alive. He was always one to do something drastic to prove a point. He'll come back at the last moment to save the day, just so everyone can love him again," said Adele, judgement ringing through her tone.

Zayn ignored her views on Invictus. Everyone had a theory about the head patron's disappearance, but they'd probably never get to learn the truth. It was more likely that it would be a perpetual mystery like "who built the sphinx?" or "is Elvis alive?"

"If you had to pick, who would you choose as the head patron?" he asked.

"Besides myself?" She chuckled. "I assume you mean from the originals. No one would choose Bannon for many reasons, and Celesse is too mercantile for my tastes. Better living through alchemy isn't always better living. Semyon is... well, he's a good person, but not always practical. The nature of the head patron's position would eat him alive.

"Which leaves—" when she spoke, the name she gave was

garbled as if it were verbally redacted. His reaction caused her to put a hand to her chin.

"Ahh, yes. I forget that he's hid his name with sorcery. I shall just name him as the Patron of Coterie. He's nearest in power to Invictus, a mage with relentless drive and limitless ambition, which is the problem," she said.

"Which leaves Priyanka."

Adele, who appeared more animated during this discussion, as if the effects of being a fire-lizard were wearing off, gestured with her hands.

"Pri, my dear, is probably the least individually powerful patron of the originals, and compromised by so many entanglements with foreign entities that it would be difficult to discern what her true motives might be. Picking her would be dangerous for reasons different than the others. Each of them have their flaws, dangerous awful flaws, but they are true to the Halls. With Priyanka, I'm afraid, we just don't know."

"That's a strange thing to say to one of her students," said Zayn, glancing up at the tall patron.

"One of my flaws is a brutal and often unsociable honesty. A side effect of spending so much time in the company of animals," said Adele. "But I would have you know that in the end, despite all that I said about her, I would still pick Priyanka over the others."

"Why?"

Adele paused at the top of a short cliff. In the distance, he could hear falling water. The cavern bent to the left and down, disappearing beyond his magic-aided sight.

"Because she is aware of and embraces her flaws, while the others have spent centuries hiding theirs. The other patrons think she's arrogant and dangerous. With names like the Mistress of Knives, or Lady Death, of course that would be their impression. But Pri's not arrogant at all. She's willing to try anything and fail, but most importantly, learn from those failures. Which is why everyone thinks she's the weakest of the five. They've seen her failures."

"But you think that's what makes her strong," said Zayn.

"Exactly." Adele motioned towards the slope ahead, where the sound of falling water was coming from. "Let's move quickly and stretch our legs. I'm beginning to feel myself again."

Without waiting for Zayn, Adele crouched down like a panther and in a perfect four-legged gait ran to the edge of the cliff and leapt, landing on a boulder, bounced off, and sprinted out of sight.

Impressed by the display, Zayn flooded his imbuement and followed, barely keeping up with Adele. The path led them past a stream cutting through the cavern. The severe slope created mini-waterfalls and slick paths, but they traversed the terrain easily.

Along the way, Zayn wondered what kind of magic sustained Adele as she bounced off the walls and bounded over obstacles as if they were children's toys.

They followed the stream as it grew until it was a few feet deep, rushing down black rock, spitting mist into the cavern. The air grew thick, and wet, mixed with a metallic tint, which told Zayn that the well of power was near.

When the land leveled out, Adele stopped on the edge of a massive lake, of which he could not see the far side.

"The Sunless Shore," said Adele. "We shall have to travel a ways over water to reach the well."

Zayn amped his senses to try to pierce the gloom ahead, but the distance and the darkness hid the well. Yet he could feel its presence. Something about it seemed off, like hearing a high-pitched ringing but not knowing the source.

"How will...?"

Zayn barely got his question out before she put her hand

on an oblong rock in the shape of a boat. The rough surface disappeared, revealing a boat with a pair of oars beneath the illusion.

"I was worried we were going to have to swim," said Zayn, scratching the back of his head.

"These waters are far too dangerous to swim in," said Adele. "I would survive, of course, but you would not."

Adele pulled the boat to the edge, letting Zayn climb in first. She took the rudder and motioned for him to work the oars. With his faez-imbued strength they were quickly making good time across the lake.

"What kind of creatures make this place dangerous?" he asked, leaning into the oar stroke.

"The proper name for them are *medusoza insanire,* but some call them man o' madness, or the jellyfish of insanity. I prefer the name Cthulhu jellies. They're drawn by the well, and faez in general, which makes them more dangerous than ones found in the wild, especially because they cluster here more. Their stings will either give you visions or drive you insane. Or both."

"Temporary or permanent?" he asked.

"Let's not find out," said Adele.

The air grew colder the further across the water they went, then as if they'd breached an invisible wall, the air started to grow warm again.

Glancing into the water, Zayn saw at first solitary ghostly blobs in the water with icy-white tendrils that descended into the deep. The closer they got, the more the jellies filled the water until there was an eerie fullness, as if they'd been drawn by their approach.

Zayn knew they neared the well long before he could see it. He felt the power tugging on his mind.

When at last he laid his eyes upon it, he knew at once that

it was both similar to the earth well, and very different. This one was on an island at the center of the lake, and like the other, wrapped in a metal shell covered with glowing runes. But while the other throbbed with intense but regular pulses, this one seemed to emit a hissing static-like energy.

Adele sensed it as well. Her lips were squeezed tight.

"Something's wrong with this well of power," she said.

While the keening of faez in his mind made him want to turn the boat around and return to the shore, the feeling tripled when he saw the well's guardian.

Plodding around the runed cylinder came a beast larger than a pair of double-decker buses. But it wasn't the size of the creature that unnerved Zayn, it was the number of heads sprouting from its enormous body.

"Merlin, that's a five-headed hydra," exclaimed Zayn.

An agonized sigh dripped from Adele's lips. "It's only supposed to have three heads."

Chapter Twenty
Undercity, March 2017
Five heads are not better than one

The hydra was a rare beast, but not entirely unknown. A small two-headed version had been caught off Mykonos island about eight years ago. Zayn vividly remembered the nets and chains around the poor frightened creature as they dragged it onto the shore.

The hydra had wailed and fought against the ropes, clearly a youngling by its size and reaction. It'd been no larger than a warhorse, the heads more giraffe sized than dinosaur. Paleontologists claimed the hydra was a version of a brontosaurus warped by magic during prehistoric times, but it was an unproven hypothesis.

"I've never seen nor heard of a specimen this size nor with this many heads," said Adele with a certain mixture of awe and wonder.

"How do they get so many heads?" he asked.

"If one gets chopped off, two grow in its place," said Adele.

"Something must have attacked it, or it damaged itself some-how."

She didn't sound like she believed the latter, and if it were the former, he didn't want to meet something that could attack a hydra this large and survive.

"This will make your job more difficult," she said.

"Let me guess, I'm the one that gets to take the sample," he said.

"After you pacify it with your imbuement," said Adele.

Zayn froze. "Did Priyanka tell you?"

Patron Adele speared him with an amused gaze. "Who do you think helped her and Percival design the imbuement? This has been a work in progress for many years. Far too many of the Halls foes are non-human, which makes the normal sorcerous methods more challenging."

Reflexively, Zayn touched his side, feeling like he was wearing a priceless piece of art rather than an imbuement.

"Merlin," exclaimed Zayn. "How am I going to deal with that beast?"

"If it is not within your ability, we can return to the surface and consult Priyanka about the next steps," said Adele.

"No," said Zayn, then a second time more emphatically. "No. I can do this. It's just not...what I was expecting."

"I will stay in the boat and protect you from the well," said Adele.

"Back in the boat? But how do I get to that island?" he asked.

"You'll swim."

"Swim? I thought you said I couldn't survive in the water because of the Cthulhu jellies?"

A broad smile broke across her face. "Then you'll have to be quick. I can lure them away from the area temporarily, but they will return and I'll be too busy with your shield to remove them again."

Zayn studied the island and the hydra's path while he undressed to his underclothes. A chuckle slipped out when he thought about the earth well.

"Is something funny?"

"At the last one, Priyanka jokingly told me I'd have to get naked to get a sample," he said.

"It won't bother me if you don't want to get your underwear wet. I have few inhibitions," said Adele with a blank expression.

"Yeah...I'm still going to wear my underwear. No offense."

"None taken," she said. "It is your choice."

When Zayn was ready to make his swim, Adele knelt down in the back of the boat and shoved her head into the water. He saw her chest rise and fall as if she were singing, but he couldn't hear anything. After a few minutes, she pulled her dripping wet head out and said, "It is safe. Now let us make your shield."

Creating the protection against the ravages of the well took longer than Zayn would have liked. He kept glancing into the water expecting the Cthulhu jellies to return. Not to mention that he'd have to deal with the hydra, get a sample, and return before then. He shoved the sample taker into his underwear as he climbed to the edge of the boat.

The water was icy cold, taking Zayn's breath away as he plunged beneath the darkened surface. He pulled himself through the water with powerful strokes, expecting the stings of the jellies at every moment.

When at last he crawled onto shore, he slammed his knee into the rocks in his haste, relieved to escape the lake. The island was wide enough that he still had some distance to go before reaching the runed steel cylinder, which meant he had time to pacify the hydra before venturing near it.

As he pulled on the hydra's essence, his head grew dizzy and his vision hazy. The nearness of the excess faez made his magic surge with power.

He had a taste of the beast's nature by the time it came lumbering around the cylinder, but unlike the kwalic, it saw him immediately, a benefit of having five sets of eyes. Zayn flowed a calming wave against the creature, but it was so large, and had so many heads, that the hydra resisted his first efforts and took a few steps towards him.

Doubling down on his efforts, Zayn tried a second time, pushing against the hydra's resistance until it stopped moving. But holding it in place was like wrestling with the ocean. Each time he tried to hold on, another head broke free.

Zayn quickly realized he was not going to be able to completely pacify the hydra, but he could slow it enough that he might be able to take the sample and escape back into the water. Which would require imbuement weaving, to distract the hydra while flooding his speed imbuements at the same time.

Grateful for what he learned in Harmony—though he was aware that Priyanka had probably planned it—Zayn broke into a jog, working in the speed imbuement slowly, while he battled the great beast. The unruly hydra fought his every effort, smashing back his attempts at control.

The hydra broke into a lumbering gait, forcing Zayn to hurry his pace over the uneven rocks, leaping ravines while weaving his imbuements. If he didn't push his speed too much, he could slowly build distance between himself and the hydra without losing control. It was a delicate balance hovering within the limits of his abilities while staying alive.

The first time he tried to take the sample, he fumbled with the mechanism with his frozen hands, forcing him to take a second loop around the island. It was on the second try that he noticed a section of the cavern floor near the cylinder glowed.

It looked like a gouge had been taken out of the earth, like a giant fist had scraped away the rock, exposing the frothing golden faez. The hole seemed to be creating the dissonance in the well's protections. The nearer he got, the more the keening rang in his head, worrying him that it might trigger a migraine.

When he stopped to take the sample from the well, he realized he might be able to stop, or at least reduce the faez leaking into the cavern if he could plug the hole. If he could get control of the hydra for ten seconds, he could convince it to move the boulders that had been ripped out of the earth to stop the leak.

Convinced that he had to take the chance, Zayn stood his ground when the hydra rounded the corner. Though he wasn't sure how he knew what to do, Zayn tapped into the well, drawing on the excess faez in the air to control the hydra. At first, the beast's five heads screamed, raising back their necks in defiance, but he bore down, focusing his attention on them.

"Come on, come on."

The creature fought against him, and he remembered that fledgling hydra on Mykonos that he'd seen on TV, and faltered for a moment, until he remembered what would happen if it reached him. He pushed as hard as he could, straining as the faez turned to sparks around him as if he were standing in a sparkler fountain.

Rather than trying to calm it, Zayn funneled the hydra's rage into the pile of boulders. The beast charged the pile, knocking boulders across the floor, only half of them going into the hole. When the first boulder tipped into the golden hole, a blast erupted, evaporating the rocks and knocking Zayn to his knees.

When the dust cleared, he saw two of the heads had been severed by debris, and the hydra was spinning around in pain, making horrible tortured honks. What was worse was that the hole was larger now, and the keening in his head so sharp it made him squint.

Not only had he not fixed the problem, he'd made it worse.

Zayn thought about what he could do to fix it, but he no longer had control of the creature, and when it regrew the additional heads, it would not be happy with him, so he sprinted to the water.

A few white blobs had returned, floating ominously near the surface, but he couldn't wait, so he shoved the sampler back into his underwear and dove in. As soon as he slipped into the water, the Cthulhu jellies converged, but he was quick enough and they were slow enough that he could outmaneuver them.

But as he crossed the distance between the island and the boat, the jellies grew more numerous, forcing him to dodge deeper and deeper into the water, which was more perilous because he had to avoid their trailing tendrils.

The breath in his lungs burned like coals and his vision grew hazy, the effort from imbuement weaving and the fight with the hydra having already drained his energy. As the jellies descended, Zayn swam further down, his ears popping from the pressure.

He paused when he realized that going further into the depths would be the end of him because he only had so much air in his lungs. The sight above was both beautiful and gut-wrenching. A dome of white curtains floated down upon him, blocking all chance of escape.

Using his imbuement only brought pain to his side, as there was no air to pull the pheromones from, which left him with no options.

Floating hundreds of feet beneath the surface, a host of Cthulhu jellies converged on him. Glistening tendrils slipped towards him, forcing him to dodge, but swimming side to side was difficult, and he barely avoided being stung. Even the Five Elements were useless at this point, because his hands were stiff from the cold and there were so many he didn't think it would make a difference.

Zayn was so busy avoiding the tendrils, he didn't notice the jellies started swimming away until there were half as many as before. Only then did he hear the wavering song floating through the water, calling them away. The tug of Adele's voice had no effect on him, but he could feel its trembling power like a song through a thick wall.

With his air running out, Zayn didn't wait for the jellies to completely vacate the area. He swam upward while the air burned in his lungs. There were still many jellies above him, but he spied a narrow path back to the boat. He pushed himself upward, swimming through the torturous hole, squeezing his lips shut because they desperately wanted to take air.

He didn't see the Cthulhu jelly until it was almost on him. It was so small, so delicate, no bigger than a quarter, with tendrils no longer than his forearm, that it escaped his notice. Only a few strokes from the boat, Zayn slipped past the baby jelly, and he pulled himself over the gunwale the moment he felt a sting on his left leg. Rather than pain, Zayn experienced a warmth traveling up his leg.

Adele, head pulled from the water, glanced over at him.

"Did you get stung?" she asked, eyes wide with worry.

As the feeling crept up his leg and into his midsection, he was going to say yes, but inexplicably he said, "No, no stings. It was close but I got through them thanks to you."

"Did you get the sample?"

He pulled the brass container from his underwear.

"There's another problem," said Zayn. "A hole near the cylinder that's leaking faez. That's what's causing the runes to flicker."

"It's not good if the faez is leaking outside of the well, but I'm sure Priyanka will know what to do," said Adele.

"I hope so," muttered Zayn as he grabbed the oars and started them back toward the distant shore, wondering when the effects of the sting would kick in, but the further he got from the island, the more he was convinced that he never got stung and the strange feeling going up his leg was his imagination.

Chapter Twenty-One
Eleventh Ward, April 2017
Creature Feature

For the first five months in Invictus, Neveah barely had enough time to shower, let alone explore the city or do any other frivolous activity, due to the constant demands of the food truck business. Between preparing for the next day, or serving her customers, the only extra time she allotted for herself had been spent investigating what had happened to Zayn.

So when the Cease and Desist order was served by Celesse D'Agastine's lawyers, and Neveah had to shut down the food truck, she was faced with more time than she knew what to do with.

She'd made enough money that she didn't have to leave the city right away, assuming she cut back on meals and didn't run her propane tank, but thankfully the weather had been good on the second part. As for food, she knew how to stretch a dollar, so cheap ramen and crushed cracker pizzas became a staple.

This left her more time to figure out the identity and location of the comic book artist. The third issue of *The Spider Queen Must Die!* had come out a week ago, and she'd read it cover to cover a half dozen times in the local comic bookstore (feeling guilty the whole time that she couldn't afford to buy it), but it added nothing more to the story. Unlike most comics, each issue was pretty much the same, involving numerous people trying to sneak into her plantation home and kill her. The only thing different was the identity of the would-be killers and their methods of sneaking. All of them unsuccessful, of course.

She was convinced that she'd never figure it out when she got an email from Frank at Hilltop Comics. She was sitting in the City Library at a free computer when the email came through. She'd been in contact with him since her visit, because he thought she was an HR representative, and especially because she'd gotten them a visit from the Herald security division by posing as Melissa, the HR manager, and giving them a call.

Re: Movie recommendation

Thanks again for the rec on *The Last Unicorn*. Loved it. If you know any other good movies, I'd love to hear about them.

Frank LaBaum
66 Highwayman Drive
Invictus, IV 600600

She read the email three times because it didn't make any sense. She'd never given him any movie recommendations. It wasn't until the last line that she realized that he'd never put his address beneath his signature before, which probably meant it was the artist's address.

Her heart jumped around like a jackrabbit as she gathered her things, hoping that the artist hadn't moved, or that he or she would talk to her. She had to remind herself not to hurry, but she was closer than she'd been since she'd gotten to the city.

The artist lived in the Eleventh Ward, which would be about a two-hour walk from the City Library. But feeling like she was near a breakthrough, Neveah sprung for the train ticket to get there as fast as possible.

The three-story brownstone had a colorful purple door. From the sidewalk, Neveah could see framed monster movie posters from the 50s on the living room wall. Posters like *Creature from the Black Lagoon*, *The Giant Leeches*, and *Terror of the Haunted House* gave Neveah a good idea why this artist had been chosen.

She waited for a few minutes, knocking multiple times before deciding they weren't home. Neveah made it halfway down the street before heading to the back of the house. The alleyway led to a fenced courtyard, which was easy to scale due to a pile of concrete blocks next to the rusted blue dumpster.

Hoping the artist's neighbors didn't see her sneaking up to the house and call the cops, Neveah peeked through the window into the kitchen for signs. A mixing bowl next to a carton of eggs, a loaf of bread, and a gallon of milk sat on the counter suggesting that the artist was in the middle of cooking French toast or something similar. Pressing her face against the window, Neveah strained to see the state of the stove, which had a pan on top, but the heat light wasn't lit.

At this sign, her stomach twisted, and Neveah checked behind her, expecting to see a police officer, or worse, a Watcher from Varna. There was no way the artist had started making French toast without turning on the stove. Even the worst cook in the world flipped on the heat first thing, so the pan would be ready by the time the ingredients were mixed, especially if it were French toast.

Neveah checked the back door to find it open. The hinges creaked on the way in.

As soon as she saw the broken eggs on the floor, congealed and smelling like sulphur, she knew that whatever had happened had occurred days ago. A sniff proved the milk had curdled and a squeeze on the loaf showed the bread was hard. Whoever had interrupted the artist cooking had turned the stove off. Or maybe the artist had fled the building? But it didn't make any sense that they would drop the eggs, but take the time to turn the heat off the pan.

Neveah cringed every time the floor creaked as she crept through the house. The living room had more posters on the side she couldn't see from the sidewalk, except these had comic book covers on them, each one signed by a David Haddlesong. A picture on a side table showed a dusty-haired guy in glasses at a signing, holding up a copy of a comic book matching one of those on the wall.

Neveah stood at the bottom of the steps for a few minutes before deciding to go up. She delayed because she was afraid of what she'd find upstairs. She didn't have a weak stomach, but she had no desire to find a body either.

"Come on, Nev."

She paused again at the top of the stairs. The bedroom door had been broken in. Whoever had been pursuing David had blown through the door as if it were paper-mache, which suggested magic-added strength.

"Whatever happened was days ago," she said out loud, trying to will herself to go through the busted door.

Neveah was about to take a step when she heard a squeak from a room down the hall. It was clear as day.

Her heart leapt into her throat. Her mouth was dry.

Neveah backed towards the stairs when she heard a second squeak.

She held her hands up, fingers poised to send a fire blast—one of the Five Elements she could do most of the time without fail—but when something short surged from the room, racing towards her, Neveah abandoned her plan and fled down the stairs.

She hit the ground floor, heading straight to the back of the house, the slap of feet chasing her. The thing was quick, and when she reached the kitchen she grabbed the pan from the stove and turned on her assailant.

"I'll bust your head in," she said with the pan raised.

The thing that ran into the kitchen came up to her waist. It had wide amphibious eyes, ridges on its head, and webbed feet. Neveah was about to smash it with the pan when she realized it was a miniature version of the Creature from the Black Lagoon, an enchanted toy, and once she realized what it was, she couldn't help but see its rubbery head and seams where it'd been manufactured.

"You gave me an awful fright," she said, pointing the pan at the Creature as it waddled back and forth on its webbed feet as if it were expecting a command. "I guess I should be glad that David didn't have a thing for clowns, or I would have run right through that door."

The Creature toy made no more moves towards her, so she felt comfortable enough to pass it—keeping the pan at the ready—and head back upstairs.

"To think I used to love scary movies as a kid," she said.

Back in the room, she found what she'd feared, the artist's body sprawled across the floor, a wide-eyed look of fright still on his face. There was no obvious wound on his body, but that didn't mean anything in the age of magic.

"Who killed you? Was it one of the Watchers? Or did they

send something to get you?" she asked.

Without touching anything, she looked around, hoping to find evidence of who might have hired him. It appeared whoever had killed him had done the same, as his papers were scattered across a side table.

Neveah startled when she noticed the Creature waddling closer to her.

"You shouldn't sneak up on me like that," she said, holding the pan up, but the Creature ignored her and kept moving into the room.

It stood by the body as if it were waiting for instruction.

"I'm sorry, little buddy. Someone killed your owner," she said. "We're both shit out of luck. I'm out of leads and about out of money. Maybe I'm going to have to accept that I can't figure out what happened to my brother. Maybe nothing happened to him. Or maybe it's me."

She slapped the pan against her leg. "But I *feel* so close. I need more time. More money really." She sighed. "Maybe I'll just head back to Varna. I doubt that Celesse lady will bother shutting me down back there, and I won't have to worry about permits, or where I sleep, or if I get a bath...this week."

Neveah spun around, lifted her chin, and spoke to the air. "I wish I knew what to do next, Zayn. I know something's wrong. You've always had something buried deep, some secret you've been hiding. Everybody in Varna was surprised when you joined the Academy, everybody except me. I'd seen you practicing, heard you mumbling to yourself when you didn't realize anyone was listening. You have a plan, for what, I don't know, or I'm afraid to think about. But you left yourself, and came back somebody else. I know it. I just have to figure it out, because it's eating you alive..."

No answers came while she stared at the body, so she put the pan back in the kitchen, after carefully wiping away finger-prints, and returned to her food truck. Since the moment she stepped into the city of Invictus, her mind had been whirling like a mixer on high, but now that she'd decided to return to Varna, it was like the oven was hot and ready to go, but she had nothing left to cook.

Chapter Twenty-Two
Harmony, April 2017
Weaving his way to oblivion

The cool air of the mountain jungle had been banished, replaced by an oppressive heat that seemed like it was squeezing the moisture from the air, dripping it over him. Even the mist, which normally sat in the valley like a witch's cauldron, had retreated until he could see a river that cut through the verdant space.

The good part about the heat was that there was no chance the mystdrakons would venture to his elevation, a worry that kept him looking over his shoulder whenever the mist grew thick. But that didn't help him with Priyanka's training.

Zayn wiped his face with the back of his hand, trying to clear the paint from his forehead and catch his breath, while Priyanka paced beneath the poles. He looked down at the mess of colors across his chest and legs. It looked like Willy Wonka had vomited on him.

"You should be further along than you are," said Priyanka, hands on hips, lips squeezed to disappointment. "I've seen what you can do. This shouldn't be that hard. Are you holding back, or is something wrong?"

"It's hotter than it's been in the past, I guess," he said, shaking his head.

Priyanka had been having him cast force bolts at rocks on a ledge fifty feet away while jumping from pole to pole while she shot a paintball gun at him. He'd dodged maybe one in three.

"That's a load of crap," she said, stomping away, before spinning right back around. "It's that attitude that's behind your failure. When you were an underclassman, you didn't care about little things like heat and being tired, you leapt off buildings without thinking about them. It's like you're...it's like you're not the same person, that you've given up on whatever was driving you before."

While she was speaking, he felt a pang of recognition. *I don't feel myself these days*, he thought, but he couldn't say it.

"Maybe I need something more challenging," he said, cringing, because he realized how it sounded, but she didn't react negatively, only nodded.

"Go on," she said, crossing her arms with an eyebrow raised.

"Like you said, I'm..." at that moment, the words caught in his throat as he saw a person standing down the slope from them. He recognized the red bandana and the beaded braids of his sister, but when he blinked to take a second look she was gone. "I'm...not performing as I want either, but maybe I need to be pushed more, not that you're not pushing me, but maybe I need a challenge that seems too difficult, like trying to make the purple path leap on my first run."

Priyanka glanced down the path to where he'd been looking a moment ago. He couldn't tell her about the migraines, and he definitely wasn't going to say anything about the visions he'd been seeing since he got stung by the Cthulhu jelly. He knew that if he got sent to Golden Willow they'd unravel the knot in his head and he knew in his gut that it was bad, even if he couldn't put his finger on why.

"You're the first student I've ever had tell me I wasn't being hard enough on them," said Priyanka.

"If it makes you feel any better, I'm not asking you to be harder on me, just give me challenges I probably can't do," said Zayn.

"Let's see if you keep this opinion after your task." She flicked a bug off her arm. "If you get yourself killed, I'm going to be very cross with you."

"As will my parents."

Priyanka squinted at the sky. "Today's probably a good day for this challenge, what with the heat. You know how we've been sticking to the clearing, not going into the jungle where the maulapines live? Today that changes. You're going to take the pole path into the jungle, through their territory, and into the valley." Priyanka unhooked a pouch from her belt and handed it over to him. "So I know that you made the trip, and to save me one, you're going to pick a moondew plant from the river's edge and bring it back. Celesse has been bugging me for a new one."

"I thought that's where the mystdrakons are," said Zayn.

"Having regrets?"

"No, but I want to understand the dangers."

She nodded. "It's a hot enough day that they'll be deeper in the mist. They weren't given that name for nothing."

"Any last advice?" he asked.

"Don't die."

Zayn stepped to the first pole, looked over his shoulder at her, and said, "That quote would look great on one of those inspirational posters with a cute animal on it."

The corner of her lip quirked. "In this one it would be a fierce kitten flipping you off. Go on. Get to the river and back. And don't forget my moondew."

Zayn climbed the successively higher poles with leaping strides. The gaps between them would be impossible for a normal human, but the imbuements allowed him to make each jump as if he were out for an afternoon jog.

Had he only needed to keep up a good pace, the trip to the river would have been easy, but once he'd developed a rhythm, he weaved a round of sensing into his routine. In the jungles of Harmony, maulapines and mystdrakons weren't the only dangers. Awareness was the first line of defense.

When he reached the edge of the maulapine territory, he slowed his pace and searched the trees for the creatures. During his first visits to Harmony, troops of them had watched him practice, but over time, fewer and fewer showed up, bored by his presence. That would change now that he'd entered their territory.

Zayn saw the first maulapine, an older specimen with gray streaks and white ear tufts, in the canopy of a deaddropper tree. The older members of the troop were usually left with guard duty, since they knew the dangers of the jungle the best. As the spines on its back bristled to attention, the maulapine made a high screech that traveled over the trees and deeper into their territory. Moments after the warning cry, other voices returned the call, indicating his intrusion was being responded to.

Letting his sensing imbuement drop, but maintaining the physical one, Zayn sampled the older maulapine's pheromone. He reached out, calming it enough that it stopped its screeching.

It was good to know that it would work on them, but Zayn worried about how many were approaching. They'd stopped announcing their approach, but Zayn sensed, even without his imbuement, that many were on their way.

He saw the first one through the trees, running along the long connecting cable vines that stretched through the jungle. The short powerful strides conveyed a buried anger, waiting to be unleashed upon the creature foolish enough to enter their territory.

While maintaining his speed, Zayn sent his calming force towards the maulapine. He was proficient at juggling two imbuements, so the creature immediately slowed, then stopped on the cable vine.

"That wasn't so bad," he said.

Four more maulapines showed up. The first two had been easy, and adding four more wasn't hard, but he was beginning to sense that he would quickly test his limits if he got more than a dozen.

Focused on movement heading his way, Zayn missed the maulapine hiding in the foliage on the pole path. He threw himself to the side, launching into the empty air, barely getting his hands out to slow his fall by snatching branches and limbs on the way down.

Zayn hit the jungle floor.

"Oof."

Maulapines were coming from all directions, at least two dozen. Zayn quickly hopped to his feet and sent out the calming force. Since he wasn't moving, he was able to still their advances, but now he was stuck on the jungle floor.

While keeping them mesmerized, Zayn craned his head to see how he could get up to the pole. As he spied a path, he heard crashing through the undergrowth at his level. Not wanting to find out what it was, Zayn started climbing the nearest tree. The maulapines hooted and screamed, as they desperately wanted to come after him, but he was preventing them.

He made his way back to a pole, counting the maulapines that surrounded him. There were at least thirty that he could see, far more than he could manage if he wanted to leave the area. He thought about returning to the jungle floor, but the dangers there were much worse than in the trees. It was the reason for the pole path, so Priyanka could venture into the valley without having to battle every creature.

"I asked for this," said Zayn, trying to give himself a pep talk.

When a few maulapines made tentative steps towards him, he knew his calming touch was losing effectiveness. It didn't help that a boiling rage hid beneath the spines and fur— he could feel it through the connection.

As the tide broke against him, Zayn took off into a full sprint, abandoning his influence on the maulapines for speed and sure-footedness. The next phase of his journey became a massive game of tag, except if he lost this one, the game would be over for good.

The unrestrained maulapines hooted and screamed as they chased him through the jungle canopy. Zayn varied his defenses, sending short force bolts at maulapines that got near enough, or if two or more were in the same place, he twisted their minds to attack each other. Through all this, he managed to keep his sensing imbuement on alert.

Zayn thought he might get away from the troop until he saw a group of five maulapines racing parallel on a massive cable vine that allowed them to outpace him. Their path would intersect his ahead. While he'd been able to fend off one or two maulapines at a time, five posed a significant challenge, especially with so many others on his heels already.

The five maulapines leapt onto his poles, blocking his path through the canopy. Mesmerizing or force bolting them wouldn't work, because they were too spread out, and too many were right behind.

The first maulapine bristled into a defensive stance, facing him with a back full of deadly spines. At the last possible moment, Zayn switched into the Veil, leapt to the left, onto a deaddropper tree limb, and scurried over the five maulapines. He switched out of the Veil as he landed, increasing his speed now that there were no maulapines ahead of him.

The creatures screamed, a chorus of anger rising through the jungle, sending birds into the sky, as they pursued him. He ran full out across the poles, feet slapping hard enough the edges bit through the soles of his shoes, barely keeping enough sensing ahead, pouring every ounce of faez he could into speed, but the maulapines were keeping up.

Zayn ran for what seemed like a half hour but might have only been two or three minutes. It felt like trying to breakdance on a high wire while juggling knives. He kept expecting to miss a pole or have one snap beneath him, flinging him into the jungle.

The cries and screams were all around him. It was an avalanche of sound following him. After a while he stopped trying to check behind him.

A small part of him worried about how he was going to actually pick a moondew with the maulapines all over him, but his worries evaporated the moment he realized the maulapines no longer followed him.

One moment they were there, the next they were gone. The silence was imposing.

Zayn slowed his pace, increasing his sensing, finding that the maulapines had stopped back a ways. There were no other dangers around him, none that he could detect, and after climbing a tree, he realized he was deep into the valley. He must have left their territory.

Moving more methodically, Zayn sensed a change in the air. The heat had broken and the mist returned to the valley. Beneath him, mist swirled between the trunks. It wasn't so thick he couldn't see the jungle floor, but its presence left him jittery.

When he reached the river's edge, Zayn wiped away the sweat around his eyes with his fingers, scanning the area for creatures. If it weren't for what the cool air brought with it, he might have considered it refreshing by the river.

Mystdrakons weren't the only thing to worry about in the valley. Brightthorn wasps, which were stinging insects as large as hummingbirds, could do serious damage to him in swarms.

Staying in the canopy, Zayn moved south along the river, looking for moondew plants. They grew along the edge, glowing as if they contained a shard of moonlight.

He had to travel further down the river than he wanted, noting how the mist thickened the longer he stayed. It felt like it'd lured him into the valley with promises of an easy journey.

He spied the moondew in a thicket of plants that looked similar to cattails, in a little oxbow pond. The still water was dotted with dead foliage from the jungle upon which small insects buzzed around. The water reflected the hazy sky, which had lost the radiance of the day. He'd have to leave the safety of the canopy to reach the moondew plant, so he took extra care to scan the surroundings before moving out of cover.

Dropping down to the cushiony jungle floor, Zayn slipped into the Veil to cross the brief coverless space to reach the oxbow pond. Back out of the Veil, Zayn stayed crouched by the water, scanning the jungle's edge as he pulled a trowel from the pouch Priyanka had given him. He carefully freed the plant from the soil without damaging too many roots and gently placed it into the pouch after wrapping it in linen cloth.

His hand was moving towards the pouch, to place the

trowel back inside, when a snout broke the surface of the water.

Zayn froze.

The snout was pale and long.

It was a mystdrakon, and it was only ten feet away.

He'd missed it because the reflection on the water hid what lay beneath, but now that the creature disturbed the surface, he could see its long powerful body submerged in the oxbow pond. It'd probably jumped in the water to cool off.

Zayn kept perfectly still, but he didn't know if it would matter. Using his fourth imbuement wouldn't work, because the creature would attack him before he could calm it. And if he slipped into the Veil, the mystdrakon was close enough to hit him unerringly.

Assuming it'd noticed him.

That part he wasn't sure about. The mystdrakon faced to his left. Its forward-facing predator eyes roved back and forth, but he was right at the edge of its vision.

He didn't even let himself swallow, though it was what he wanted to do.

A pair of black biting insects landed on his right arm. They were as big as his thumb, like horseflies, but meaner. Priyanka like to blast them out of the sky with her paint gun when they came up to the training area.

But he had no such defense. The first bite felt like he got jabbed by a syringe. The second bite was like getting pinched by pliers.

The mystdrakon crested the water, and the disturbance chased the biting insects away.

Priyanka had described them as a Komodo dragon crossed with a dragster. Her description was right on. It had powerful back legs and a long slightly triangular body.

The mystdrakon stayed crouched in the water, half its

body sticking out like a crocodile on a patrol. The biting insects came back. This time one landed on his neck, while the other was on his forehead.

It took all his self-control not to slap his neck or forehead when they started biting him.

By the third or fourth bite, Zayn's vision wavered. He couldn't close his eyes, not even a blink.

Past the mystdrakon, on the canvas of the mist, Zayn saw a building rise up: white columns beneath a canopy of oaks at the end of a long road. He saw himself walking inside, a blade in his hand and rage in his throat. He wanted to shake away this vision, but he couldn't, even though he knew it was more dangerous than where he was standing.

No, I can't, he thought.

The mist and the tension squeezed this vision from his mind, as if it could only take so much.

Zayn fought against it, pushing away those thoughts, knowing them as dangerous even though he couldn't remember why.

I gave that up, he thought. *I gave that up. They'll all die.*

Mired in his vision, Zayn forgot about the nearby mystdrakon when an insect bit his neck and he crushed it beneath his hand.

Water exploded around him, as if a starting gun had fired. He was sprayed with the contents of the pond—bugs and dead leaves—as the mystdrakon sped along the river's edge toward a squat pig-like creature that had come for a drink. The pig-like creature was at least a hundred feet away, but the mystdrakon crossed that space in a single heartbeat.

Stunned by the speed, and that he was still alive, Zayn let the other insect bite him again before he crushed it.

The mystdrakon ended the pig-creature's life with a powerful bite, then threw itself into the water, cooling in the slow current of the river as steam rose around it. Zayn reached out with his sensing imbuement, feeling the heat rolling from it as if it were a raging fire.

He didn't want to draw the creature's notice while he made it back to the jungle, so Zayn pulled the packet of novelty runes from his pocket, fished around for a flat rock, and rubbed a couple of them onto it. He still didn't understand why there were so many runes, when only a couple of them actually did anything. The ones that had no function were of a different design.

Before slipping into the Veil, Zayn added faez to the runes, then he stood up and launched the rock high over the mystdrakon's head to land on the water's edge. Immediately, a spray of flowers erupted from the rock like a fountain, sending colorful petals in all directions.

When the mystdrakon surged to the flower-erupting rock, Zayn slipped back into the Veil and made his way back to the jungle and climbed up to the cable vine.

The whole way back, Zayn couldn't get his mind off how close he'd come to death. Between the migraines and the visions, one of them was going to get him killed, and even if they didn't outright, Zayn felt like the pressure in his mind was going to shear away. He feared what might occur if that was allowed to happen.

His trip through the maulapine territory was easier on the way back. He avoided their guards, so was able to get past them quickly before they could assemble. Zayn reached the cliff stairs without further incident.

He entered the Aerie as the sun passed over the mountain, casting the place in shadow. Priyanka was in the kitchen with a glass of whiskey in one hand, twirling a thin knife with her other hand.

"Something happen down there? You look like you saw a

ghost," said Priyanka.

"Mystdrakon," he said. "I walked right up on it."

Her eyebrows arched. "And lived to tell the tale." Her gaze fell upon the welts on his arm. "Ran into some biters, eh?"

Zayn recounted his story, minus the vision, while he pulled the moondew from the pouch carefully, lying it on the counter.

"That was a close one," she said. "But now you know more about our friends in the mist below."

"Now I know why you avoid them," he said.

"Never fight a battle you can't win."

Zayn tilted his head. "But what about 'Nothing is impossible, only improbable'?"

"That too," she said, raising her glass momentarily before taking a drink.

"A little contradictory, don't you think?" he asked.

"Maybe," she said, pouring him a glass and pushing it towards him.

"Or maybe you just say whatever you think will motivate us," he said.

Priyanka winked. "Drink up. You should always celebrate a win, even if it came because of luck."

After clinking their glasses together, Zayn took a long pull from his drink, grimacing at the bitterness of the whiskey. As he set the glass down, he noted the way Priyanka was studying him, as if she were trying to see into his mind. When she poured another round, Zayn pushed it away, not daring to let his inhibitions down around his mentor.

"Has anything happened with the dragons? The meeting is only a month away," he asked.

The way Priyanka glanced sideways told him it was not going well. "Preparations are being made."

"You've picked a successor?" he asked, spinning his glass

clockwise.

"Of course not," she said.

"Then war?"

Priyanka looked him straight in the eyes. "We won't let it get to that."

The thought of what the original patrons could muster in defense of the city made him shudder.

"I should get back," he said. "Keelan and I are sparring in the morning. I don't want to have a hangover."

He wasn't sure if he detected a twitch of disappointment when he told her that he didn't want to stay and drink, but she nodded her head, then led him back to the portal.

Chapter Twenty-Three
Tenth Ward, April 2017
The prophecy of tacos

A knock on the side of the food truck woke Neveah from her daze as she stared at the open tome in front of her. She was going to ignore the knock until it happened a second time, so she threw the book closed and opened up the metal window to find a Hispanic-looking guy and his girlfriend, both wearing touristy Hundred Halls hockey-style jerseys.

"Yeah?"

"When are you making the tacos?" asked the guy in a Canadian accent.

"There are no more tacos," said Neveah as she reached up to pull the window down.

The guy shared a look with his girlfriend. "No tacos? My cousin told me about your truck when he was here over holiday break. He said they were the best tacos in the world, and that I had to try them. We came all the way down from Pittsburg to have them."

A heaviness weighed on her heart. "I'm sorry. I can't make them anymore."

"The way my cousin talked about them, I'd pay triple or quadruple to try some," he said.

"I would if I could, but I can't," she said, closing the window on the two disappointed would-be customers.

Neveah sank back onto her cot and put her head in her hands. She'd gone to the lawyers three times in the past week, begging for them to give her a reason why her tacos had violated some stupid intellectual property of one of the richest people in the world.

The only reply she got was that she would need to challenge the cease and desist order in court, but of course, she didn't even have the money for gas back to Varna now, let alone pricey lawyer fees.

Neveah fished into her front pocket and pulled out her remaining cash. She had three small bills and a handful of change. If she was going to make it back to Varna, she'd have to sell something, or contact Keelan or Zayn to borrow the cash.

Neither of those options was appetizing. She loved her brother and cousin, but they'd always treated her like the "annoying little sister," so there was no way she was going to go to them for cash. Then she'd have to explain everything with the cease and desist order, and why she'd been in the city for months while not working.

The real problem was that she didn't want to give up on Zayn yet, even though everything seemed to indicate that she should. The comic book artist was a literal dead end, befriending Uncle Larice with Jamaican treats had gained nothing, and she didn't even really know if something was truly wrong with Zayn. It'd been eight months since she'd seen him last, and he could have fixed whatever was wrong with him.

Neveah was well aware that what she'd been doing probably looked to an outside person like she'd gone crazy, the very
thing she'd worried had happened to her brother.

Even Keelan had warned her away.

How do you believe something as true if no one else shares
that belief? She felt like reality was gaslighting her.

There was one thing left that she knew she could do, but
it wasn't going to be easy.

Neveah pulled the tome off the counter and set it in her
lap. *Brewer's Delight: Divinations & the Divine* was a gift Zayn
had given to her after his first year at the Academy. Cooking
and alchemy were a lot alike, he'd told her, so he thought she
might enjoy it.

But she'd never really looked through it until this week.
Neveah had never desired to join the Hundred Halls, so learning to brew potions seemed pointless, and as she'd learned this
year, it was fraught with legal pitfalls.

There was a potion in the tome that might point her in the
right direction if she brewed it. It was a bit of a Hail Mary pass,
but she was out of useful options. The only problem was that
she was out of money. And the rarer ingredients—silver dust,
satyr hoof shavings, a faeila eye—weren't cheap. She'd priced
them at a local alchemy store, and the only way she'd be able
to afford them was if she sold Sojourner.

A deranged chuckle slipped out as she thought about sell-
ing her beloved food truck. She didn't even know if the potion
would work. She assumed her brother had bought a real spell
tome, but what if it were one of those crappy novelty ones?

Or she could just go home.

She missed her parents, the twins, the little lioness Imani.
She missed the Stack.

She didn't miss Varna, except that her family was there.
That place felt like a prison, and now that she'd had a taste of

freedom, she never wanted to go back.

What she wanted was her family to be free. To go where they wanted to go, live where they wanted to live. Was that so much to ask?

"Go home or do something incredibly stupid?" she asked herself, knowing in an instant that if she went home and something happened to Zayn, she'd live with regrets for the rest of her life.

Making that decision let her release the breath she'd been holding.

"I'd rather fail than quietly suffer, but oh man, this is going to hurt," she said, caressing the inner wall of the truck lovingly.

At first she researched places to sell the food truck, but then she realized she would need a kitchen to brew the potion, so she turned to a sketchy short-term loan place in the thirteenth ward called Cash & Hatchet. The terms were gross. If she couldn't pay the principal and interest back in two weeks, she'd lose the truck. The truck was worth more than what she was getting but it was the only collateral she had. And the owner was going to let her continue to stay in the truck while it was parked in his rune-protected warehouse, which made it the best and worst possible deal.

She had the money for all of about two hours, the time it took to get from the Cash & Hatchet to the alchemy store in the third ward. By the time she got back to the food truck, it was getting late, and she practically ran through the ward to get to the warehouse.

Sequestered inside her truck, Neveah laid out the ingredients on her foldout prep table. She'd bought enough for one and a half potions, not because she wanted to make that many, but because the ingredients were sold in portions larger than the recipe called for.

She read the instructions until she could recite them backwards, because once she started the process she couldn't pause for long or the divination potion would be ruined.

The satyr hoof shavings had to be boiled for three hours, so she put them into water and turned on the propane tank to heat the pot. When they were finished, they would be turned into a paste that would provide the base for the potion.

Next she placed the faeila eye, which looked like a small ruby gemstone, into a walnut cracker and crushed it. Afterwards, she carefully picked out the wire-like threads contained within the shattered eye. From the notes on the brewing, the faeila eye threads were important because creatures in the Eternal City had to navigate by intention, which meant they had minor divination abilities. Neveah didn't quite know what that meant, but she followed the directions explicitly, making sure to use only threads that were black, not peppered gray.

The silver dust had to be sprinkled into the hoof paste when it was finished and stirred under heat. Over the next hour, a silvery liquid formed on top of the mixture, which she carefully scooped off with a brass spoon and deposited into a vial.

When she finished around ten o'clock that evening, she was left with a potion of divination and a pan of dregs that had eaten away the non-stick lining. She dumped the pan into the trash and collapsed onto the cot, cradling the cool vial in her hands. It smelled like peppermint.

"I hope you are worth it," she told the vial.

Her plan had originally been to wait until the morning when she was refreshed enough to drink it, but now that it was finished, she knew she'd never be able to sleep if she didn't find out if it'd worked.

Neveah took a quick look at the picture of her and Zayn on the food truck for inspiration before she threw the silvery liquid down her throat.

"Down the hatch."

It burned like a chilled hot sauce, conjuring beads of sweat onto her forehead as a glow formed in her stomach. Neveah gripped the cot as her vision grew hazy.

"What's going on with Zayn?" she asked aloud.

With the words spoken, the mist in her vision thickened until she could no longer see the interior of the food truck. Though she had no sense of movement, her body felt like it was hurtling through space, as if she were riding a rollercoaster while her mind was in a stationary place.

"Tell me, dammit, tell me," she pleaded as the mists swirled in her vision.

She sensed something right behind her potion-added sight, a vague unrecognizable outline. Neveah squinted, willing the form to resolve.

"Come on, please."

But rather than refine, the haze thickened, blotting out any hints of what was there, followed by gut-wrenching vertigo and a sudden return to the food truck.

When Neveah was aware again, she found she was lying on her back on the stainless-steel floor of the truck. Her vision was dotted with black spots, which over time disappeared.

Finally able to sit back up again, Neveah climbed onto the cot. Her stomach ached as if she'd been throwing up all night. Her body felt feverish and sore.

"It was right there," she said as she lay on her side. "I could see it. The answer."

But the potion had failed her. It wasn't powerful enough, and she only had enough ingredients to make another half potion. If a full wouldn't work, then a half wouldn't even be worth the effort.

Neveah pulled her blankets around her shoulders, staring

blankly at the empty vial on the countertop. All her life's possessions for a stupid potion that didn't work.

She looked around the food truck. If she'd been able to figure out what happened to Zayn, losing it would have been worth it.

"Why are things never easy?" she asked the empty air. "And why couldn't you have worked, you stupid potion. I can make tacos that make people drive from far away to try them, but not a simple divination potion from a crappy budget spell tome."

Neveah thought about her secret ingredient, the little bit of faez she added to her cooking to bring out the flavor. She wasn't sure how it worked, but it turned everything she cooked from high quality to gourmet level. What if she used that technique on the divination potion?

"It'd probably get me killed," she said in response to her thought, but she couldn't push the idea out of her mind.

She'd been warned from an early age not to experiment with magic. It was full of unintended consequences. Just last week, there'd been an explosion at one of the halls. Two students were dead, and one had been turned into a living pile of gray goo. Tinkering with an established potion recipe was a sure way to end up like one of them.

"Or it might work," she told herself. "I mean, it's not like I know how much faez to use, or if it will change the way the potion works, but I do have half a potion's worth of ingredients."

A surge of energy filled her when she realized she was going to try again. Neveah started by brewing up a fresh pot of coffee, running through the recipe in her head while she downed the first cup.

It was already midnight. Once she got the boiling water going, she dumped the hoof shavings in and started working on the faeila eyes. After sorting through the crushed gems for threads, she didn't have as many black threads as the recipe called for, so she went back through again, pulling out a few that were close enough except for a spot or two of gray.

A flash of despair hit her when she realized she didn't have enough silver dust either, but she pulled out a pair of silver earrings and shaved off the remaining weight with a knife.

During the stirring of the hoof paste, when she added the silver dust, Neveah poured faez into the mixture in the same way she did when she was cooking.

Descriptions of faez usage had always imagined it as a well in the mind that the raw stuff of magic was drawn from. Neveah had never thought that analogy described how she used it. Her faez always came from the gut and through her hands. Magic to her was primal, instinctual. She'd always struggled at simple things like the Five Elements, despite having superior dexterity to her brother and cousin, because the faez came out of her differently.

As the golden stuff oozed out of her hands and into the mixture, Neveah focused the idea in her mind that the potion would give her the answers she sought. It felt like a golden river flowing through her and into the paste. By the time the silvery liquid started forming on top so she could spoon it off, the whole pan was glowing reddish-gold.

By the time she finished, it was around four in the morning. Her eyelids barely held themselves open no matter how much coffee she drank.

Neveah held up the potion when she was finished. It had an inner glow as if it'd been filled with moonlight. She was too tired to drink the potion, but planned to do so the next day after she'd rested. She hated not knowing if it'd worked or not, but she didn't want to screw it up either.

With the divination potion stoppered and safely placed inside the refrigerator, Neveah stepped outside for fresh air.

It was a clear night, and she could hear dogs barking in the ward. She stretched her arms upward. She yawned so deep it made her shake her head when she was done.

Suddenly, the horizon lit up a couple of wards away. The air glowed with electricity as if a powerline had been struck by lightning, but the sky was devoid of clouds. After a few seconds, the glow subsided, and the city skyline returned to its early morning darkness.

"Somebody's having a bad night," said Neveah, glancing back towards the place where the electricity had exploded.

She climbed back into her food truck, content she'd done everything she could. Tomorrow when she woke, one way or another, she'd have *an* answer. It was all she could do.

Chapter Twenty-Four
Ninth Ward, April 2017
Failure is always an option

"There's a demon loose in the ninth ward."

These were the words that Instructor O'Keefe woke them with in the middle of the night.

Zayn gathered his team and set off toward the park where it'd been sighted.

"What the hell is a demon doing in the city?" asked Vin as they stood by a playground area filled with slides, swings, and mulch.

"Summoning gone bad," said Skylar with a shrug. "Probably a dead mage somewhere nearby. We just need to banish it."

"Not this time, lads and lassies," said Instructor O'Keefe, who hadn't bothered changing out of her pink unicorn silk pajamas. "This one is the kind they call a tall demon, and nobody with any sense summons those. Eh, this one somehow slipped into the city of its own volition."

Instructor O'Keefe glanced at him, and Zayn knew exactly what she was implying. It'd come through the thinning at the well of power, since the water well was located below the ninth ward.

"Is this the park with the big mermaid fountain?" asked Zayn.

"Aye, lad. This is the park."

"Shit, it's probably trying to damage the well so more demons can come through," said Zayn, thinking about what the dragons had said about the city. The Council of Scale meeting was in another month. It wouldn't be good if they found out about the demon.

"I used to be frightened of places like this when I was child," said Portia.

Lampposts lined the concrete pathways leading through the park but they were dark. The air smelled like burnt ozone.

"Why can't one of the Coterie take care of this demon? Don't they specialize in crap like that?" asked Vin, peering into the darkness.

"We're here, and we're going to take care of it," said Instructor O'Keefe.

At that, a spray of sparks burst from the center of the park, briefly silhouetting the trees.

"How do you kill a tall demon?" asked Skylar.

"Going to have to lure it into a salt circle," said Instructor O'Keefe, "close it up behind it, and then try banishing it, but since it came here directly, that might not work."

"Great," muttered Skylar under her breath.

"What did you bring for us, Keelan?" asked Zayn.

Keelan slipped his backpack off and started digging through it. He handed everyone except Instructor O'Keefe a short empty darkwood tube with filigree designs on the outside suggesting webs.

Portia put it up to her eye, peering through it like a spy-glass.

"What's it do?" she asked.

"I wouldn't do that if I were you," said Keelan.

"Gonna give me a black eye or something?" asked Portia with the tube still against her face.

"It's a web launcher. There are hundreds of tiny spiders living inside, making webs that you can spray. It might be a way to hold this demon so we can do real damage to it."

Portia pulled the tube away from her face. "Whoa, you should really warn me first."

Keelan smirked.

Instructor O'Keefe cleared her throat. "Alright. You five move up there and take out the tall demon before it leaves the park."

"Us five? What about you?" asked Portia.

"I'm going to try to put some protections around the park, make sure no one comes in, and I'll be the last line of defense if the tall demon makes a break for it," said Instructor O'Keefe.

Zayn led his team into the park. They spread out, keeping about ten feet between them. Zayn kept the web tube in his pocket so his hands remained free. They hadn't bothered with a light source, since there was enough ambient city light that their imbuements allowed them to see clearly.

A grunt, followed by another fountain of sparks into the sky, urged them to pick up their pace.

When they reached the center of the park, they found a large mermaid fountain. Rather than coyly lying on a rock spitting water from a pitcher, the mermaid wore scaly armor and held a trident from which the water erupted.

On the far side, a tall humanoid shape smashed a staff into the fountain as it mumbled phrases in an ancient arcane language. As the staff hit the brass fountain, ripples of faez traveled through the metal, illuminating it as if it were going through an x-ray machine.

At first glance the tall demon looked like a man wearing stilts and a costume, but the longer Zayn watched it strike the fountain, the more the details came into focus: legs bent backwards like a praying mantis, double-jointed arms snapped with each blow, a black ichor sprayed from its jackal-like maw.

Zayn motioned to his teammates, giving them the signal to set up the circle on a section of asphalt with five plastic horses on springs. Skylar pulled a cannister of salt from her pouch and started drawing out the circle, but didn't finish it, so they could capture the demon.

Using the secret language they'd developed over their years in the Academy together, Zayn told them to prepare a stunning strike. Five sets of arms rose and then five sets of body-numbing energy flew through the air at the tall demon.

His hopes that the fight would be over quick were dashed when at the last moment, the demon turned its staff towards them horizontally and reflected the strikes back at them. Zayn barely got out of the way of the blowback. Vin and Skylar weren't so lucky.

The tall demon hissed out a war cry, raising its staff above its head, and ran-bobbed towards them. At each step, its body sunk nearly to the ground, before catapulting up as it rose into the next step. The whole crazy gait made it look like the tall demon was pistoning towards them.

The speed of the demon surprised Zayn, and only Keelan's quick action saved Skylar from getting impaled on the staff. Keelan leapt to the front, slapping away the strike with his bare hands. The battle between them blurred with speed, until the demon caught him with its staff, throwing him thirty feet away into a copse of bushes.

Zayn had no time to wonder how his cousin had been able to withstand a head-to-head battle—maybe being a Watcher had given him additional abilities—because the tall demon attacked them in earnest with whipsaw motions.

Recovered from the stunning blowback, Skylar sent ribbons of shadow at the tall demon, confusing it and blocking its vision, while Portia threw flaming knives that seemed to appear out of thin air.

Zayn ran over to his cousin around the time he was climbing out of the bushes.

"You okay?"

Keelan nodded and raced back to the battle.

The five of them fought the creature to a stalemate. It couldn't get away, nor could it hurt them, but they didn't seem to be able to contain it either.

Zayn motioned to the others to pull out the web tubes, when a stab of migraine forced his hands to his temples. Only Keelan seemed to notice the grimace and shot him a worried glance, but Zayn shook him off and continued with the massage.

He figured if they could tangle the tall demon in the webs and haul it to the circle, they could give it a proper banishing before it could break loose.

"One, two, three!"

White sticky material exploded from the tubes, capturing the creature. From close range, and multiple directions, it wasn't so much a web, but a ball of sticky goo that had stuck to the springy demon. It fought against it, but the stuff stretched and expanded, rather than breaking. It looked like the tall demon was trying to climb out of a giant half-melted marshmallow.

"How long will that hold it?" asked Zayn.

Keelan gave him a one-shoulder shrug with his face

scrunched up.

"Then we better get it into the circle fast," Vin said, rubbing his ribs where he'd been smacked with the staff during the battle.

"I'm not touching that thing," said Portia, pointing a flaming dagger at it.

Skylar waved her arms and billowing cloth made of shadows wrapped around the demon. She tugged on them, but the black cloth broke into mist.

"It's too heavy, or something," said Skylar, a frown tugging on her lips. "I can't move it."

Zayn glanced back to the salt circle on the playground. They were twenty feet away.

"What about a circle here?" asked Keelan.

"The ground is too uneven," he said.

"I know," said Vin, raising his hand as if they were in class. The gesture made Zayn smile because it reminded him of their first classes in the Academy. "Let's blast it over using force bolts."

While they moved into position, tendrils of electricity slipped from the tall demon's knees and elbows, charring the sticky goo to black dust.

"Hurry," said Zayn. "It won't hold it much longer."

They raised their arms together and knocked the demon towards the salt circle. Sparks popped and danced around it, crisping the air.

"Again!"

The second blast pushed it almost to the middle of the circle, but it also shattered the sticky white paste that had hardened from the electricity.

Released from its prison, the tall demon exploded into action, swinging its staff in wide, circular arcs. A force bolt from Portia was reflected right back, knocking her head over heels.

Zayn thrust the web tube towards the tall demon but nothing came out.

"It's a one-shot item," shouted Keelan over the clicking of the demon's joints and their grunts and arcane words.

He didn't think it would work, but Zayn opened up his fourth-year imbuement. The foul scents of the tall demon punctured his concentration. It felt like he'd been punched in the nose with a bucket of sewer garbage.

Collapsed to his knees, Zayn retched.

"Are you okay?" asked Keelan as he dodged the demon's staff.

"Bad idea," said Zayn. "My imbuement doesn't work with demons."

"I have one more thing I can try," said Keelan, pulling a small bead from his pouch. "This might knock it out, but it also might blow up the whole park, us included."

"What is it?"

"Think of it as the tactical nuke of magic," said Keelan. "If this doesn't knock it out, nothing will. Everyone back up."

On the same count, they all leapt backwards. Keelan threw the bead at the demon, who tried to smack it back towards them, but when it contacted the staff, the bead exploded into a shimmering ball of light that surrounded the demon momentarily, before turning into a mushroom cloud of electricity crackling into the sky like a million fireflies.

The concussive blow knocked Zayn to his back, and the remnants of the flash remained in his vision, but when he looked back to the center of the park, he saw the tall demon prone on its back.

"It worked!"

Using the staff, which had fallen into the grass, Zayn rolled the demon towards the salt circle. Once it was inside, Skylar poured out the last portion.

"Everyone together," said Zayn.

While they didn't know the more complex spells taught at Coterie or Arcanium, they knew a simple banishing spell—assuming they could keep their movements and words in lock-step—that would be effective enough to get rid of the demon. Or so he hoped.

Speaking the spell was like trying to tie a knot in a cherry stem using his tongue. The arcane words required linguistic dexterity, but he managed them well enough. Their chorus of spellcasting rose and fell together. They were in sync, and the edges of the salt circle began to glow with accumulated faez.

As the spell crackled air around the park, sending out flecks of electricity, a strange mist rose up in Zayn's vision, clouding his mind. His fingers felt like they'd turned to noodles. The words in his mouth felt like they were expanding until they didn't fit out his mouth anymore.

Across from the demon and the springy rocking horses, he saw two figures. The first was his sister in her red bandana, reaching towards him as if she were casting a spell. The second was Watcher Sabrina, who stood with fists bunched at her sides.

The world fell away from him. He was only vaguely aware of the shouting, and a spray of ichor across his jeans.

He could see Neveah and Sabrina as if they were as real as the trees and the colorful springy rocking horses.

"What's going to happen?" he asked them.

A flat line blurred over his head, but he ignored it. They'd come to tell him something important: maybe why they were a danger to him, which he didn't understand. *How could my sister be dangerous to me? She's back in Varna with the rest of the family.*

"Are you here, Nev?" he asked.

His sister mouthed words but no sound came over the din

of battle.

Zayn opened his mouth to speak again, but something heavy slammed into him, throwing him against the jungle gym.

He groaned. The mist no longer crowded his vision, but now Vin was lying unconscious on him. Zayn rolled him off and climbed to his feet while Skylar shook Vin awake.

The others, including Instructor O'Keefe in her unicorn pajamas, were staring at him. The salt circle had been scattered, and a nearby tree had been ripped in half, the soft wood bent and broken.

Their hunched foreheads and tight lips told him they were both worried and disappointed in him.

"It got away, didn't it?"

A helicopter with a spotlight flew right over the park, straight down an avenue. Sirens filled the night air, and through his imbuement, he heard the crash of steel in the distance.

Instructor O'Keefe dismissed the others with a wave of her hand.

"Take Vin to the Honeycomb and have Alliette take a look at him, at all your injuries. I need to have a word with Mr. Carter," said Instructor O'Keefe.

Tensed and solemn, Zayn waited for his teammates to gather Vin and limp away from the park. It felt like he was waiting for the executioner, but also that he was the one holding the axe.

"Do ya care to explain?"

Zayn glanced at his shoes. There were bits of gooey paste on them, and splatters of ichor.

"I wish I knew," said Zayn.

Instructor O'Keefe's eyes roved across him, studying him as if she expected him to transform into a demon at any moment.

"You stopped casting the spell, right when they needed you. The demon got away, and there's a good chance someone's going to get hurt tonight because of you," she said.

"I understand."

"No, clearly you don't, because otherwise you'd take care of whatever's ailing you. Are you hiding something? Did you pick up a curse, or a disease that you're ashamed of admitting? Don't be a fool if you need help—we've all been there et some points in our lives. Gawd knows I've had to have Pri bail me out of a jam or two," she said.

"I didn't, and I don't know what happened. I swear. Maybe it was the demon's ichor," he said, gesturing at his jeans.

She crossed her arms and sighed. "I'm gonna have to tell Pri about this."

He nodded. "I understand."

Her words came out heavy. "No, lad. I don't think you do. Since we couldn't stop the demon before the police had to step in, everyone, including the dragons, will know about it. It will only give them more reasons to shut down the Halls."

Instructor O'Keefe left him in the park, alone. Zayn didn't go back to the Honeycomb. He wasn't going to be able to sleep anyway. Instead, he went walking through the streets, mulling over what had happened and why it felt like something was wrong with him. The answer never came, even though he knew with growing certainty that they were right.

Chapter Twenty-Five
Tenth Ward, April 2017
The ghosts of the past

Neveah didn't wake up until the next afternoon. She had fallen off her cot and was lying on the stainless-steel floor, curled up around her pillow. Her neck cracked as she sat up, and aches radiated up her back from her work the day before.

"Yuck," said Neveah as she smacked her lips.

When she'd drank the first divination potion, it'd tasted like peppermint spiked with hot sauce. Almost a day later, the flavor had disintegrated into chalky chili paste that had sat out in the sun too long.

Neveah rummaged through her little refrigerator for something to wash away the leftover taste when she saw the second vial, the one she'd made late in the night. She stared at it for a moment before reaching into the back and collecting a barely chilled bottle of orange juice, which she threw down her throat.

"If I never drink you, I never have to know if I was wrong," said Neveah as she pulled the vial from the refrigerator. "And I don't get a second round of this awful taste. Yuck."

She peered out the front window, forgetting she was in the warehouse, rather than the street in the seventh ward, which only made her remember that she couldn't just drive back to Varna and forget everything that had happened.

"I could sell this potion," she said. "Maybe even get my money back."

But even though she said the words, she knew she wouldn't.

"Might as well get this over with."

Neveah crawled onto the cot, leaned against the wall of the food truck, and cradled the vial in her hands. The stopper made an audible pop when she opened it, and the first pungent whiff made her a little dizzy. She didn't know if her addition of faez had changed the properties of the divination potion, but she knew that whatever it was, it was much stronger than before. Much.

The potion burned with cold when it went down as if it were liquid nitrogen. Neveah gasped, holding her chest as the pain radiated out.

She was reaching for a bottle of water on the counter when the vision hit. One moment she was in her food truck, the next she was catapulting through her mind. It felt like she'd been launched from a slingshot.

"Zayn," she whispered, "what's happened to you?"

The world was encased in mist. Neveah flew through the swirling gray fog catching glimpses of things she didn't understand: an ancient blade dissolving into someone's arm, a man-shaped creature made of glass, bottles shattering against the concrete, a neon pink dildo covered in sparkles dancing through the dark, a white Cadillac speeding away, a dead girl lying against a wall with a blade in her gut...

There were others but they flew by so fast her mind could

barely keep up.

Then the acceleration slammed to a stop. The change was so abrupt it felt like being woken from the dead.

Her innards twisted as vertigo reigned, but through it all she stayed focused on what was before her: a glass door etched with a familiar name. There was a Closed sign hanging from the handle.

She traced her fingers across the name of the store: Howling Madwoman Fortunes and Spells.

Before she could push through the door, the vision dissolved around her, returning her back to the inside of the food truck with her hand hanging in the air, finger extended.

It took her about thirty minutes before she could move again. Any little movement brought back waves of vertigo, but eventually the nausea passed.

Neveah washed up before leaving the truck. The tenth ward wasn't too far away.

The store looked the same as it had in her vision. She pushed on the door, knowing it would be locked.

"Dammit," said Neveah. "How am I going to get in?"

With the hotel next door, there was enough traffic that busting through the window would only get her thrown in jail, so she headed to the back alley to see if that might offer a way in.

A metal door with chips of rust blocked entrance to the store from the rear. Neveah banged on it with her fist in frustration, kicking it one last time for good measure.

Neveah had started walking away when something spectral came through the door.

"I thought I told you not to use this door..."

The ghost girl stopped in mid-sentence. Neveah, frozen with concern, couldn't decide if running or trying to mangle a spell was her best option.

The girl stared back, the corners of her eyes creased with growing understanding. She had punk hair: shaved on the sides, a Mohawk flopping into her face. Her sleeveless shirt revealed her fit arms as if she were a rock climber or a...

"Are you...?" asked Neveah, the stories from her brother filtering through her shocked brain. There was a lot he didn't tell them when he came back for the summer, but Keelan had let things slip about the ghost of a dead girl.

"Katie. And you must be Neveah. I can see the resemblance."

Neveah nodded. Her whole body was covered in goosebumps. She'd never stood face-to-face with a ghost before.

"Why...?"

Neveah didn't really know what she was asking, the appearance of the dead girl had scrambled her thoughts.

"This is my home, of sorts," said Katie, "or at least the place I'm most connected to in the real world."

"You're, like, buried here?"

Katie nodded.

"And you and Zayn...were dating?"

Katie looked away. "We went on a date and then some stupid things I did caught up to me. But then"—her eyes glittered with thoughts—"things changed."

"If you knew my brother, maybe you have some answers for me," said Neveah.

"I might, though there are some things I cannot speak about." Katie looked up the alleyway at the passing cars. "Go around. I'll let you in the front."

When she went back to the street, the door clicked open, even though she couldn't see anyone. Neveah stepped inside the store, and Katie reappeared. The place was surprisingly clean except for the empty bottles of Mage Blaster lined up on the counter.

"I didn't know ghosts could drink," said Neveah.

"I don't. My band practices here. It's the place easiest for me to affect the real world," said Katie.

In the back of the store, behind rows of empty shelves, a set of drums and a trio of amps sat on a carpet. Half-burnt candles sat on the walls and amps, the drippings giving the space a Gothic feel.

"You're in a band?" asked Neveah.

Katie's face brightened, and for a moment, she almost looked real. "We're called the Sticky Wickets. We play gigs around the city. We're the only band with a ghost girl drummer, so we bring in a pretty good crowd."

"I...I didn't know ghosts could be in bands," said Neveah, feeling like there were levels of magic that she'd never experience as a non-mage.

"It's kind of a special case," said Katie, tilting her head to one side so her hair flopped over and touched her shoulder. "I owe your brother for it."

"Right," said Neveah, glancing around while shaking her head. "If he wasn't my brother, I'm not sure I'd believe it."

"He talked about you when we hung out," said Katie, a faded regret threading through "when we hung out" as if she still had feelings for Zayn.

"Probably only as his annoying little sister," said Neveah.

To her disappointment, Katie said, "Yes," but then she added, "but he said you were the smartest in the family, the one that could do anything she put her mind to."

A warmth filled Neveah's chest at hearing the compliment. She hadn't realized her older brother noticed her that much, except for when he was hungry. Of course, he always seemed like he was in the middle of a million plots, so when did he actually have time?

"Right now I'm putting my mind to figuring out what's

wrong with him," said Neveah, glancing around the room. "I came here for information—I'm guessing that it's you who I'm supposed to talk to."

Katie's translucent forehead wrinkled. "Something's wrong with Zayn?"

"He's not...himself," said Neveah, after searching for the words. "It's like part of him got erased, or buried. And he's been getting headaches, bad ones. I came because I'm worried."

"You must love him a lot," said Katie, her expression soft with wonder.

An ache formed in her chest at the thought of articulating her feelings.

"He's my brother...and in Varna, we don't have much except each other. He always looked out for me. Him and Keelan saved me when I was a fool child. I don't know, it's hard to put it into words. He'd do anything for me, just like I would do anything for him," said Neveah.

"You put it into words just fine," said Katie.

"That's all well and good, but what I need are answers," said Neveah.

The ghost girl sat on a speaker and knocked a piece of hair away from her face. "I'm sorry. I don't know anything. I haven't seen him this year, at all."

"At all?"

Katie shook her head. "I'm sorry."

Neveah put her hands against her face and massaged the bridge of her nose with her fingers. "I don't understand. I was supposed to come here. Are you sure?"

Katie looked pained as she shrugged. "I think so."

Neveah let out a big sigh. "He left for his third year the same ol' Zayn, and then when he came back last summer, he was different, all normal and not scheming like he always did.

A regular Dr. Jekyll and Mr. Hyde."

At those words, Katie sat straight up. "Like maybe he drank a potion and changed into someone else?"

Neveah hunched her forehead. "Yeah?"

Katie stood up and walked straight through a wall, heading deeper into the building. The sudden change made Neveah stiffen with surprise. She'd gotten used to talking to Katie as if she were a real girl, but walking through a wall completely dispelled that illusion.

A moment later Katie reappeared, except this time she came through the door that went into the back.

"Follow me," said Katie.

The area behind the door wasn't what Neveah expected it to be. There were plants and trees and the smell of rich earth. In a normal business, the back area was for merchandise storage, but whoever the "Madwoman" of the shop had been, she had used the space to create a garden.

In the center of the thirty by forty room was a raised bed about two feet high in which bushes and small trees swayed in an unseen breeze, surrounding a larger tree that scraped the ceiling with its canopy. Grow lights provided ample light and heat.

There were two other doors leading out of the room: one in back clearly leading to the alleyway and another in the corner that looked like a janitorial closet.

"Are you...?"

Katie nodded.

"Why here?" asked Neveah.

"I wish I knew. You'll have to ask Amber, or your brother," said Katie as she led her to the janitorial closet.

"I have a feeling he doesn't know or remember," said Neveah. "Do you even know why this garden is here?"

"I think it was something to do when she wasn't working, because she was bored." Katie glanced at her transparent shoes. "But that's the stuff I can't talk about."

Neveah motioned for Katie to continue. She showed her the door in the corner, indicating she should open it.

The janitorial closet had been converted into an alchemy lab. It wasn't a high-end lab, like the kind Neveah had seen in magazines and TV shows, but it had clearly been used by someone who knew what they were doing. The whole area was neatly kept, organized with labels and drawers, except for a mess on the far side of the table.

Neveah poked through the ingredients, but nothing stuck out. It was like whoever had mixed a potion had forgotten to clean up. While she was reading the labels, her foot crunched a piece of paper that had been knocked under the table.

She recognized her brother's patient scrawl the moment she laid her eyes upon it. Zayn had thoughtful penmanship.

But what was he doing?

There was clearly a potion recipe on the crumpled paper with ingredients like crystalline zinc nitrate, dried siren blood, and blue mountain flyberries. But there were no tomes in the room. She got on her hands and knees to see if the book had been knocked there too but she only saw dust bunnies and a few dead bugs.

"Is it what you're looking for?" asked Katie, wide-eyed.

The dead girl's voice startled Neveah, as she'd been puzzling over the purpose of the potion.

"It is. It's his handwriting, though I don't know what it means," said Neveah, shaking her head.

"I'm sorry," said Katie. "I thought this might be important."

"It is," said Neveah, biting her lower lip. "It tells me that he did something. Made a potion. For what reason? I don't know, but I know what's in it, and that's a start."

"What will you do now?" asked Katie.

The answer came fully formed to Neveah right away. She knew someone who knew a thing or two about alchemy.

She folded the potion recipe and shoved it into her back pocket as she said, "I need to talk to someone. I just hope I don't get thrown in jail first."

Chapter Twenty-Six
The Honeycomb, May 2017
Uninvited

With a week to go until the second Council of the Scale, Zayn grew worried that he hadn't heard from nor seen Priyanka. He expected to journey to Iceland with her and wanted to be prepared, so when he heard she was in the Honeycomb offices, he knocked on her door.

"Come in, Zayn," she said through the closed door.

He glanced around for cameras or visible scrying enchantments, but saw nothing obvious. He wouldn't have been surprised to learn she'd just guessed at his appearance. Even the instructors talked about her preternatural ability to sense things she shouldn't be able to. Which probably explained why she'd lived so long in a dangerous profession.

When he stepped inside, Priyanka was behind her desk, sharpening a knife with a whetstone. The stone against metal made a soothing scraping sound.

Her hair was pulled back into a businesslike ponytail and the exhaustion she'd displayed at the beginning of the year had returned in the form of dark circles around her eyes, which flitted to him briefly before returning to her work.

"What do you want?" she said.

The confidence he had as her mentee dissolved against the tone in her voice.

"I...I was wondering when we were going to Iceland? The council meets in a few days," he said, clearing his throat when he was done.

Priyanka paused with the whetstone halfway up the blade. The spearing look she gave him made him feel like a first year again.

"You're not going," she said, before returning to her blade sharpening.

"May I ask why? I assume that's why you've been training me all year, to help when the time comes," he said.

"Even if that was the case, which it was not, you're too much of a risk to bring to Iceland. I can't be wondering if you're going to screw it up," she said.

Zayn wanted to shrink into himself, but he didn't want her to see how much her words had affected him, so he kept his shoulders back and his chin level.

"You're speaking about the demon in the park," said Zayn.

Before she spoke, the muscles in her jaw pulsed with anger. "Of course I'm speaking about the demon in the park. But I'm also talking about your training in Harmony. And the headaches that you won't deal with. And any of the other signs that you are compromised as an agent of the Academy."

"Compromised? I'm not compromised," he said.

Priyanka blew a breath out her nose, sighing at the same time.

"I know when one of my students is not committing to the

task. Whether it's because they have competing allegiances, or they don't believe in the mission, or can't put aside personal issues for the sake of the team, but either way, it means compromised. Which is what you are, plain and simple. Therefore, you will not be coming with me to Iceland, and it's likely that you'll need to find a new mentor for your fifth year."

The pronouncement was like having a bucket of ice water dumped on his head. To his surprise, rage rose up from his gut.

"But you trained me all year with the imbuement. It's for the dragons, to help if things get bad. And I can control it. I proved that in Harmony when I got the moondew plant. You need me," he said.

A twitch formed at the corner of her mouth. "I appreciate the passion, but it's not going to happen. It's probably best for you, since I'm taking the instructors and a number of other patrons, the ones good in a fight anyway, and it's likely that our visit will end in a battle, one that we're unlikely to win."

"Why would you do that if you thought you were going to lose?" asked Zayn.

"I don't plan on losing, but I'm prepared to deal with the consequences if I must. Which is all I'm asking for you to do with whatever it is you've got going on inside that head of yours." Priyanka squeezed her lips tight. "I'm sorry, but you really need to go now. I have preparations to make. You might as well enjoy these last few weeks. If the dragons get their way, there won't be a Hundred Halls much longer."

When Zayn closed the door behind him, an emptiness opened in his chest as vast as space. It wasn't so much what Priyanka had said, but how she'd said it. Try as he might, he couldn't help but hear the grim determination in her voice. She expected to go to Iceland and die. He didn't want that to happen, but he didn't know how to help either.

Zayn looked into his palm and rubbed it with his thumb as he thought about the battle in the park. Would the dragons still want to close down the school if the tall demon's escape hadn't been splashed all over the news? Probably. But he couldn't help think it was all his fault.

Chapter Twenty-Seven

First Ward, May 2017
Everyone hates lawyers until they need one

The firm called Black Pyramid was on the most expensive street in the city, commonly called M-Street—or Mage Street—due to the high-priced lawyers, lobbyists, and financial institutions that made it their business to service the Hall's mages. A glossy black granite pyramid towered outside the building, forcing pedestrians to walk around it, while inside the atrium the jackal-faced statue of Anubis stood over the receptionist desk as if it might come alive and defend the firm against intruders should it come to that.

The place oozed money and power. It was the kind of law firm in which the partners traveled by portal in the city, and had half the patrons of the Halls on their Rolodex. It was the kind of place that ran like a well-oiled machine, with every moment scripted and calendared, dozens and dozens of low-level mages operating behind the scenes. It was the kind of place that had authored treaties between realms as favors to Invictus, or argued cases about demonic contracts gone wrong.

The Black Pyramid law firm had seen all kinds of things, but it had never seen a young woman in a red headscarf pushing a cart full of cooking gear into its atrium as if she were attending a family cookout. Neveah's entrance surprised the receptionist so much that she dropped her cell phone as she tried to hurry out behind the desk.

"Young Miss, Young Miss. You can't bring that here," said the receptionist. "You can't *be* here."

Neveah ignored the woman and went right through the door into the next room. She expected a waiting room, but was shocked to find a huge mahogany-choked lounge with doors leading to privacy chambers.

The receptionist tugged on Neveah's arm, while she surveyed the room, looking for a place to set up.

"Young Miss, excuse me. You're not supposed to be here," she said.

Neveah turned on her. "Yes I am."

The response brought an openmouthed jawing, as if she were a fish gasping for air.

"But...the stuff, here, you're cooking," said the receptionist.

Neveah gave the woman her sweetest smile, the one that usually made her brothers and sisters suspicious. "I have an appointment. 12:45 pm. Neveah Carter. I'm here to discuss a cease and desist order with Abraham Bolten and Ralph Newsome."

The receptionist reached towards the cart of equipment, so Neveah slapped her hand away.

"It's not nice to touch things without asking," she said.

"I'm sorry. I mean, you can't have that in here. We're not a restaurant and...and I have to make sure there's nothing dangerous in there," said the receptionist, who was looking like she'd rather be at home reading a book.

"If I'd brought anything dangerous into the Black Pyramid, the firm's protections would have sounded the alarm, not counting the seers and oracles this place probably pays a pretty penny to for protection," said Neveah.

"But you're supposed to wait outside until I call you," she said, rotating back and forth while pointing to the door to the atrium.

Neveah tapped on her wrist, which didn't contain a watch. "It's time for my appointment—why don't you send for Misters Bolten and Newsome. I don't have all day."

The woman, though she probably had ten years on Neveah, took one look at her determined expression and probably decided it wasn't worth the effort, as she headed straight back to the receptionist desk.

"Thank you," said Neveah to the woman's back.

When she was gone, Neveah sighed. It was rather jerkish of her to barge in like she had, but she knew there was no way the receptionist would have allowed her in with her cooking gear otherwise.

Neveah pushed her cart into one of the privacy chambers, which contained a big table surrounded by a dozen leather-backed chairs. She parked the cart along the side and started pulling out the grocery bags filled with food, pots, and a blender. The back of her thighs ached from pushing the cart across the city, but at least she knew she wouldn't be taking them back with her. Even if this ploy worked, the equipment and food would stay. It'd taken the last of her money to purchase it.

The lawyers, Abraham Bolten and Ralph Newsome, showed up ten minutes later. The short bald lawyer, Ralph, cleared his throat as soon as he walked in, as if there was some possibility that she wouldn't notice him. Abraham stayed near the door, practicing his best grandfather clock impersonation.

"Maggie made a mistake when she let you in here," said Ralph, eyeing her equipment set out on the table with practiced derision. "Frankly, you shouldn't have even been given an appointment. You misrepresented yourself when you inquired about meeting with us. It'd be best if you collected your stuff and took it back home with you, otherwise we'll have to call security and do this the hard way."

In her gut, she wanted to lecture them about the pettiness of a cease and desist order for a taco food truck, that was primarily designed to force her out of the business since there was no way she'd be able to afford a lawyer. But she knew that approach wouldn't get anywhere. Lawyers, and the ilk that hired them, only respected one thing: power.

Neveah carefully reached into her back pocket—she didn't want them to get the wrong impression—and slid them a photograph. It was the one of her and Zayn on the food truck after painting it.

Ralph scrunched up his face as if he'd smelled something bad before sliding the picture back across the table.

"Am I supposed to know who that is? Or care?"

"It's my brother, Zayn Carter. He's a fourth-year student at the Academy of the Subtle Arts," said Neveah.

"So what, my cousin graduated from Coterie about a decade ago, but you don't see me flinging pictures around as if it was my dick," said Ralph.

"It's not that he's currently enrolled in the Academy. More, it's because as a first-year student, he broke into Celesse D'Agastine's R&D facility in the tenth ward. You're probably not aware of it, even though you represent her, because it was quietly suppressed. A loss of security protocols, especially to a first-year Academy mage, is not the best publicity for her publicly traded company. Nor would it be good for your firm, who represent her, especially when they find out you put a cease and desist order on a food truck. Not a great look if you ask me. But we don't have to go that route, if you give me a chance to prove that I'm not violating any intellectual properties."

Neveah motioned towards the cooking station set up on the table. The two lawyers stared back at her without a trace of expression on their faces. They gave nothing away, but neither did she.

Neveah knew there were a lot of ways this could go. She was well aware she might have bitten off more than she could chew. Both Zayn and Keelan had insinuated that the world was a lot darker and more messed up than it appeared to be. For all she knew, they would bring in a high-priced unscrupulous mage to have her memory wiped, or worse. In some ways, getting thrown in jail would be the best option. At least in that one, she'd have no choice but to give up.

"Give me a few minutes to make a call," said Ralph, who gave her no indication which way it was headed.

Ralph left the room while pulling out his cellphone. Abraham stayed near the door, gaze trained on her as if she might sprout wings at any moment. Neveah tried to cultivate a bored expression, but her heart was beating like a thousand butterflies.

When Ralph returned, Neveah squeezed her hands into fists behind her back. Though the room was icy cool, beads of sweat broke down her neck.

"She's coming here," said Ralph with a tiny shake of his head indicating his surprise. "She'll be here in a few minutes."

Neveah blurted out, "She?"

"Celesse," said Ralph, "or is that not who you were hoping to speak to?"

Neveah composed herself. "Of course that's who I wanted

to speak to."

Shit. Celesse D'Agastine. One of the wealthiest and most powerful people in the world. Her alchemy-based product empire was ubiquitous. Which was probably why she sent her lawyers after any possible future competitor. It would have made Neveah laugh at the ridiculousness of it, if it wasn't her whole livelihood tied up in that food truck.

A few minutes later, an elegant blonde woman—any blemishes smoothed away by enchantment—stepped into the room. Though she had high cheekbones, perfectly sculpted eyebrows, and lips that any model would die for, there was an airbrushed quality to her features that would have turned her exquisite looks mundane if it weren't for her eyes. The soul of someone who had lived for centuries stared out from those grey-green eyes: the color of moss on an old stone.

When Celesse stepped into the room, the two lawyers left, closing the door behind them. The blonde patron stared at Neveah without comment, leaving her trembling inside, but she kept her gaze matched with the woman's. Neveah wanted to speak, but the woman's presence seemed to suck the oxygen from the room.

Eventually, it grew to be too much—it was like staring at the sun—and Neveah looked away. A twitch of some emotion passed across Celesse's lips as she examined the cooking setup.

"You're as bold as your brother," said Celesse, placing a long fingernail against the plastic on the blender.

The compliment seemed to break the tension in Neveah, allowing her to respond.

"I didn't know who you were when you stopped by my truck that first time," said Neveah.

Amusement passed through Celesse's eyes. "You don't seem frightened of me."

No, I'm actually terrified of you, she thought, but she said, "I'm used to living with danger."

An expression of sadness rose to Celesse's face, one little used by the powerful mage. It settled there briefly before being pushed back below.

"You live in Varna," said Celesse. "Pri told me about the place many years ago."

Neveah nodded. *Pri.* Even though her brother studied under Priyanka Sai, it was strange to hear her nickname bantered about. The weight of who she was talking to settled on Neveah's frame, but she did not stagger. In fact, this acknowledgement of their humanity seemed to dispel the illusion of their invincibility for her. They were people like any other, albeit with vast and dangerous power, but not without flaws and feelings.

"What is your proposal?" asked Celesse.

Neveah gathered herself internally before speaking. "You accused me of stealing your intellectual property. I can prove that I have done no such thing."

"And if I believed you, why would that matter? If you cannot prove it in a court of law, then you have no legal standing," said Celesse.

If there was any doubt she was dealing with a predator, that was annihilated in that moment. Celesse might be amused, or intrigued by what was happening—maybe she thought of Neveah as a curiosity—but she would only respect power.

"But if I went to the press with my story, and the one about my brother, it would be terrible PR for your company. I have connections at the Herald. They would run my story," she said.

Celesse chuckled. "If anyone else had said that, I would have thought they were bullshitting me, but between your brother's stunt and this one, I believe you." She examined her fingernails briefly. "But know that I could have your story buried in a heartbeat. Camille Cardwell sits on my board, and we have lunch together every other week. Don't make threats unless you're sure they have teeth."

A pit opened up in Neveah's stomach. She'd given Celesse her best shot, and the woman had shrugged it off. She felt like a fool.

A secret smile formed on Celesse's lips. "Don't go soft on me now. The only reason I'm even standing here listening to a food truck short-order cook is because you were bold enough to challenge me."

Neveah forced herself to stand tall. The woman had seen right through her doubt.

"There are other outlets than the Herald," said Neveah.

"I'm sure you could find one that I couldn't intimidate, but it'd be small enough that it wouldn't break the daily news cycle," said Celesse, staring at her with intent.

Neveah almost had the impression that the patron was rooting for her, but also wouldn't give up lightly. Celesse was intrigued, and Neveah couldn't quite figure out why, and then it hit her.

"You ate some of my tacos," said Neveah.

"Of course, I'm a connoisseur of good food. When I see a long line day after day, week after week, I know there's something there. I sent someone down to grab me a plate, and when I ate them and could think of nothing else other than when I would eat them again, I realized you must be stealing from me. Honestly, I don't know how, or using what to do it, but I have patents on most food additives, so I figured it was something of mine."

"Which is why you came," said Neveah. "If I was truly stealing something from you, I wouldn't have bothered to set this up. Plus, my brother's previous involvement with your R&D facility."

"Though he broke into my facility, he was trying to stop a dangerous drug on the streets of Invictus, which suggests there might be something more to you as well," said Celesse.

"I think I should cook something for you now," said Neveah.

Celesse pulled back the edge of the grocery bag and spoke with a little bit of longing. "No tacos?"

"Too difficult to haul across the city," said Neveah. "I thought I'd make something simple. A nice cucumber gazpacho."

Celesse raised an eyebrow as she motioned for Neveah to proceed.

A gazpacho was a chilled soup made from fresh vegetables. It was the simplest thing she could think to make that wouldn't require a lot of equipment. The blender she'd bought was from the sale section of the store, nothing like the kind that she had at home.

Neveah pulled out the cucumber, tomatoes, green onions, jalapenos, garlic, oils, and spices. She expertly chopped the vegetables, throwing them into a bowl to cool over a pot of dry ice, along with the spices. Then she mixed up the oils and chopped tomatoes, and placed them into the blender.

When she did this at home, or in the food truck, Neveah had gotten used to pushing the faez through the blender and into the food. But she wanted to make it more obvious what she was doing, so she placed her hand on top of the blender without a lid, closed her eyes for effect, and started it at the same time she pushed faez into the mixture.

She ran the blender until it was a puree, which she could tell by the pitch of the blades, and then turned it off. When she opened her eyes, Celesse was staring at her in a way that chilled Neveah to the bone.

"How did you learn how to do that?" asked Celesse in a cold and dangerous way.

"No one taught it to me," said Neveah. "It just came naturally."

"I see."

There was a threat beneath that simple phrase, but Neveah ignored it, and went back to making the soup. She poured the puree into the bowl of chopped veggies, seasoned with pepper and salt, and set the stainless-steel bowl over a bed of dry ice. Normally, a gazpacho had to chill for a few hours, but she needed to force cool it. Neveah did the trick with the faez again, this time directing it into the dry ice, which made it react more intensely. A tight-lipped Celesse watched her the whole time, studying her as if she were watching surgery on her favorite pet.

When Neveah was finished, she poured out a bowl of gazpacho and handed it to Celesse with a spoon.

"Bon appetit."

Celesse stared the gazpacho as if it were a bomb, before dipping the spoon inside and taking a taste. Her eyes fluttered closed as the soup went into her mouth, and a little moan escaped her lips.

When she was finished enjoying the first spoonful, she set the bowl down as if she were afraid for her self-control.

After a quick and traitorous glance at the bowl of gazpacho, Celesse asked, "What now?"

Neveah set the bowl on the conference table. She'd hoped the demonstration would have been enough, but Celesse clearly wasn't going to give up easily.

"I want the rights to my food truck back," said Neveah.

"That's it? That's all you want?" asked Celesse, almost disappointed.

"No. The food truck isn't even really why I came, but I want it back just the same. Now that you know what I can do, you know I'm not ripping you off. I bet I could walk into any restaurant in the city and get a job, but that's not what I want," said Neveah.

"Then what do you want?"

Neveah pulled the list of potion ingredients that she'd rescued from Amber's shop and handed it over to Celesse.

"What is this?" asked Celesse.

"I don't know. But I need to find out. It's important," said Neveah.

Celesse's eyes creased as if she were going to ask a question, but then it seemed she decided against it.

"What are you offering in return if I tell you?" asked Celesse.

What am I offering? At first, she didn't know what she was going to say, and then she realized why Celesse had been so shocked at the cooking display.

"I won't tell anyone your secret, how you make your potions better than anyone else's. And I won't try to compete with you, or monetize what I can do, aside from any food trucks or restaurants that I open," said Neveah.

Celesse bunched up her lips. "That seems like quite a deal for me."

"I'm not done with my requests. I think I know what that potion does, and I want something that counteracts it." Celesse didn't make a motion, so Neveah kept going. "And I want some other things, nothing too much. Personal protection since I'm not much of a mage."

"Why not join my Hall? You'd be better than anyone else I've ever had the pleasure to teach. Or are you too old?" asked Celesse.

"I'm nineteen. But I don't want to be a mage," said Neveah.

"I'm afraid I don't understand. The world is a dangerous place. Clearly you know this because of what you came here to ask me. The Hundred Halls would give you that power," said Celesse.

Neveah looked her in the eyes. "I know this might seem strange to you, but I don't want it. It would change me, and who I am. What I want is freedom, but you can't offer me that. If I came to the Halls, I wouldn't get to use what I learned for me, but for someone else. If you talked to Priyanka, then you know why this is true."

Celesse paused before nodding respectfully.

"And even if I could join the Halls on my own terms, I don't know that I would. It's not who I am," said Neveah.

Celesse looked her over, smiling wistfully. "I believe you. And I wish I could offer you freedom, but power comes with limits. But know that I would have taken you as my personal assistant if you would have joined Alchemists. You are that talented."

A wellspring of pride opened up in Neveah's chest, giving her an idea of how Zayn or Keelan felt as a member of their Hall.

"Thank you. But all I want now is to know what that potion does and how to counteract it." Neveah blinked. "And my food truck back."

Celesse handed the paper back. "It's a personality distortion potion. I don't know why someone would take it—it's only used for psychotic patients who might harm themselves—but clearly someone had a reason. It's extremely dangerous and only given in extreme circumstances."

"Is there a counter to it?"

"There's always a counter, but yes, I could make one for you relatively easily. But the cure might be worse than the disease. Whatever is being suppressed by this potion, it could break their mind if you give them the counter," said Celesse gravely. "Especially without the care of a psychiatrist."

"That's my problem," said Neveah.

"Clearly," said Celesse, studying Neveah intently. "But if it's what you wish, I will make it. I just hope you know what you're doing."

"I do too."

Celesse held her hand out. Neveah hesitated until she realized she was offering a handshake. She took it, pleasantly surprised that Celesse's hand wasn't cold. Part of her almost expected the woman to be inhuman.

"We have a deal," said Celesse. "I won't bother with paperwork, since I trust you as a woman of honor."

"Thank you," said Neveah, wondering if she could trust Celesse, but deciding she'd probably pushed things as far as it could go.

"Are you sure you don't want to join Alchemists?" asked Celesse.

"I'm honored, but I wouldn't," said Neveah.

Celesse opened the door and summoned the lawyers.

"Tear up the cease and desist. We won't be bothering Miss Carter anymore," said Celesse.

They looked perplexed, but nodded.

"Please make Neveah comfortable while she waits. I'll send a courier with some things. It'll be a few hours."

They nodded again, their confusion becoming more pronounced.

"Oh, and have that soup sent up to my house. It's divine," she said with a wink as she walked out the door.

Left alone with the lawyers, they stared at her as if they were trying to figure out if the whole setup was a trick.

Neveah snapped her fingers at them. "You heard her.

Soup, courier, make me comfortable. Or do we need to call her back?"

As if he'd startled out of a dream, Ralph shook his head. "No, that'll be unnecessary, Miss Carter. We're very sorry for the trouble. We'll get right to it. Please have a seat. We'll send Maggie in to get you anything you might desire."

When the two lawyers left, Neveah felt a huge weight lift off her shoulders. The whole encounter had been both thrilling and exhausting, giving her a window into her brother's life as a Hall mage.

Neveah dropped into a leather-backed chair.

"I hope I'm doing the right thing, Zayn."

But there was only one way to find out.

Chapter Twenty-Eight
Seventh Ward, May 2017
Connecting the runes

Zayn was in the city the day that Priyanka left for Iceland. He'd gone for a run to clear his head—the fact that Priyanka was no longer his mentor was like acid on his bones. He hadn't been able to concentrate, and headaches had been coming more frequently.

He went by the team house in the seventh ward for company. With finals coming up, everyone had been studying or spending time with their mentors.

"Hello? Anyone here?" asked Zayn after clearing out the protective enchantments.

Marley wandered from the kitchen after pushing through the swinging door. He looked like he'd been sleeping on the refrigerator again since his fur was matted around his face.

"Hey Marley," said Zayn. "Any of the others here?"

The callolo sat on his haunches and signed his response. Zayn's ASL wasn't great but he got the gist of it.

"I forgot they were going to do that today," he said wistfully.

Since all the instructors were out of the country with Priyanka, the rest of the team was going to a show about a fictionalized early history of the Halls at the Orpheum Theater in the second ward.

He sighed and was about to leave again, when a stabbing headache blinded him with pain. He reeled for a few endless seconds, nearly blacking out before finding himself on the carpet with Marley sitting a few feet away.

The callolo's eyes were as wide as saucers. Zayn slowly became aware that the kitchen table had been sliced in half and the sword that he kept behind the cabinet was sticking in the ceiling, surrounded by painted runes.

Zayn okay? signed the callolo.

He pulled himself up while trying to ignore the nausea in his gut. Some of the runes looked like the ones on the novelty rub-ons.

"Not really."

The headaches were getting worse, which only made what Priyanka had said more meaningful. She was right to keep him from the Iceland trip. He was a liability. He just wished he could understand why he was getting them.

"I can't keep doing this," he said.

The room became stifling, so after leaving a note with an explanation about the table, he headed back into the city, wandering aimlessly. It'd rained that morning, so the streets were still wet. Unfortunately, the rain hadn't washed away those stupid runes. After a year of them, the novelty had worn off, and the lines had disappeared at the purple kiosks, but the damage had been done. He'd heard the city was going to vote on a law preventing future products like them, but they were entirely too late.

He walked past a green trash box that had been plastered with the runes. Competing for space on the painted box, the runes had been placed in various orientations. As he glanced at the runes, a stab of familiarity hit him. He'd been getting these feelings since the first time he'd seen the runes, but this time he actually remembered that he'd seen them before. It was the upside-down rune that had reminded him.

"I took a picture," he muttered as he pulled out his cell-phone, quickly swiping through his photo album to earlier in the school year when he'd gone to Iceland with Priyanka.

Vaximarillion.

He'd snapped a covert picture of the massive dragon to show his teammates. The tail was covered in runes.

Zayn zoomed in and examined the designs, and then he squatted down and compared the runes to those on the green trash box.

"Oh no."

A shiver went down his spine. He'd thought the extra runes were extraneous, unnecessary. He hadn't recognized them. No one knew what they were because the dragons guarded their runic secrets, and no dragon was older than Vaximarillion, who knew the most ancient of runes.

"The city is one big spell," he said.

The pieces fell into place: the damage to the water well wasn't accidental, nor was the hydra's loss of two heads.

"And Priyanka and a bunch of patrons are headed to Ice-land. Funny how that works. They set a date so they knew the most dangerous patrons would be out of the country," said Zayn, shaking his head.

If he had a way to get hold of her, he would have sent a message, but his privileges with Priyanka had always been one way. Not that it would have mattered. Whatever was going to happen was going to happen today. Even if he could get hold of her, it would be too late.

"What does this spell do?" he asked himself.

He knew the answer right away. The dragons had said as much at the council meeting. They wanted to seal up the city, block it off from the demonic realm, even if that meant destroying the Hundred Halls.

Knowing what he did about the dangers of the world, he knew it would be a catastrophic disaster. As long lived as they were, the dragons were shortsighted about this solution. Sure, they'd keep the demons from entering the world, but they'd set up a hundred other problems by destroying the Halls.

Zayn glanced up to the towering Spire at the center of the city.

"There's no one to stop them."

Zayn headed into the fourth ward. It was the closest Garden Network portal. He would take it back to the Honeycomb and see if there were any other students that might be able to help. It wasn't much but it was the only thing he could think of.

His problems multiplied when he walked past a comic book shop, nearly falling over. It wasn't a migraine this time, but a comic book display in the window.

"The Spider Queen Must Die!" he said, feeling a yawning pit open up in his gut. "Not now, not now."

There was something both familiar and dangerous in the white plantation and the towering oaks shown on the front of Issue #5. He knew what they were meant to signify, even if he didn't want to know why.

A tectonic shift in his mind triggered another migraine. Zayn collapsed against the windowpane, the world blacking out, only coming to when an elderly gentleman shook him awake.

"Are you okay?" asked the old man, eyes white with concern. "Your hands caught fire before you screamed and fell to the ground."

Zayn checked his hands to find them unburnt, though there was a lingering burnt smell.

"I'm fine," said Zayn, then catching himself, said, "but thank you."

He stumbled away from the shop, trying to put the comic out of his mind. There was an answer he didn't want to know.

Zayn pulled out his cellphone, typed a message to his teammates, and pressed send. He waited for a few minutes, but when no reply came, he realized they must be at the show and have their cellphones turned off. A quick check on the internet revealed that the show wouldn't be out for another four hours.

"Shit." He slammed his fist into his leg. "Double shit."

He put his hands on his head and spun around, thinking about the runes and the spell.

"How do you cast a spell as big as a city?" he asked.

The runes helped a lot. People had been putting them on everything, feeding them with faez, priming the pump for the real deal. But Zayn knew from his spell theory classes that triggering a spell like that would take a huge amount of faez. An amount so large that no one, not even a dragon, could manage it.

"Unless there was a lot of excess faez in a certain chamber beneath the city," he said, a cold hand clenching around his heart.

Everything made sense in that instant. The dragons had damaged the water well so the chamber would be filled with enough faez to trigger the spell. It wasn't just to release a few demons into the city, to give the dragons more justification, it was to further their plan.

Zayn sent a second message to his teammates, letting

them know his theory and where he was headed. If he was wrong, then it would be a nice distraction going into the Undercity. If he was right, then he expected to find some evidence at the water well of power.

Lost in his thoughts, he didn't hear Watcher Sabrina's approach until she was directly behind him.

"Zayn Carter."

Seeing a familiar face on that difficult day brought a burgeoning smile to his lips until he caught her nothing-but-business expression.

"Is something wrong?" he asked, feeling the sudden need to flee.

Despite the warmer weather, Watcher Sabrina wore a heavy trench coat and dark sunglasses. Her hand was hidden beneath the coat, clearly clamped onto something.

"I figured out what your plan is," said Sabrina grimly. "You're coming with me to Varna."

Before he could flood faez into his imbuement, she opened the coat briefly, revealing a handgun the size of Kansas. There was no doubt in his mind it was filled with mage-killing bullets. As fast as he was, she was just as fast, and there was no way he could outrun a bullet.

With her other hand, she reached into her coat and threw him a collar.

"Put that on, or you're not taking another step ever again."

Chapter Twenty-Nine
The Black Pyramid, May 2017
Gifts from above

The fifth-year student from The Order of Honorable Alchemists looked utterly confused when she brought the equipment bag to the conference room in the Black Pyramid law firm.

"Neveah Carter?" she asked, wrinkling her face at the bowls and cooking supplies left on the table.

"Expecting someone else?" asked Neveah.

The girl blinked, glancing around. "No, I guess...anyway, here."

Neveah knew what she thought. She'd come to the law firm expecting a celebrity or high-powered diplomat, or other such "important" individual. There was no way that Celesse would brew up a batch of potions for anyone but a person like that. So she didn't take offense, because she would have probably done the same thing if the roles had been reversed.

"Can you tell me what they do?" asked Neveah as she

looked into the bag.

"Uh, yeah," said the girl, who kept glancing back to the bowls of leftover gazpacho mixture with suspicion. "In Alchemists, we call this one the 'Superhero.' It does all sorts of things—make you stronger, faster, etcetera. But this one should be extra juiced, because, you know, the queen."

"Right, light blue is Superhero," said Neveah.

"This next one is a general purpose regenerative. If someone's hurting, this will get them back in the game." The girl handed a crimson vial to Neveah. "Here's another that will turn up your senses, and another that will help you find someone, but make sure you concentrate on who it is before you drink it."

Then the girl pulled out a syringe, eyeing it with a frown on her lips. "This one, I don't know what it is, but it doesn't look friendly."

"I actually know what that one is," said Neveah, taking it carefully out of the girl's hands and placing it back into the bag. "Thank you, you've been a big help."

After the girl left, Neveah put the vials and syringe in her backpack.

Ralph was waiting outside the conference room, twitching as if he were expecting Celesse to come back and char him into bits at any moment.

"Is everything in order?" he asked, a genuinely concerned expression on his face. She knew his concern was about his well-being and not her, but whatever got the job done.

"Yes. Everything's good. Well, actually, there's one more thing," she said, thinking about her impounded food truck. "I need a couple thousand dollars."

"Excuse me?"

"Do I need to have Celesse come down again? Or are we clear that she brewed me a bag of potions that are worth a small fortune? I think she would want you to give me the money," said Neveah.

Ralph blinked a few times, clearly weighing the risks of calling her bluff with the loss of funds. When he reached into his pocket and produced a leather billfold, Neveah had to hide her surprise that he had that kind of money already on him.

"You did the right thing," she said.

"Anything else?" he asked tersely, his nostrils flaring.

"No, that will do. You've been a big help."

Outside the Black Pyramid, the day seemed much brighter. She'd walked into the most powerful law firm in the city, maybe even the world, and had come out with a bag full of answers. Tracking her brother down and administering the potion didn't seem like it'd be that hard compared to the first task.

Neveah pulled out the gritty greenish-brown potion, swirling it before her eyes. It was supposed to help her find him. She thought about delaying drinking it for another day, but the vision she'd had in the food truck had felt imminent. And there wasn't much time left in the school year. Whatever was going on with him, she needed to deal with it before he returned to Varna, so she placed the image of her brother firmly in her mind and uncorked the vial.

"Bottoms up," she said, throwing the potion back and instantly regretting it.

"Augh, that tastes like coffee grounds mixed with rotting baby food," she said, spitting a few times to clear the flavor from her mouth.

Neveah didn't know what to expect from the potion, how it might tell her where Zayn was, until she felt a tugging on her forehead pulling her westward. She pulled a city map out of her pocket and traced the direction to see it either led to the fourth or the thirteenth ward.

After calling a taxi, she told the driver to take her into the fourth ward. He didn't seem to mind when she had him make random turns as she triangulated her brother's position—after all, she was paying by the mile. When she saw her brother talking to a Watcher from Varna on the corner of an intersection near a Wizard's Coffee, her blood ran cold.

"Take me near those two people talking and park like you're waiting for a new fare," said Neveah.

"Whatever, lady, the meter's still running," he said with a shrug.

As the taxi approached, Neveah rolled down the window and sunk onto the floorboards. The taxi driver parked about twenty feet away, which was close enough for her to hear her brother without straining.

"...if we don't stop"—a nearby car blared its horn, annihilating a few words—"there won't be any more Varna. If you want to protect the Lady, you need to listen to me."

Zayn's statement was met with silence. Neveah desperately wanted to peek above the backseat of the taxi, but didn't trust that her brother or the Watcher wouldn't see her with their supernatural senses.

She also didn't understand why he would care about the Lady. If there was one thing she knew about her brother, it was that he despised the Lady. But was that what had happened to him? Did they change him somehow? In the same way the Watchers seemed drained of their personalities once they graduated? Her brother had insinuated that he had a special job once he was done with the Halls. Could he have meant the Watchers?

Neveah was so intent on solving the conundrum that she barely missed that they'd wandered away from the taxi. It was only a chance change of wind direction that brought Zayn's fleeting words to her ear.

"Dammit," she said, sitting up and almost getting out of the taxi until she remembered the fare. "How much do I owe?"

When he answered, she grimaced, but produced the bills, throwing them into the front seat and then hurrying to the corner to see where her brother and the Watcher had gone. Whatever was going on with him, it seemed to be coming to a head. Why else would he be reporting to a Watcher?

But around the corner, she didn't see or hear her brother. They'd disappeared completely.

The tugging on her forehead pulled her forward, but she didn't see them.

Neveah ran recklessly down the sidewalk, turning her head like an oscillating fan to figure out where her brother was headed, only to learn they'd cut down an alleyway. She threw herself behind a brick wall when the Watcher glanced backward.

With her breath caught in her throat, Neveah debated running back the way she had come, in case the Watcher wandered back to investigate. It wouldn't be good for her or her family to be caught spying on the Lady's henchwoman.

When a few seconds passed and she realized that the Watcher wasn't coming, Neveah fished into her bag and produced the sensing potion. She couldn't risk running into them again, but needed a way to make sure she could stay close.

This potion was a refreshing change from the previous as it tasted like a nice seltzer water with lime and cherries.

"Ahhh," she said, her enjoyment deepening as the potion kicked in. "Ahh...ohh, crap."

It was like the world had been turned up a few notches. Suddenly the world drew in around her as a canvas of sound and heat. Her vision was a little overwhelming as she could see every pore on the brick wall and every freckle on the face of a woman waiting to cross the street fifty feet away.

Neveah was so lost into the sensations she almost forgot what her purpose was, but quickly reoriented herself towards the alleyway, catching snippets of conversation at the far end.

She sped after them, using a combination of the sensing and tracking potions to keep her brother at a reasonable distance without losing him.

It seemed the pair was headed to a courtyard behind the apartment building, protected by a tall wrought iron fence. Neveah ducked behind a rusted blue dumpster as her brother approached the gate. There was a squeaking of hinges, and a muttered password, which she easily heard.

Neveah waited for a minute before following. When she reached the wrought iron gate, she said, "Rumpelstiltskin," and opened the gate, which swung lazily open, revealing a circular space with no exit and a large black obsidian pillar at the center. Neveah quickly examined the small space for a way that her brother and the Watcher could have left without her notice, but there was no visible sign or hidden door that she could discover.

Neveah put her hands on top of her head, looking all around. "Where did they go?"

Chapter Thirty
Fourth Ward, May 2017
The enemy of my enemy

The collar in his hand was cold despite the warm day. He looked down at the clasp, seeing that once it was around his neck, he'd never get free again.

"No," said Zayn.

Sabrina shifted the gun forward, poking it out of the trench coat.

"I think you'd be wise to listen to me. It's my duty to protect Lady Arcadia, and I finally know what it is you're planning. When I take you back to her, you'll confess everything," said Sabrina.

A double-decker tour bus passed them, the guide's droning voice carrying over the street noise as the tourists with their phones held high and set on record craned their heads in all directions.

"...up the avenue is the famous Invictus City Library with its extensive collection of..."

While the bus meandered by, Zayn held the collar to his stomach while the gun slipped back into the trench coat. He could have used the opportunity to escape—he didn't think she'd shoot him with so many witnesses—but this wasn't a problem he could run from.

"You look like you dressed up as a budget FBI agent for Halloween in that coat," said Zayn.

Sabrina scowled. "I'm not here for games. Put the collar on."

"I'm not putting it on, and before you shoot me, I'll tell you why," he said.

"Put it on, now," growled Sabrina.

It didn't take his imbuement to see how agitated she was. The pulse in the vein in her neck was pounding away. She'd probably expected a fight, and his refusal was confirming it. He needed to convince her—and fast.

"Last year, I went with Priyanka to Iceland to meet with a group of dragons that were deciding whether or not to take over the city. They gave us until today to decide if it was going to be a peaceful takeover, or not," said Zayn.

"What does this have to do with anything?" asked Sabrina.

"I'm getting there." Zayn nodded towards a lamppost that had a few runes etched onto it. "See those runes? Wait, never mind, you're not going to look away from me, are you? But you've seen the runes all over the city. The dragons pulled a fast one on Priyanka. They told her they would give her an answer, so she took a bunch of patrons to Iceland to stop them. The problem is that they've been preparing the city with these runes all year. They're going to shut everything down, which will destroy the city in the process, and along with it, the Hundred Halls."

Sabrina blinked a few times and took a furtive glance at the runes on the lamppost. "Back to my previous question.

Why do I care? You're a talented fourth year, but still, only a fourth year. Even if the dragons pulled a fast one on Priyanka, what are you going to do about it? I still think you should put that collar on and come with me, or I'm gonna have to put a few holes through you."

"But I *can* do something," said Zayn, calming himself after he realized he was yelling. "I know what they're going to do, and where. But I can't do a damn thing if I have this collar on and leave with you."

Sabrina gave an exasperated sigh. "I don't know, Zayn. This sounds like one of Pennywhistle's gambits. Well, this is a bit more farfetched than the kind of stuff she taught us. I mean, who thinks up a conspiracy of dragons at the drop of a hat, but I know you're good, I wouldn't put it past you."

"Great, I never thought being *good* at something would backfire on me."

"Why hasn't anyone else figured it out? These runes have been scattered around the city of sorcery for nine freaking months. Surely one of the hundreds of arcane scholars would have known what they were going to do. Why you, of all people?" asked Sabrina.

"Thanks for the vote of confidence." He sighed. "And why me? Because these aren't runes that anyone in the Halls knows about. And how do I know? Because I was with Priyanka when she went to Iceland. And I got to see Vaximarillion in dragon form."

Sabrina wrinkled her face. "Vaximarillion? I thought he was a legend."

Zayn shrugged. He wasn't up on his dragon lore. "Beats me. But I got a picture of his tail. It wasn't until, well, today that I realized the runes on his body were like the novelty runes."

Making sure to move slowly, he pulled up the picture on

his cellphone and threw it to her. While keeping half her attention on him, Sabrina studied the photo.

"By the holy web, that *is* Vaximarillion," she said breathlessly.

When he looked at her strangely, she shrugged a single shoulder. "If I hadn't been born in Varna I would have joined Animalians. I always wanted to work with dragons."

"Look, Sabrina. I get it. It's a bit much, especially when you've got a gun trained on me. But if we don't stop the"–a car horn blared—"dragons, there won't be any more Halls, which means there won't be any more Varna. If you want to protect the Lady, you need to listen to me."

She stared at him for a good ten seconds, before giving him a slow nod, indicating that she was going to let him go. He moved past her, heading towards the Garden Network portal, but she caught up to him, matching his stride.

"I'm coming with you," she said.

"I guess I could use the help," he said, knowing he had no way to really refuse her.

Sabrina wrenched the collar from his grip and shoved it into an inner pocket.

"See, trench coats have uses," she said with a huff.

He gave the password at the Garden Network, touching the stone as he said the word. The portal took them into the Undercity, where they layered up enchantments before traveling.

Sabrina kept glancing over at him and her hand never strayed far from the inside of her coat where her gun was hidden.

"There are a lot more dangerous things than me down here," said Zayn.

"We're both trained in the Academy, so don't try to pull your tricks with me," she said.

Zayn turned on her. "Either you're here to help, or you need to leave. We can't be mistrusting each other. Not now."

Sabrina pushed him forward, a scowl on her lips. "Just lead us to wherever it is you're taking us."

He started walking because he didn't want to delay. Who knew when the dragons would complete the spell, or even if there was anything they could do about it?

"We're headed to a well of power," said Zayn over his shoulder, his voice echoing through the cavern.

"You say that like I should know what you're talking about. Not all of us were Priyanka's pet during our time at the Academy," said Sabrina, not hiding her bitterness.

A quip formed on his lips, but he swallowed it. He needed her on his side, or at the very least, not suspecting him. Not only for the dragons, but for afterwards, when he'd have to deal with her desire to take him back to Varna in an imprisonment collar.

"This is all I know, which isn't much, because Priyanka only tells me bits and pieces. The city was built in a place that allowed mages to use more faez naturally, but the more we used it the more it opened the pathways to faez, which eventually damaged the earth, and in turn, made it easier for other realms to connect with us. It's why the portals work well in Invictus, or to other realms, but you can't, let's say, hop a portal to Paris. Anyway, some time ago, they funneled the excess faez into wells, put protections on them, including guardians, and have been monitoring them ever since."

Sabrina was so quiet, he had to check behind him to make sure she was there. She seemed deep in thought.

Eventually she asked, "So where do the dragons fit in?"

"Without Invictus, who helped make the wells, I think, the barriers between this world and the other realms are thinning. Especially with the demonic one. They're afraid that the dam will burst and the demons will come flooding in, ruining this world and all the others. So they want to block the wells, which will in turn destroy the city and the Hundred Halls."

"It's like a nuclear plant that's getting too hot and they're wanting to shut it down and fill it with concrete," said Sabrina.

"Yeah, I guess," he said, then froze when a familiar mental signature pinged of his mind.

He held his hand up in the universal sign to freeze, and extended his senses forward into the cavern they were about to pass through. Though they were still a hundred feet away, he could hear the soft scraping of claws on stone.

Zayn leaned against her ear and whispered, "Modrats. We have to find another way around."

Her nose wrinkled, suggesting she'd never heard of them, but she nodded, accepting his assessment of the danger. Then she tapped on his shoulder and pointed to the left, where a passage headed perpendicular.

"This place is a labyrinth," whispered Zayn. "I know the modrat cavern goes where we need, because I can smell water, but we'll have to see if that one gets us where we're going."

They worked their way in the new direction, moving slowly and carefully, as to not make a sound. It wasn't hard for them, as they each moved with the grace of a panther, but they didn't want to take chances.

A few minutes later, when they were well down the passage, they heard a chorus of squeals from the previous cavern as if the modrats were chasing after something. They both paused with ears turned as the ruckus built to a crescendo before dropping into a low level of activity.

"I guess they got whatever was back there," said Zayn.

"Think someone was following us?" asked Sabrina.

"No," said Zayn, thinking that it was too early for his teammates to be out of the play. "If it were a dragon, they wouldn't have been worried about a bunch of rats, and no one else knows where we are. It was probably a random denizen of the Undercity. Whoever or whatever it was, it's probably dead."

Chapter Thirty-One
Fourth Ward, May 2017
One-way journey

Neveah banged her fist against every portion of the wall, trying to dislodge a secret door or hidden passage. The whole thing was very strange to her. She'd been sneaking through garbage-laden back alleyways, and now she stood in a perfectly clean circular space with a huge obsidian stone in the middle. The place even smelled like lavender as if she were in a high-end boutique.

A quick knock on the obsidian stone proved that it wasn't hollow. The glossy black surface reflected her like a funhouse mirror.

Frustrated that she couldn't figure out where they'd gone, Neveah sat on the ground, leaning her back against the stone.

"What am I thinking trying to follow them? They've got all this magic and knowledge, and I've got a few potions and no idea what I'm doing," said Neveah.

The obsidian stone was cool against the back of her head

at least.

"And what kind of a password is Rumpelstiltskin?"

The moment the word left her lips, Neveah thought a hole had opened up and sucked her backwards. She closed her eyes against the vertigo, only opening them again when the world was no longer spinning around her.

She was in pitch-black darkness.

This is not good.

Using her heightened senses, Neveah could tell she was in a large cavern, and from the darkness, the smell of mold, and the chill, she deduced it was probably underground. She rubbed her arms for warmth.

It was no secret that the city had huge underground caverns beneath, but no one went there because they were dangerous. She was okay with the idea of following her brother through the streets, but not in the Undercity where she was unequipped to deal with the dangers.

Neveah placed her hands against the cool stone and said, "Rumpelstiltskin."

Nothing happened.

"Shit."

It dawned on her why she was down here and why the password didn't take her back. She'd thought the password had been necessary to get into the little space with the obsidian stone, but really it'd been to activate the portal. There was probably a different word to get back up.

Neveah realized she had two options. Stay here and wait for her brother to come back and face those consequences, or try to follow him.

"I'm not giving up, Zayn."

As she pondered the next steps, she realized that she could barely see. The only light was from phosphorescent fungi in the cavern that gave off dim illumination.

Thankfully, there was only one path forward, which Neveah took, head craning in all directions for potential dangers. She moved rather quickly, worried that she'd fallen too far behind Zayn, when she heard them talking not far ahead. She couldn't hear what they were saying, but she could tell where they were. She realized if she kept them at close distance, she could follow and avoid most dangers.

This worked for the first twenty minutes. Neveah moved through the caverns, keeping watch where her feet where placed so she didn't accidently scuff some loose gravel and notify her brother and the Watcher of her existence. It helped that they were chatting, which hid her minor mistakes.

Then as easy as they were to follow, suddenly it seemed like they'd disappeared completely. She couldn't hear them, and when she moved up the passage, she couldn't see them either.

The fungi that had provided light in the earlier sections had disappeared, leaving her nearly blind.

Without her brother to lead her, she wasn't sure she could even find her way back to the portal. A sense of panic gripped Neveah as she realized she was alone in the dark, in a vast and treacherous place.

Think, Neveah, think, she told herself.

She'd always found that if she had a cooking problem she didn't have a solution for, she would explain the issue to an imaginary friend, and the answer would usually present itself.

I'm in the dark, in the Undercity, I can't see, and the fungus that helps me see isn't in this cavern, so I need to...bring the fungus with me!

Neveah hurried back to the previous cavern, found a thick patch of it, and scraped it away with her pocketknife, forming a large enough ball that she could use it like a lamp.

When she returned to the place she'd lost her brother and

held the fungus ball up high, she saw that her problem had multiplied. There were at least three different passages leading from her location: a large cavern straight ahead, a smaller one to the right, and a leftward passage.

The center one seemed the most likely, especially because she smelled water. Her brother had mentioned a well earlier, so that seemed the likeliest course. She took a step forward, only to catch the sound of scrabbling claws ahead. It wasn't just one or two sets of claws, but dozens, and it sounded like they were headed towards her.

Chapter Thirty-Two
Undercity, May 2017
The enemy revealed

The perpendicular passage, after winding around for a half hour, brought them back to familiar territory. As he hopped down from a ledge, landing on angled rock, he remembered the vision he'd had in the Starwood Mirror involving Watcher Sabrina and his sister. It occurred to him that the mirror might not have shown him danger *from* Neveah, but *for* Neveah. It made more sense, given that she was back in Varna, while Watcher Sabrina was in Invictus with him.

If he'd been taken back to Varna in a collar, would she have done something reckless to save him? He wouldn't put it past her. In her own way, she was like him. Had she been a few years closer in age, he could have seen her deciding to attend the Halls. He needed to understand the danger, not only for himself, but for Neveah.

"When again did you graduate from the Academy?" asked Zayn.

"A gentleman never asks a lady her age," said Sabrina, catching up to him since the passage was wide enough for two.

Zayn chuckled. "Neither am I a gentleman, nor are you a lady. People that sneak around in the dark with sharp objects can be called neither."

After a long pause, Sabrina said, "Before you think—when I graduated, that is."

"I guess there are some benefits to working for the Lady," said Zayn.

He expected a response, so her lack of answer was unnerving. He realized that by talking about the Lady, he was reminding her of what she'd intended to do before he'd convinced her to come into the Undercity. He searched for a topic to switch to, so he might defuse the tension, when he heard someone curse from off to their right.

"By the Mother's Wings," said Akhekh, who was climbing down a slope backwards in a white three-piece suit.

Zayn pulled Sabrina into the shadows. When Akhekh neared their position, they both slipped into the Veil. Sabrina was focused on the intruder, which left Zayn a moment to examine Sabrina. She had a strange secondary aura around her and a purple thread that went up and out from her back. His gut tightened when he thought of Keelan as a Watcher.

After Akhekh left the cavern, Sabrina asked, "Who was that?"

"Akhekh. He's one of the dragons that was at the council last time. He's probably the one designated to trigger the spell," said Zayn.

Sabrina looked internally conflicted. "We're going to have to kill him?"

"If we can or at least stop him," said Zayn. "We'd better hurry. Once he gets to the lake, he can leave us behind. We're going to have to take him before then."

They'd been moving methodically up until that point, but now that they had a purpose, they moved with precision, using their imbuements for silence and speed. Zayn internally scolded himself for not taking the opportunity to attack Akhekh when he'd passed them, but he hadn't had a chance to tell Sabrina, and he knew a simple dagger strike wouldn't deal a fatal blow.

His concerns that he'd missed his chance disappeared when he got to the cavern, finding Akhekh on the edge of the water, waiting for them.

The white three-piece suit was untouched by dirt or grime. He held his darkwood cane under his arm with his hands clasped before him.

"You knew we were there," said Zayn, feeling foolish for not being quieter earlier.

"I had to make a bit of noise just to get you to shut up. I was hoping you'd try to attack me as I passed, but alas, you stayed in that damned Veil," said Akhekh.

"You can't do this," said Zayn. "Destroying the Halls will cause destruction across the realms."

Akhekh pulled his cane from beneath his armpit and leaned on it with a smirk on his lips. "Not necessarily. I mean, there will be a period of adjustment, but the Halls, or some other such organization, will rise from the ashes like a phoenix, or a dragon, if you prefer, which I do."

Something that Akhekh had said when he met him in Iceland came back to Zayn.

"This isn't a plot of the dragons, this is *your* plot. You funded the kiosks personally, didn't you? You're wanting to set up your own Hundred Halls in Vegas. What do they call it now? Little Invictus?"

Akhekh nodded his head to the side as he adjusted his expensive clothing.

"You're beginning to see the big picture," said Akhekh.

"Yeah, I do. Not only do you take over for Invictus, but you get to be the one that solved the problem for dragonkind, one that you probably brought to their attention."

"Not directly," said Akhekh. "It took some time to maneuver Sphyianna into bringing it up. She's such a hothead. It was only a matter of time. But yes, in the end, I will have solved the problem and set myself up as the head of a new school, the name of which I have not decided, thus increasing my status within the Circle."

"And making a tidy profit from the lives of millions," growled Sabrina.

She glanced at him with fierce determination. Whatever feelings she had before, they were set aside while they dealt with Akhekh.

"Let the world toil while the dragons remain," said Akhekh, showing his teeth.

"Asshole," said Sabrina.

"Now," he said, producing a blade from his jacket while Sabrina pulled her gun.

Zayn took off towards Akhekh with Sabrina at his side. Her gun went off in rapid succession, but Akhekh spun his cane like a propeller blade and the bullets ricocheted through the air. After the first couple deflections, Sabrina threw her gun to the side and produced a blade of her own.

The casino mogul stayed in an en garde position until they were strides away, then he leapt into action, using his cane to deflect their blades.

Amped up on faez, Zayn moved lightning quick, punching through the air with his blade, but every time he thought he had Akhekh, he slipped out of the way. Zayn began to wonder if they would be able to take him, given that even Priyanka had to dose up with super potions to battle Jörm.

In a rare pause in the action, Sabrina muttered, "Head-long Zipper."

Though the sparring forms were mostly used for training, as real battle happened far too quickly for preplanned attacks, this specific technique would provide an opportunity for a second fighter. He threw himself at Akhekh, arms pinwheeling in a forward attack meant to push the defender backwards, and Sabrina used a Flying Rickshaw. The double attack nearly worked, as Akhekh backed all the way to the water, before he punched his fists forward, blasting them with an unexpected force shield.

They quickly responded, but it was clear they'd lost what little advantage they'd briefly enjoyed.

Zayn switched to a different tactic. He kept up his attacks, but diverted faez into his fourth imbuement. He couldn't overpower the dragon, but maybe he could force him into a critical error that they could take advantage of.

Weaving the imbuements in the middle of battle felt like juggling a dozen chainsaws while trying to sing opera. Akhekh seemed to sense his distraction, and the defense work of his cane switched to offense, revealing a blade at the end of the darkwood shaft.

The change caught Zayn off guard and he barely stayed ahead of the blade, dodging dragon-strength blows that would have cut him in half. Caught up in the fight, he didn't realize he was being pushed backwards until his heel caught a rock edge and he tipped backwards.

The blade headed straight for his heart, but somehow missed, nicking his shoulder instead.

Akhekh looked down at his hands to find them encased in webs, which had come from Sabrina somehow. His blade flew at her, but the momentary pause gave Zayn a chance to recover his balance and slam Akhekh with his imbuement.

The casino mogul's eyes shot wide open when he felt Zayn enter his mind, and for a moment, Zayn thought he might be able to take control, or at least interfere with his defenses enough, but just then, a migraine slammed through him.

Black spots filled Zayn's vision and he caught a kick from Akhekh, sending him across the beach to land on hard rock. One-on-one, Sabrina was no match for him, and she wisely backflipped out of the way of his cane attacks.

With the both of them away, a strange smile plastered itself onto Akhekh's lips.

Before either of them could do anything, Akhekh transformed, his human-size shape expanding rapidly, growing until it was a bronze-gold colored dragon the size of a city bus.

Transfixed by the dragon's presence, Sabrina didn't move when Akhekh reared back his head. Zayn sprinted toward Sabrina, narrowly dragging her out of the way when the blast of sand and heat came from Akhekh's toothy mouth, stripping the rock of any soft material.

Tumbled into a pile, Zayn barely had time to get to his feet when the dragon beat its wings, raising its scaled body into the air, and then with the lumbering grace of an elephant, slowly turned toward the center of the lake, flying over the water towards the well of power.

Chapter Thirty-Three
Undercity, May 2017
What you don't see can kill you

With a host of scrabbling claws seemingly headed towards her, Neveah resisted the urge to flee, knowing that her flight might incite being chased if they hadn't noticed her yet. Neveah took deep breaths and concentrated on her senses. The potion allowed her to draw in the way ahead as she listened for the sounds of the small creatures bouncing off the rocks. She also sensed they had a psychic ability, as she kept feeling pressure on her thoughts.

Whatever they were, they were milling about the cavern, chewing on little mushrooms that had grown on the rocks, but after calming herself, she realized they weren't headed towards her. Neveah looked around her to see the tiny toadstools clinging to the sides of the gray-black stone that they were eating.

Neveah considered the tools she had and formed a plan. She started by taking a sip of the Superhero potion. She didn't know if she wanted to down the whole thing, but she wanted a little more oomph if she needed to run for her life.

Immediately, she felt like she'd drunk a half dozen energy drinks, but not in a shaky way. She felt positively alive.

I could get used to this.

Then she gathered the little brown toadstools, collecting a big handful of them, and dripped a few drops from the syringe on them while pushing as much faez as she could through her hands and into the toadstools. She didn't know if it would work, but it was worth a try. If the antidote was dangerous for someone trapped by a cogitative construct, it would probably be worse for a bunch of small psychic creatures.

After squishing the ball of loaded toadstools together, Neveah pulled back her arm and launched the mushrooms into the cavern. As soon as they hit, the creatures reacted as if she'd thrown a bomb into their midst.

They descended onto the toadstool ball in a host of squeaks, drawn by the faez she'd infused it with, which like her tacos, had turned an ordinary meal into something transcendent. As the first creatures fought over the toadstools, they started turning on each other. Their tiny screams filled her with dread, but at least they weren't attacking her.

As they fought, she started to see them, as if their natural camouflage had left them. They looked like mottled rats, but with mole-like eyeflaps instead of eyes. One of the larger rats, after being bitten, leapt away from the crowd, headed towards the right passage, while the others followed.

Using the distraction, Neveah hurried forward, her back prickling with worry that the creatures might turn on her at any moment. But once she was through the cavern, she sensed that she'd successfully escaped them.

With the psychic rodents behind her, she used her ball of fungus to light the way, but even with her senses turned up, she felt blind. Her progress was slowed when she had to climb down difficult slopes, stuffing her fungus ball into her backpack to leave her hands free.

Her progress slowed even more, as she had to stop and listen every thirty seconds to make sure nothing was following or preparing an ambush.

After a half hour, she thought she heard the sounds of gunshots, but it was distant, and she couldn't make it out. The noise put a hurry into her step, and she risked ambush. Along the way, the sounds of battle changed to a high-pitched noise she couldn't make out that slowly retreated.

Finally, she came out into a massive cavern filled with a dark lake that she could easily see in because of a strange light coming from the far end, almost like an underground sunrise.

Neveah had expected to find her brother, or at least other people, or creatures. What she wasn't expecting to find was nothing at all.

Cupping her hands around her mouth, Neveah called out, "Hello? Is anybody here?"

Chapter Thirty-Four
Undercity, May 2017
Fly me a bird

The bronze-gold dragon winged his way through the vast cavern, slowly disappearing from sight, leaving Zayn alone with Watcher Sabrina.

"You're bleeding," he said, pointing to the deep cuts in her shoulder where she'd hit the rocks.

Her gaze flashed over him. "You too."

Zayn touched his shoulder where the cane-blade had gone into his flesh. It hadn't hit any arteries or tendons, which was good, but he had no way to close the wound.

Sabrina approached and examined the hole in his shoulder. "You know how to fix that, right?"

"Not really," he replied.

"I've heard Priyanka can close her wounds just by concentrating on one of her imbuements, but for us mortals, we need to do it the old-fashioned way," said Sabrina, producing a flame in her palm.

The prospect of using flame near his face was less than appetizing. "You wanna do the honors?"

Sabrina smirked. "I thought you'd never ask. Off with the shirt."

Once it was off, he caught her examining him with a leering eye.

"You might want to look away, mostly so I don't burn off your eyebrows," she said, concentrating on the flame in her hand.

As soon as he turned his head, she thrust her hand forward, and a spike of pain went through his shoulder, followed by the smell of burnt flesh.

"Thank you," said Zayn, grimacing. "Now we need to get to the island, though I'm afraid we'll be too late."

He touched the illusionary rock, which revealed the boat beneath it, and he pulled it along the shore to where they could climb in.

"I could help with that," said Sabrina as she glanced at her shoes.

"Unless you can fly, I don't think you're going to be much help," he said.

Sabrina cleared her throat.

"You can fly?" he asked.

"I can, but I'm not sure I can carry you," she said.

"How does this work? Is it an anti-gravity spell or something?" he asked.

"Remember when I said I wanted to be in Animalians? When it came time to pick my fifth-year imbuement, I had to get special permission from Animalians for a shape-changing spell. Luckily for me, Adele owed Priyanka a few favors, which she cashed in so I could transform."

"Don't tell me that you can turn into a dragon," said Zayn, shaking his head.

Based on her suddenly sheepish behavior, he knew that wasn't the case. "No one is allowed to shape change into a dragon. They've made that explicitly clear. To do so would be to earn a death sentence from the Circle of the Scale."

"Then what? A hawk? A condor? An eagle?" he asked.

Sabrina looked a little ill. "When you become a Watcher, the Lady gets approval on all fifth-year imbuements, for the obvious reasons. My request to be able to transform into a flying creature was granted, but the Lady did not approve my original idea."

"What is it?"

She blushed and wouldn't meet his gaze. "It's a hawk, but not the kind you'd expect. We'd better hurry. The dragon awaits." She looked up at him. "Oh, and make sure to bring my clothes. I'd rather not fight naked."

Zayn turned around so she could disrobe in private. He used the moment to throw his shirt back on. By the time he had it back over his head, he heard a heavy buzzing.

He turned around to find an enormous insect hovering in midair. Her body was jet black with a massive stinger hanging from her glistening body. Zayn was both horrified and impressed.

"A tarantula hawk?" he asked, recognizing the insect because of Keelan.

Sabrina answered, or at least he assumed it was an answer, by nodding her head. Zayn didn't want to think that the Lady had chosen this form, especially in a Watcher.

"I'm ready," he said as he gathered up her clothes.

Before he could do anything else, the Sabrina-insect flew over him and grabbed him by the shoulders with her legs, cradling him. At first he wasn't sure she'd be able to lift him, but then the buzzing increased in frequency and his feet lifted from the rock.

Sabrina-insect flew across the water, barely keeping above the dark surface, which teemed with Cthulhu jellies. If she dropped him, he'd be stung to death before he made it halfway back to shore.

As they neared the island, the concentration of faez grew overwhelming. The burnt-ozone smell burned the inside of his nose and made the back of his throat ache as if he'd inhaled hot smoke. Sabrina-insect dipped closer to the water, as if the raw magic in the air was distracting her from the task.

It was only then he remembered that his two earlier approaches to the cylinder had required protective magics from a patron. In his hurry, he'd forgotten about it. He hoped the effects wouldn't be too terrible before he could put up protections.

The rune-covered cylinder surrounding the island pulsed with crimson-gold light as it worked to contain the well which had become damaged. Zayn couldn't see Akhekh, either in human or dragon form, but the hydra raged near the front of the island, its seven heads gesticulating in all directions like cattails in a windstorm.

Hoping she could hear over the beating of her wings, Zayn yelled, "There's an outcropping on the left side which can hide us while we prepare. Land there. It might give us a chance to plan before the hydra attacks."

It was also the closest they could land without Akhekh seeing them. He didn't want the dragon to know they were coming.

Sabrina was worn out from the journey, or she misjudged the final stretch, as she nearly slammed his lower half into the rocky ledge. Zayn yanked his legs up just in time to clear the edge, before she dropped him. He managed a roll, which dissipated the worst of the impact, but his back was left with scratches.

Sabrina-insect collapsed onto the rocks, morphing back into the naked woman on her hands and knees. Zayn brought her the clothes he'd kept cradled in his arms, and helped her dress, while keeping an eye out.

Shaking with exhaustion, Sabrina looked ready to pass out, when a wave of raw faez rolled off the runed cylinder. The air seemed to singe his skin, and breathing was difficult. He was about to start the protective ritual when he felt the ground vibrate, so he climbed to the top of the outcropping as the enraged hydra came barreling over the rise, its seven heads striking.

Chapter Thirty-Five
Well of Power, May 2017
Rocking the boat

The rocky shore was empty except for a small wooden boat with two oars. Neveah found shell casings on the rocks, which led her to a pistol with runes along the barrel. She turned in all directions, expecting to see something, but there was no one.

"Where'd everyone go?"

An ominous light at the far end of the cavern seemed to suggest a direction. She couldn't see its source, which told her the cavern was larger than she thought.

Neveah shoved the gun into her backpack, climbed into the boat, and shoved into the water. As soon as she took a few strokes, she remembered the Superhero potion. She downed it in one gulp, and overwhelming warmth radiated from her midsection. Earlier, when she'd taken a sip, the feeling had been bearable, but this time she felt like she was holding a supernova inside.

Upon the first stroke of the oar after the potion, she knew why it was called Superhero. The little boat flew across the water as if it had an outboard motor. Each dip of the oar thrust her over the dark lake.

After a few minutes, she felt the strain on her body. She wasn't much of an athlete, sweating in the kitchen was the only kind of exercise she knew, so her muscles weren't made for the extra effort.

When Neveah slowed to give her shoulders a chance to warm up, the cavern shook, followed by a beastly roar and a pressure wave that slammed into her back ten seconds later. The burnt ozone smell of raw faez choked her as her eyes watered.

Random sparks popped in midair, leaving Neveah unsure if she should keep going or turn back. But she knew if there was trouble ahead, her brother was sure to be there, so she slipped her oars back into the water, and ignoring the pain, kept going.

The further she went the more the air burned her skin and eyes and nose. It felt like she'd stepped into a forest fire, except this one was made of magic.

Neveah wasn't sure she could go much further when the cavern shook again, and a low gong filled the air, like a city-sized bell being rung. After the sound, the oppressive pressure from the raw faez dissipated as if it'd been suddenly sucked into a huge vacuum.

The change allowed her to push her speed again, and a minute later, she caught her first glimpse of the island. Her oars faltered. Having spent the last eight months in the city of sorcery, she was used to seeing magic, but she'd never seen a construction like the one on the island. The massive cylinder blazed with runes as if it were about to switch into overdrive.

Facing the island, Neveah witnessed an explosion of white flame ripple off the cylinder, and it headed her way. She watched the way the wave sizzled across the water, and sensing she would not survive its passing, kicked her shoes off and dove into the underground lake.

Chapter Thirty-Six
Well of Power, May 2017
The final mistake

Zayn leapt from the rocks as the hydra struck, speeding over the island in a faez-imbued run as the air burned his skin. It felt like he was breathing fire, but the massive creature in pursuit gave him no chance to protect himself with magic.

Sparks sizzled in the air as Zayn slipped through the Veil to dodge through the hydra's legs, coming out the other side as the beast crashed into the edge of the water. He ran back towards Sabrina, staying along the outside of the island because getting too near the well would be fatal.

Clothed and waiting for him, Sabrina glanced towards the hydra, which was pulling itself from the lake. Her forehead was knotted.

"This is awful. It feels like my skin is on fire," she said, blinking away the pain.

"It's the well. I thought I'd be able to protect us once we got here, but that hydra's not going to give us a chance," he said.

"A seven-headed hydra," she said, shaking her head. "It's bad enough we're facing down a dragon, but a hydra too? I should have taken you back to Varna."

"Focus on what we can do," said Zayn. "Do you think you can distract it in wasp form?"

"Hawk," said Sabrina, frowning. "And I guess, but those seven heads are going to be hell to avoid."

"Do you have another idea?" he asked, checking behind them to see the hydra was on the way.

"No," she said as she pulled her shirt back off. "I hope you know how you can stop Akhekh."

"Me too," he said.

The hydra was coming too fast, so Zayn threw a firebolt at it to get its attention, before heading the other direction while keeping to the edge of the island. He weaved his speed imbuement while distracting the heads by filling them with rage and confusion. He could only manage two or three heads, but it was enough to keep it engaged with him.

Zayn spied the far cliff wall and was wondering if he could get on top so he could spy Akhekh and whatever he was doing with his ritual, when the well of power exploded with energy, a white wave rolling forth.

He threw himself behind a rocky outcropping, barely avoiding a direct impact of the concentrated faez. But the impact triggered a migraine, filling his vision with spots, leaving him helpless on the ground.

It felt like spikes being driven into his skull through his eyes. He was aware that he was moaning with pain, and that nearby, a hydra was ready to strike, but he couldn't move a single muscle.

As the migraine slowly dissipated, he heard an angry buzzing, followed by a chorus of roars. He looked up to see a giant tarantula hawk stinging the unprotected backside of the hydra.

The hydra spun, nearly trampling Zayn in the process, as it snapped at Sabrina, who flew towards the other end of the island. The great beast pounded after her, shaking the island in its fury.

"Oh, thank Merlin," said Zayn, giving Sabrina a thumbs-up, even though she probably didn't notice.

The air was different now. The blast had blown away the worst of the concentrated faez.

Or the ritual was nearing completion and Akhekh was sucking up the faez in the room, he realized.

Zayn growled with concern as he poured speed into his legs, churning over the island to reach Akhekh. As he rounded the massive runed cylinder, he saw the bronze-gold dragon crouched over the glowing hole in the earth. His voice rumbled in an ancient dragon tongue that was almost too low for Zayn to hear.

He thought he might rush in and disrupt the ritual until he saw the protective circle around the dragon. He'd placed a warding before starting the ritual.

With no time to disable the warding, he realized there was only one way he was going to stop Akhekh.

Zayn stopped at the edge of the circle, closed his eyes, and reached out with his imbuement.

Usually, his experience with his imbuement was like reaching out a spectral hand and gently nudging the subject in the direction he wanted. This time, as his "hand" neared, it was slapped away with considerable force.

A spike of pain went right through him, and he gasped, his eyes flying open.

From inside of the circle, Akhekh kept speaking, but his menacing eyes glared at Zayn, a promise of what was to come after the ritual was complete.

Zayn refocused himself, closed his eyes, went back to work.

This time, when he reached out, he steeled himself for the impact, mustering all the faez he could manage.

Their wills hit with great force, the reverberation knocking his eyes open, but not ending his imbuement. Zayn pushed.

The dragon pushed back.

He knew he only had a chance because Akhekh was busy with the ritual.

He thought about what would happen to his Hall, and his friends. Used that for inspiration and pushed harder.

The battle between them shifted in his favor, slightly.

The air sparked around him from the effort.

Zayn strained with all his might and he felt the dragon's resistance crumbling.

But as he pushed further, spots formed in his vision.

No!

A migraine.

Just a little longer.

He pushed.

Something in his mind split like a cleaver had struck his skull.

One moment, he was standing, and the next, he was entombed in darkness, trapped in a world of pain.

Chapter Thirty-Seven
Well of Power, May 2017
The answer to her question

Neveah crawled onto the island, exhausted and trembling from the mad swim through the water. She had no idea what those pale jellyfish would do if they stung her, but she didn't want to find out.

A glance over the water revealed that the boat had been destroyed by the white wave.

She nearly passed out as she stood up, because the effects of the potion had left, leaving her shaky and a little nauseous.

She felt like she'd run three marathons in succession and was now asking her body to do another.

"I'm gonna be sore for a month," she said. "If I live through this insanity."

At least the air wasn't stinging her skin and eyes like it was before.

The massive rune-covered cylinder pulsed with ominous energy. It had a rhythm that suggested it was nearing a conclusion.

On the left side of the island, a seven-headed hydra was neck deep in the water snapping at a giant wasp flying tantalizingly out of reach. The way the insect was moving suggested an intelligence, but Neveah had no interest in finding out if that were true.

On the far side of the island, she heard a low rumble, like a slow-motion avalanche. Neveah mustered her will and headed towards the sound.

"What have I gotten myself into?" she said, climbing over the rough terrain.

On the far side of the well of power, Neveah saw the dragon first.

It was smaller than she expected, and also more grand. She had an urge to either run screaming from the area or throw herself onto her knees before it.

One of these two things would have happened if she hadn't seen Zayn standing near the edge of a glowing circle, arms held above him at an awkward angle.

She opened her mouth to call out his name when he dropped to the ground as if he were a marionette and his strings had been cut.

"No!"

Nevaeh ran towards her fallen brother, but there was so much ground to cover, and it looked like the dragon was almost complete with its ritual.

When she reached Zayn, he was lying on his side, twitching with his eyes rolled back into his head. He was bleeding from multiple wounds, but it was the soft moan of terror emanating from his lips as if he were trapped in a nightmare that broke her heart.

"No, Zayn," she said, cradling his head in her lap.

This wasn't what she'd been expecting to find when she

found him. Neveah pulled out the syringe.

"I don't know if this is the right thing to do." She looked at the dragon, whose scales glowed with power. "I hope I'm right."

She shoved the needle into his arm and pressed the plunger until the full potion had been injected.

Nothing happened for a good five seconds.

Then he reacted as if he'd been hit with a shock paddle, back arching painfully.

Zayn screamed as if his soul was being ripped from his body and Neveah held on with tears dripping from her cheeks.

As the scream trailed into a hoarse whisper, he looked up at her with forgiving eyes.

Then his heart stopped.

Chapter Thirty-Eight
Well of Power, May 2017
A choice

In the depths of his pain, a fissure opened in his mind. The schism was between two competing versions of himself. The surface Zayn, the one that had been in control for the last year, dutifully pursuing his studies at the Academy of the Subtle Arts, and the deeper Zayn, the one buried beneath the fictitious version of himself, the one who planned to kill the Lady of Varna.

He remembered the construction of this alternate Zayn, built from a series of potions designed to help those with multiple personality disorders. It'd been a tricky thing, he remembered, conspiring to destroy his own personality. Or at least hide it for a while.

As he recalled the bitter taste of the potions, sucked down in the back of a ghost taxi on the way back to Varna, he focused on the reason for his farce.

The Lady of Varna.

Lady Arcadia.

The ancient Entana.

A being out of history, who had survived on her wits and her unshakable poison lock on her subjects.

He remembered the way her purple eyes had regarded him when they'd met. And again later when he told her that he'd given up his quest to kill her.

He even remembered why he had to play it this way. Because otherwise, the truth would reach her and she would kill his family, down to his littlest sister, Imani.

And now that he knew himself again, knew the one beneath the lie, he knew he had a choice.

His life was balanced on a knife edge. Between the original potion and the cure, his mind was being torn apart. He could by the simple action of giving up, choose the eternal darkness, and spare his family the Lady's revenge.

But if he did so, Akhekh would complete the ritual and silence the Hundred Halls forever.

His hesitation nearly cost him.

The heart was a powerful muscle, but even it had its limits when family was involved.

The abyss opened beneath him, and for a brief second, he thought he'd delayed too long.

Then the warm tears of his sister splashed across his cheek, making him aware that he was lying in her arms—even though he didn't know how she could be there in his time of need—reminding him that if he did not act now, she would surely die.

Zayn thrust himself upward.

Back in his body, wracked with pain, he wanted to pass out. To enjoy the cool embrace of slumber.

But Akhekh was about to complete the ritual.

"Oh, that hurt," said Zayn, pulling himself to sitting.

Neveah's eyes glistened with burgeoning tears. He kissed her forehead. Thank yous would come later.

The shackles of his false personality no longer holding him back, Zayn threw himself at Akhekh.

To his surprise, the dragon was ready for him, but this time Zayn pushed harder, and he found that his limits had been extended. Dancing at death's door had given his ability more depth.

But the dragon had almost completed the ritual. He knew if he didn't overcome his resistance soon, it would be too late, no matter how hard he pushed.

Rather than doubling down, he reached out to the well of power, finding ample faez. Though he'd never considered how to access it, tapping into the seemingly limitless supply came naturally.

What before had seemed like a nearly impenetrable stone wall of resistance, turned to balsa wood as Zayn punched through it, grabbing the reins of the dragon as simply as riding a common horse.

In his haste, Zayn nearly cut the ritual off, thinking that would solve the problem, only to realize that it was far too along towards completion, and that if he ended it now, it would likely destroy the well of power, and them with it.

He needed a way to dissipate the energy and close up the hole in the barrier.

He looked across the warding and saw the answer written on the dragon's scales. Firmly entrenched in Akhekh's mind, he could understand the language behind the runes. He understood keenly how the dragon was using them to close up the wells of power and seal off the city of Invictus from its source of faez.

While keeping Akhekh under his control, Zayn spoke the words of power contained on the dragon's runes, adjusting them ever so slightly, and completed the ritual.

Then before it could trap him with Akhekh, Zayn released his control.

Akhekh's look of utter confusion and horror was only matched by his fear.

As the concentration of faez glowed with impending completion, Zayn threw his sister over his shoulder and sprinted towards the front of the island.

He got halfway across before the dragon exploded.

Chapter Thirty-Nine
Well of Power, May 2017
The end of the party

The doors to the grand kitchen opened wide, welcoming her into its embrace. Pots rattled across stoves kissed with flame, tended by cheerful workers. Neveah passed a tall, handsome sous chef with brown skin and a twinkle in his eye as he stirred a cranberry port wine sauce in a pan.

The steams and smells sent shivers of pleasure down her spine.

The chef de partie handed her a cleaver and motioned towards a pile of flaming pink dragon fruits.

The cleaver was perfectly balanced. It felt like it'd been weighted specifically for her. She expertly slammed it into a dragon fruit, revealing a creamy white center peppered with seeds.

Neveah lifted the cleaver again when she heard the shout from outside the kitchen. The words were muted. She couldn't tell who was speaking.

The doors remained open. Much to her surprise, there wasn't a restaurant outside, but a rocky cavern.

She felt some calling to return, but she sensed there would be nothing but pain.

Why return when I could stay here? *she thought.* I did what I came to do. There's nothing left for me now.

Her thoughts carried with them a kernel of truth, but she didn't know why. Her mind was filled with a pleasant fog.

Neveah slammed the cleaver down, splitting the dragon fruit in half. A spoon, cupped in her hand for more leverage, removed the soft flesh from inside the hard skin. When the first half was scoured of its edible fruit, Neveah grabbed the second piece.

A noise startled her.

When she looked back up, the door had closed.

It made her sad, though she couldn't figure out why.

Chapter Forty
Well of Power, May 2017
The Lady's revenge

Zayn woke with a collar around his neck and a bruising headache. It wasn't like the migraines from before. This one pounded through his temples, the aftereffects of channeling too much faez.

His fingers touched the collar. The steel was cold. His first instinct was to look for his sister, but as he sat up, Watcher Sabrina in human form clenched her fist and his whole body arched with pain.

"I'm sorry, Zayn," she said when the pain vanished. "I didn't want you to get any ideas before you knew the stakes. We're going back to Varna so you can face the Lady and she can judge you for your crimes."

He shoved his fingers beneath the collar, next to his neck, but there was no room. Even if he used his imbuement, he was more likely to break his own neck than to snap the steel.

"Where's my sister?" he asked, not even really comprehending how she'd gotten to the island, or if she'd really been there at all.

Sabrina's hard expression broke into a frown. She nodded to behind Zayn.

Slowly, and with great trepidation, Zayn turned around, to find the broken and limp body of his sister lying sprawled. Her red handkerchief had miraculously stayed on her head, but dark red blood pooled in the rocks.

His whole body went cold, and he collapsed to his knees, tears flowing freely from his face.

Zayn sobbed.

The sound broke from his lips like a great cleaving of the world.

She'd saved him.

Somehow, Neveah had saved his life so he could stop the ritual.

The vision in the Starwood mirror had told him a truth. He just hadn't known what it meant.

"Neveah," he whispered, knowing he wouldn't ever get to laugh with her again, never get to sit on the counter in the kitchen and watch her cook as she threw verbal barbs at him and Keelan while they needled her back. Would never get to see the look on her face like when she drove the food truck for the first time, the limitless possibilities it had given her evident in her effortless smile.

The crushing weight of realization that he would have to tell his parents about what happened dawned on him. It would destroy the twins and Imani, who loved their older sister fiercely.

When Zayn looked up at Watcher Sabrina, she took a step back.

"I didn't do it," she said, shaking her head. "She must have hit her head during the explosion. It damn near killed me too. I barely dove into the water in time to avoid it. It got the hydra at least."

Zayn took a step towards his dead sister.

"No. Leave her body be. I don't want to stay any longer than we have to. I'm done with this city," she said.

"Kill me," he said, holding his arms wide. "Do that at least for me. Better than me going back."

Sabrina's eyes creased with sadness. "I'm sorry, Zayn. You gotta face the Lady for what you were planning to do. Even if it's just so she knows how to stop it next time."

"How'd you find out?" he asked.

"That you were behind the comic? It wasn't easy. There was no paper trail and I couldn't get anyone to snitch. In the end, it was simple luck. I'd placed a surveillance spider in Camille Cardwell's office at the *Herald,* and when the last issue was published, someone asked her if the run was going to continue because it'd been so popular, but she said it'd been a special favor, and she went on to talk about it, and there was enough said that I knew it was you. Or at least enough to bring you back to Varna."

"I assume her methods are pleasant," he said.

"I'm sorry, Zayn. It feels shitty after what you did here, but my allegiance is to her," she said.

"If she dies, you die," he said.

"So do you," she replied. "For what it's worth, it was a brilliant plan. I mean, I don't know how you're going to get into her home and kill her without all of us dying, but at least the part about foiling her seers was pretty smart. In different circumstances, I'd be rooting for you."

"That doesn't make me feel any better," he said. "If you really want to help, kill me right now. Tell her I died in the explosion. You can even take credit for stopping the ritual if you want. I don't want my family to get hurt."

Sabrina looked out over the water. "I can't. One way or another she'd find out. She always does."

"But you're in the Undercity. There's no way at this distance and depth she can know what you've done," he said.

"But her seers."

He shrugged his shoulders. "Why would they know? They're there to protect her. This lie only protects my family. Please. Either let me go, or kill me."

Sabrina put a hand to her forehead. She squeezed her eyes shut for a moment.

"I can't."

Sabrina lifted her hand. He sensed she was going to debilitate him so she could turn into a tarantula hawk and fly them back to the shore. It was going to be a long and painful ride.

But then her eyes widened and her hand dropped.

An ear-splitting blast deafened him.

Watcher Sabrina looked down at her chest, which now contained a fist-sized hole.

"I..."

She collapsed into a heap.

Zayn turned to find Neveah propped onto one elbow, the handgun in her fist, blood smeared across her face. Her gaze was unfocused.

He rushed over to her, lifted the gun from her hand, and cradled her head.

"You're alive," he said, the words barely coming out.

"Only to save your ass again," said Neveah, grimacing with pain. "When I get to ten do I get a free sandwich?"

"You can have whatever you want," said Zayn, fighting back tears. "I thought I'd lost you."

"Me too," said Neveah, coughing.

"Let me fix your head. You're still bleeding," said Zayn.

He got out a pocket knife, heated it with flame, and cauterized the wounds she'd sustained from hitting the rocks.

Once she was stabilized, he dumped Sabrina's body in the water. Then he returned and carried his sister to the place he and Sabrina had landed because it would protect them from the worst effects of the faez buildup.

Using his hands to cup water, he got them both a drink until they were no longer thirsty. Then he sat back against the outcropping with her.

"I can't tell you how happy I am that you're alive," he said.

"Probably because you didn't want to have to tell Mom and Dad that you let me die," said Neveah. "Either that or you'd miss my tacos."

"That too," he said with a wistful smile.

Neveah tried to grin, but it ended in a grimace. "So how we getting off this island?"

"We're not," said Zayn. "At least not without help. I left messages with the team. Eventually word will get back to Priyanka, assuming she's still alive, and someone will come get us."

"How long is that going to be?"

He looked out over the dark water. "Long enough for us to tell some stories. Like how you got here and how you counteracted the potion."

"I'll tell you if you tell me how and why you made that comic. I overheard what you and Sabrina said, but I don't understand why," she said.

"I guess I can tell you. We should be protected from the seers because of it," he said, then continued when she wrinkled her forehead. "One of the basic problems with assassination, or other endeavors that put well-connected people's lives in danger, is that most of them have seers on hand to predict any attempts on their lives."

"Well connected," she said derisively. "You mean the rich people get special privileges and we get what we get."

"Something like that. The Lady has a particularly strong cadre of seers, which means any attempt on her can easily be thwarted."

"Wait," she said, frowning. "You're planning on killing the Lady? That's what you've been plotting all these years?"

"You can't tell anyone," he said.

"I wouldn't. Oh, hell no. That would just get us all killed, which speaking of, how are you going to solve the poison problem?" she asked.

"I don't know yet. Don't worry. I won't do anything until I have. But my plan to keep her seers from figuring out what I was doing was twofold. I had to implement a short-term solution because the real one was going to take too long."

"The comic."

"Yep," he said. "You see, if there are lots of people thinking about the same thing, it makes it very hard to see the details. The whole purpose of *The Spider Queen Must Die!* was to get so many people thinking about killing her that no seer could possibly pick me out of the noise. Which would leave me free to plot against her without fear of discovery."

"That's brilliant. Even for my older brother," she said with a wink.

"Thanks. The problem with my solution was that it was going to take too long, and the Lady wanted an answer about my allegiance before it would take effect. So I buried my true plan beneath a bunch of personality distorting potions."

"The potions that were giving you those migraines," said Neveah.

"And would have killed me had you not come along and saved me, somehow. I think we're to the part where you explain how the hell you got here," said Zayn.

Neveah told the story of her coming to the city, her struggles with the food truck, the investigation, the gambit at the *Herald*, leading eventually to Celesse and then to the Undercity.

When she was finished talking, Zayn didn't say anything for a long time until his sister asked, "Is something wrong?"

"Wrong? No. On the contrary. I think you should have joined the Hundred Halls," said Zayn.

"And risked my life all the time like you? No thank you. I prefer cooking to imminent death. Anyway, as far as I can tell, I can brew potions safely due to the Lady's poison without having to bother with all those Merlin Trials, and other nonsense," said Neveah.

Zayn squeezed his sister around the shoulders. "And that's why I love you so much, sis."

Neveah rolled her eyes. "Or tacos."

"That too."

She hugged him back, and they fell into a comfortable position against the rocks, or at least as comfortable as the surroundings would allow.

They waited for a long time, sleeping at times, speaking at others, making plans when they were feeling alert. After what was somewhere between half a day and two, a figure came striding across the water.

Priyanka wore what looked like boots made of shimmering water. At each step, the water cushioned the blow, but sprung back as if it were spongy soil rather than a deep underground lake.

Beside him, Neveah whispered, "Wow, she's beautiful."

Zayn chuckled. She was beautiful, but that wasn't why he enjoyed working for her.

When Priyanka reached the island, she pulled a little brass tube from her pocket, placed it against the watery boots, and the liquid disappeared inside.

"Neat trick," said Neveah.

"You must be Zayn's sister," said Priyanka.

"And you must be the one Zayn complains about," said Neveah with a smirk.

"Hey, that's not fair," said Zayn.

Priyanka glanced around the island. "I'm sure there's a story, but for now, I'd like to get out of here."

"What happened in Iceland?" he asked.

"Your message reached me before I got to the council. When I accused them, they grew extremely embarrassed, because they'd figured out what Akhekh was doing before we'd gotten there. They apologized profusely. While they wanted to solve the barrier issue, they did not want to destroy the Halls," said Priyanka.

Neveah pointed to the pocket where Priyanka had put away the brass tube. "So do we get to wear water-walking boots?"

Priyanka smiled, producing an ornate cube from the same pocket. "No. We get to ride in a boat like normal people."

"Bummer," said Neveah.

Priyanka tossed the cube towards the water. It expanded into a decent-sized rowboat with two oars.

"After you," said Priyanka, motioning towards the small watercraft.

The three of them left the island, and eventually the Undercity.

Chapter Forty-One
Thirteenth Ward, May 2017
Compound interests

After a few days of sorting things out at the Academy, Zayn took his sister to get her food truck back. She'd been staying at a hotel in the fourth ward, paid for by Priyanka. They'd taken the Green Line into the thirteenth ward near the Enochian District.

"Are you sure you don't want me to pay the fees for you? I've got extra," said Zayn.

Neveah's gaze glittered with pride. "I appreciate it, but no, I borrowed the money, I want to pay it back."

"It's like you're all grown up now," he said, laughing when she punched him in the arm.

The thirteenth ward had seen better days. Zayn had to step over trash on the way to Cash & Hatchet, but it didn't impact his buoyant mood. Neveah seemed to have it as well. It'd been so long since he'd gotten to spend time with his sister that he'd forgotten how much he missed her.

He was about to tell her as much, when prickles of danger formed on his back.

Zayn shielded her with his body as he spun around.

"What's wrong?" she whispered.

He sent his senses out in all directions, catching a familiar scent on the wind. Then he saw her, a young woman with dark hair wearing designer jeans and a K-pop band T-shirt walking their direction on the opposite sidewalk.

"Who is she?" asked Neveah.

"Stay here. I'm going to go talk to her. If things go bad, run as fast as you can," said Zayn.

"What? Is this bad?"

He turned his head and growled under his breath, "She's a dragon."

Zayn crossed the street after a white delivery truck rumbled past.

"Hello, Ne Yong," said Zayn, keeping faez at the ready.

Ne Yong's glossy pink lipstick was a contradiction with her ageless gaze.

"There's no need to fear me, young man. I'm here to talk." Ne Yong glanced over his shoulder. "Your sister can relax. I'm not going to eat you, as delicious as you look."

He couldn't tell if she was making a joke, but he allowed himself to visibly relax, while keeping the faez loaded like a bullet in the chamber.

"Why are you looking for me?" he asked.

"You have something that doesn't belong to you," said Ne Yong.

He searched his memories for something he might have taken, but unless it was lost during his memory wipe, he didn't think he had.

"I'm sorry, you must be mistaken."

"You took it last year," said Ne Yong. "It's on your phone."

The picture of Vaximarillion.

"Oh," he said, handing it over after unlocking it.

She swiped through his pictures until she came upon the ones with the great dragon. "Are these the only ones?"

"Yes. I didn't send them anywhere else," he said, sensing that if he had, this encounter might have been much different.

"Good." Her eyes glittered with amusement. "I believe you."

"I'm sorry about Akhekh," he said.

"I'm not. Fool put profit above the well-being of our race. There are far too few of us to take such a risk," growled Ne Yong, a heat rising to her cheeks.

"Let the world toil while the dragons remain," he said without thinking.

Ne Yong's eyes widened. "Where did you hear that?"

Zayn touched his throat.

"Akhekh."

"Doubly arrogant fool, then," she said.

She narrowed her gaze at him, making a noise in the back of her throat.

"If you know any more you should forget it. Never speak of it again," said Ne Yong.

"I'm trying to forget it already," he said, which was the truth. The words had spilled out of him like a fragment of song that hadn't quite been erased.

Ne Yong stared at him for an uncomfortable minute as if she could see inside his soul. Zayn stared back, if only to have somewhere to look, because looking away would have been worse.

Eventually her eyes widened and she exhaled, hissing slightly through her teeth while shaking her head slowly. Ne Yong pinched his cheek like an old woman greeting her grandson.

"You are a paradox, Zayn Carter. Good luck, it appears that you're going to need it," she said, as if it were a private joke.

Ne Yong handed him back his cellphone and kept walking, leaving Zayn bewildered. He returned to his sister, who had been waiting at the corner, watching with considerable interest.

"What was that about?" she asked.

"Family pictures," he said.

Neveah raised an eyebrow, but wisely didn't ask a question.

Cash & Hatchet was a few blocks further. Neveah paid the owner a fee that made Zayn raise his eyebrows. They went into the storage yard, beyond the barb-wired fence. The food truck looked the same as when he'd seen it last.

After his sister climbed in and started the engine, his phone vibrated in his pocket. He checked the message, then tapped on the hood to get his sister's attention.

"You can head on back to the hotel. I've got a quick errand to run," he said.

Neveah adjusted her red headband in the rearview mirror. "It's okay, Zayn. You don't have to babysit me. I took care of myself just fine all year."

"That's not why I'm..." His words trailed away as she gave him her *look*. "Fine, I just wanted to make sure you were safe. Are we still all riding back to Varna together?"

"Three days, older brother. Right after you finish your finals, or whatever you freakshow assassins do in your secret lair. That'll give me time for a little project in the city," she said.

"Project?"

She gave him a big smile. "You'll see."

Neveah pulled out of the yard and Zayn headed out behind the food truck, taking a slow jog. He got to Empire Ink about ten minutes later.

The store was empty except for three people: Percival, Priyanka, and Adele Montgomery—the patron of the Animalians Hall.

The three of them were chatting quietly until he came in and then they turned towards him. He only had to see Priyanka's amused expression coupled with Percival's pinched face to know that his request had been accepted.

"Into the chair, young man," said Percival, a barely contained sigh hovering beneath his words. "We've got a lot of work to do today."

Chapter Forty-Two
Fourth Ward, May 2017
The Taco Witch returneth

The five-star hotel with all the amenities had been wonderful—Neveah had taken three showers a day and ordered room service for every meal—but climbing back into the food truck felt like home. She'd lived in the six-by-eight-foot space for nearly eight months, and despite the cramped quarters, it'd been a joyous experience. Mostly because of the reception her food had gotten on the streets of Invictus.

But that time was coming to an end. She'd come to the city of sorcery to figure out what was wrong with her brother. It'd been a strange ending to what had seemed like a simple problem, which told her what living in the city would have been like if she'd joined the Halls.

As blood-pumping as it'd been, she preferred the heat and excitement of the kitchen. Which was why she threw herself into her work once she was back in the food truck. With only a few days left in the city, she wanted to go out in style.

After making a couple of stops, Neveah spent the rest of the leftover cash from lawyer Ralph on food. It took two baggers to carry everything into the back of the truck.

The permits for Sparrowhawk Park were easy to acquire after she made a call to the Black Pyramid. Their fear of Celesse carried over to minor legal matters, but she didn't know how much longer she could push it. And to prove that she wasn't that mean-spirited, she sent a couple of fliers for the party to the firm.

The day before the event, Katie's band helped set up the stage, the speakers, and the tent in case it rained. While they hauled the gear, Neveah caught snatches of incorporeal green light flitting between the trees in the park.

Once the event stage was set up, Neveah got right to work on the tacos. Knowing she wouldn't be hassled by Celesse anymore let her throw herself into her cooking. It'd been weeks since she'd really been able to work in her kitchen, and as soon as the crockpot of carnitas started steaming, a weight lifted off her shoulders.

Neveah worked until midnight before crashing on the cot, her hands numb from the constant chopping. Sleep was absolute, and she woke as dawn slipped through the front window of her truck. After a quick sponge bath and a change of clothes, including a bright new red handkerchief, she got right to work on the final preparations.

By late morning, the tacos were ready. She was a little drained from the lack of sleep and the faez use, but it was a contented tired.

Katie appeared outside the food truck when Neveah climbed out.

"Are you sure anyone will show up? Not that I'm knocking the idea, but it seems pretty random to throw a party in the middle of the week right around finals at the Halls," said Katie, her Mohawk flopping into her eyes.

"We'll see," said Neveah, humming to herself. "Is your band ready to play?"

Katie twirled a ghostly drumstick. "Always."

Neveah took a walk around the park, stretching her legs one last time before she climbed back in the truck. If things went as planned she'd be busy for the next twelve hours.

By the time she got back, there were a few customers milling around the truck. Neveah gave them a wink and climbed inside, taking a long drink from a huge bottle of water before sliding open the metal window, which rattled when it hit the top.

"The Taco Witch is open for business," she said triumphantly.

Cooking had always been a mixture of science and art for Neveah. Seeing customers wander away from her truck, possessively clutching their plate full of tacos spilling with spicy carnitas, caramelized onions, cotija cheese, cabbage, and salsa made her smile.

By the time she served the first dozen customers, the line to her food truck went around the corner. The Sticky Wickets started up a little after that, filling the park with jazzy hip-hop beats. The music brought more people, who were probably just on their way for a lunchtime errand and got curious about the gathering crowds.

After an hour, Neveah looked down to find a group of lawyers from the Black Pyramid waiting for tacos. She gave them an extra heaping for their help with the park permits. Ralph even said thank you, and slunk away sheepishly as if he still felt guilty for delivering the cease and desist.

As the afternoon rolled on, more food trucks showed up as if they'd heard the word on social media, but they didn't put a dent into her monster line. Many of her customers had traveled from the tenth ward to relive the taco experience, since she'd put up her fliers in that area.

Though her hair was wet with sweat, the work never-ending, Neveah served every taco with a smile on her face.

"Do we get a discount since we're family?" asked Zayn when he showed up with Keelan and the rest of their team.

"Only if you pay for your friends," said Neveah, giving them a wink.

The shorter Latina girl that Neveah recognized as Portia said, "Oh, I like her."

"You're gonna like her more after you try her food. She's the best chef...she's the best chef. Period," said Zayn.

Her brother and his team stood off to the side making obscene noises while they ate their tacos. The tall broad-shouldered one, Vin, leaned into the window, his eyes wide with wonder, almost to the point of tears.

"Those tacos are better than a heist," he said.

Neveah wrinkled her nose. "Umm, thanks?"

Vin wandered away with the rest of the team.

"Great party, sis. See you in a few days," said Zayn, waving.

The rest of the team said their goodbyes, and while she was serving the next customer, she heard them chastise Zayn for not introducing them earlier.

As the sun dropped below the skyline, a cool breeze washed through the truck. Her taco fixings were running low, so she started limiting the number purchased. By this time, the park was packed with students from the Halls, dancing before the stage. In between sets, they DJ'd dance music. The students, mages from the various Halls, filled the air above the park with sparks and illusions and random spells.

Neveah was so busy enjoying the latter antics, she didn't notice the semi-familiar customer until she heard her voice.

"I'm glad everything went well with your errand. Were my potions helpful?"

Neveah looked down to find a woman that looked like Celesse, but not quite. Her nose seemed slightly crooked, her hair was a dirtier blonde and pulled back into a ponytail, and she wore running clothes.

"Yes," said Neveah. "Slumming it?"

Celesse tugged on her spandex tights. "When your face adorns billboards, you have to take certain precautions, especially when you have a hankering for tacos from a certain witch."

"Hankering?" asked Neveah with a chuckle. "That word seems out of character for you."

Celesse winked. "You'd be surprised."

When Neveah handed over the plate of tacos, extra portions and sides, Celesse handed back a slim tome.

"Recipes," she said. "You might find some that are useful."

"Thank you," said Neveah enthusiastically.

"And if you ever want to come back to the city and work for me, I can always find a place for someone as talented as you," said Celesse, right before she stuffed a taco into her mouth and moaned.

After wiping off her grease-stained hands on her apron, Neveah peeked inside the tome to find various alchemy recipes written in what she guessed was Celesse's handwriting. An inscription at the beginning noted:

For my new favorite witch, tacos or otherwise, thank you for what you did for the city and the Halls. These recipes should come in handy wherever your adventures take you. They are unique to a couple of tough broads who don't know when to quit. I know you'll make great use of them.

With great regard,
Celesse D'Agastine
P.S. – If you open a restaurant anywhere in the world and don't invite me to be your first customer, I will burn it to the ground. <3

Neveah reread the inscription a couple more times, barely comprehending that it was real.

"What is my life?" she muttered.

"Excuse me, are there still tacos?" asked the next customer.

Snapped out of her trance, Neveah gently placed the recipe book on the front seat before returning to her taco making.

"Absolutely, hun. What can I get you?" asked Neveah with a smile.

It was the best day of her life.

Chapter Forty-Three
King of Prussia, May 2017
Truth and Consequences

A few days later when finals were over, Neveah picked them up outside their house in the seventh ward. Zayn took the front seat, while Keelan had to use the edge of the cot on account of him losing their quick game of Five Elements.

As Neveah put the truck in gear, and the engine rumbled to life, Zayn took a tentative sniff.

"What gives? I thought this place would smell like tacos the whole ride back." Neveah raised an eyebrow. "Not that I'm complaining, because I wasn't looking forward to smelling what I couldn't have, but it's completely sterile in here."

"The kitchen is the laboratory of a good chef. Since the party, I've been scrubbing every nook and cranny to remove the layers of grease," said Neveah.

"That was a swag party," said Keelan, leaning his head between the front seats.

"It was," said Zayn. "Everyone at the Academy is asking

if you're coming back next year. Even the people that didn't have the tacos are wondering, mostly out of jealousy I think."

A rosy glow rose to his sister's cheeks. She could be so serious while working in the kitchen, it was nice to see her enjoying a compliment.

"I don't know," said Neveah as she tapped on the steering wheel. "I wanted to spend the summer at home, and then decide where I'm going next." She glanced back at Keelan. "Assuming I'm allowed to leave again."

"I'm not a Watcher yet," said Keelan. "But if I can put in a good word, I'll try."

"Thanks, Kee."

The drive was going to take them around fourteen hours, assuming they only made a few stops. No one talked about the events of the year, the conversation stayed on safe topics like childhood remembrances, or places Neveah might take the food truck next year.

Occasionally, cars or trucks passed them with a honk and a wave, usually followed by the driver or passenger miming eating tacos and adding a thumbs-up for good measure. It simultaneously made Zayn proud of his sister, and hung a heavy load of guilt on his heart that if his plans for next year went wrong, none of it would matter. But he hated the idea that Neveah and the rest of his family had to ask permission to leave the city, and that it could be revoked at any time based on the whims of the Lady.

When they arrived in Varna, they headed to the Gardens first. Buford waved them through cheerfully. Zayn noted that in this day and age, there were spells or technology that would serve the same purpose, but he knew that having a live guard was a reminder of the different classes in Varna.

The manicured streets of the Gardens glowed with enchanted light, basking the neighborhood in an idyllic dream, but all that came to an abrupt end the moment they saw the Speaker standing outside Keelan's house in her blinding white pantsuit.

A cold chill blew through Zayn. Neveah's hands gripped the steering wheel tighter before she pulled into the driveway.

If he had any doubts that Keelan was becoming a Watcher, they were gone in that instant. He was sure that the Speaker had known about their arrival through his cousin.

"Keelan?" he asked, but he wouldn't meet his gaze, busying himself with gathering his gear.

"I'm tired, man. I don't know what she wants."

Keelan slipped out the back of the truck and hurried inside his house after going right past the Speaker.

When Neveah moved to open her door, Zayn put his hand on her arm. "She wants to talk to me. Just stay here. I was expecting this."

He was expecting that someone from the Lady would talk to him about Watcher Sabrina, but he wasn't expecting it to be so soon, or that it'd be the Speaker. It indicated the importance of his discussion and the many potential landmines that awaited.

The Speaker seemed entirely unchanged from when he'd seen her last at the Ceremony nearly four years ago. Sorcery smoothed away any wrinkles or signs of age, leaving her features airbrushed. Her steel-white hair had been coifed into a cobra's hood and her dark eyes sparkled with purple highlights as he approached.

"Good evening, Mister Carter," said the Speaker in a rich Southern accent.

Usually when he came back home, he slipped into his accent, but he found himself forcibly stripping it from his speech.

"Good evening, Speaker. I wasn't expecting to see someone so soon," he said.

"But you *were* expecting to see someone. Why is that, Mister Carter?" she asked as she tapped on the buttons of her coat with long pale fingernails.

"Because Watcher Sabrina is dead," said Zayn, letting the news sink in.

To her credit, the Speaker did not react, which either meant that they already knew, or she was a good actress. As much as Zayn wanted to use his sensing imbuement, he didn't want to give any impression he was trying to hide anything.

After a long uncomfortable silence, the Speaker said, "I assume you're going to tell me what happened."

"She died saving the Hundred Halls, deep in the Undercity," said Zayn.

The Speaker's trim eyebrows narrowed at the center. "And why do you suppose that we would believe that?"

"Because it's true. Get one of your truth scorpions if you don't believe me. Or check with Priyanka. We fought a dragon, and by the grace of Sabrina's sacrifice, we won," said Zayn.

The Speaker's lip curled with displeasure. "An unlikely event. There's no way that two mages, talented as they may be, could win a battle against a dragon. Not even a fledgling one."

"Yet, it's true. Sabrina kept it distracted as a tarantula hawk while I managed to disrupt the ritual he was performing. So technically, we didn't kill him, but the blowback from his ritual failing did," said Zayn.

The Speaker lifted her chin and looked down at Zayn. "And which dragon did you kill? There are few in this realm, so it will be easy to verify."

"Akhekh, the casino owner in Vegas. There's more to the story, including a trip to the Circle of the Scale, and other intrigues, but those are details of the Academy. I'm sure if the Lady wants to hear about them she can ask her friend

Priyanka."

She blinked a few times. "I see."

"Please tell the Lady and Sabrina's family that I am very sorry for their loss. She died valiantly, and in service of the Hundred Halls, the Academy, and by connection, the Lady of Varna," said Zayn.

The Speaker glanced to the side. "Very well. I will pass along your condolences." Her gaze returned, hard and direct. "But know that we will follow up on your story, and if there is even a hair out of place, that you will be making a final visit to the Lady's plantation."

"Understood," said Zayn, meeting her gaze.

She didn't seem like she was done, but Zayn desperately wanted to climb into his bed in the Stack, so he asked, "May I leave now?"

"Yes," said the Speaker, clearly disappointed the conversation hadn't gone the way she'd wanted.

With his heart leaping around in his chest, Zayn climbed back into the food truck. Neveah silently put the truck in reverse and pulled out of the driveway. The Speaker watched them the whole way, and Zayn didn't let out his breath until they'd left the Gardens.

"Everything good?" asked Neveah tentatively.

"I think so."

Neveah sighed, rubbing her forehead. "Well, I'm awake now."

"Me too."

The woods around the Stack were alive with the sounds of crickets and frogs. They drove with the windows down, letting the evening breeze caress their faces.

As they pulled into the gravel parking area near the Stack, the lights blinked on, and the door opened immediately, revealing the rest of their family, who'd been patiently waiting for them to get home.

Before they reached the food truck, Zayn reached out to Neveah and clutched her hand.

"Thank you for saving me."

With tears in her eyes, and a grin the size of the moon, Neveah said, "Anytime, big brother. Anytime."

§ § §

Read the thrilling final book in the Reluctant Assassin Series

THE
WEBS THAT
BIND

April 2019

Also by Thomas K. Carpenter

HUNDRED HALLS UNIVERSE

THE HUNDRED HALLS
Trials of Magic
Web of Lies
Alchemy of Souls
Gathering of Shadows

City of Sorcery

THE RELUCTANT ASSASSIN
The Reluctant Assassin
The Sorcerous Spy
The Veiled Diplomat
Agent Unraveled
The Webs That Bind

Special Thanks

My wife Rachel and I have a tradition when we go out to see a movie. After the feature presentation is finished, when most people are leaving the theater, we stay to read through the credits. The reason is that everyone one of those people has contribuited to the final work and we want to acknowledge their part in it.

In fact, we've watched so many credit scrolls that years ago, we started to recognize familiar names. One of those names was Mo Henry, a negative cutter. It was mind boggling how many films that he'd been a part of, even though we really didn't even know what a negative cutter was! Eventually, we looked him up to find that the original Mo Henry had long ago retired and that the name had continued as a small company of his assistants that wanted to carry on. I hope you'll view the names below in the same way.

So to all those people that helped make this possible: thank you! People like my wife Rachel who helps me craft the stories that you love, Ravven who conjures the covers from her imagination and skillful craft, my editor Tamara Blaine who fixes my absurd word choices and makes the reading experience more pleasant, the beta readers (Tina Rak, Carole Carpenter, Paula J. Fletcher, and Patty Eversole) who give me great feedback while dealing with an error filled manuscript, to the Vanguard (Elaine Stoker, Jennifer Beere, Tami Cowles, Lana Turner, and Andie Alessandra Cáomhanach) who catch those final gremlins that plague every book.

Your time and effort have helped bring to life this moment of joy in readers' lives. Thank you!

ABOUT THE AUTHOR

Thomas K. Carpenter resides near St. Louis with his wife Rachel and their two children. When he's not busy writing his next book, he's playing soccer in the yard with his kids or getting beat by his wife at cards. He keeps a regular blog at www.thomaskcarpenter.com and you can follow him on twitter @thomaskcarpente. If you want to learn when his next novel will be hitting the shelves and get free stories and occasional other goodies, please sign up for his mailing list by going to: http://tinyurl.com/thomaskcarpenter. Your email address will never be shared and you can unsubscribe at any time.

Made in United States
Orlando, FL
06 August 2024

49985423R00193